Restored

KARI JENKINS

WESTBOW
PRESS®
A DIVISION OF THOMAS NELSON
& ZONDERVAN

Art Credit: Megara Keener

WestBow Press books may be ordered through booksellers or by contacting:

WestBow Press
A Division of Thomas Nelson & Zondervan
1663 Liberty Drive
Bloomington, IN 47403
www.westbowpress.com
1 (866) 928-1240

ISBN: 978-1-5127-9412-0 (sc)
ISBN: 978-1-5127-9414-4 (hc)
ISBN: 978-1-5127-9413-7 (e)

Library of Congress Control Number: 2017910997

Print information available on the last page.

WestBow Press rev. date: 06/20/2019

For my family—my amazing husband, spectacular four boys, and phenomenal mother.

CONTENTS

CHAPTER 1

Winter in a Waiting Room

Adin

The officer pushes me through the door into a small waiting room, arms secured tightly behind my back. Rolling my eyes, I scan the all too familiar surroundings and let out a loud, obnoxious sigh while being dragged right next to the multi-colored plastic chairs that are always scattered in disarray. There is one desk near the front where an old man sits reading a newspaper. By the looks of him, I'd say he'd fit in better greeting people at Walmart. I could probably make it to the street before my state-appointed bodyguard catches up, but the handcuffs would eventually slow me down.

The nostalgic Christmas music plays from overhead as if the merry tunes could suddenly make me forget my life and transport me into one of the fairytale Santa-fixes-all cinemas. I am once again being *taken care of* by the state of Pennsylvania.

Seriously, I'm tired of case workers thinking that they know what I've been through, and I'm over everyone else believing that I'm nothing but bad news. I can figure this out—I've gotten this far, haven't I? I don't need other people to take care of me just so that they can feel better about themselves, like they're doing me a favor. I just need to get out of here. Now, if only I can figure out how to lose my overweight bouncer…and these cuffs.

"Adin Taylor," a nasal voice says over the intercom, interrupting yet another upbeat Christmas melody.

My aggressive bodyguard stands, forcing me to rise with him. He still hasn't taken his iron grip from my arm. Did I rob a bank? I mean what kind of reward is this guy going to get for bringing me in? An extra candy-cane? The temptation to run becomes stronger the tighter his fingers dig into my arm.

I allow him to drag me along through a set of doors next to the geriatric patient reading the paper. I roll my eyes again when I hear the old geezer chuckling, probably assuming my scowl is some type of "stage" that teenagers just go through instead of the authentic anger that develops based on what this system does to unwanted kids. It takes every bit of self-control I have not to growl at him in frustration when passing.

A few seconds pass before my eyes adjust to the hallway lighting as we continue to walk down a long corridor, meeting another set of doors. The fluorescent lights are barely working, giving me a mental picture of what a prison must be like. I'd definitely like to keep the reality of that possible future far away for as long as I can, thank you very much.

I hate state buildings. How much money would it cost to get good lighting? Another blatant sigh releases from my lips. Officer Aggressive turns his head sharply in my direction, his eyes slit into tiny lines while he stares down at me, clearly meant to project his own frustration.

At the next set of doors, we stop, so he can press a button. After a loud buzzing sound, the doors jolt open. I take this opportunity to peer around to his nametag, reading: *John Anderson*. Good, so Officer Anderson has been to One Park Building. He must have been here before to know where we are going. I've been here a few hundred times, and it is still a mystery to me as to how I wind up in front of my case worker's door.

Ms. Watts will be annoyed to see me; she will want to know why my last home didn't work out.

"Why didn't you call me, honey?" she will ask, her nasal-high voice making my ears want to bleed.

If there were a hint of sincerity in her question, instead of the sugar-sweet fakeness covering the formalities, I might care to answer. The system is all about protocol, at least what I've seen of it.

Yes, I have my game plan in check. I'll just nod at everything. If that's not good enough, I know a few hand gestures that could get me locked up in juvie. No, no, Adin—deep breath here, girl—you are going to behave. These people will never understand; just keep your head down.

Officer Anderson knocks once on the door that we abruptly stop at. He looks down at me as if to make sure I am still here. I pop my eyes out at him, so he gets the message loud and clear: "What are you looking at?!"

I hear a muffled, "Come in," to which Officer Anderson opens the door.

Well, if you've been in one state run office, you've been in them all. I'm starting to wonder if there are just a hundred ways to arrive at the same door in this building. The distinct smell of old cigarettes still lingers, and the vintage 1970's desk and chair are still just as puke green colored and dusty as every other time I've been here. The only surprise in this office is that the woman behind the desk is not Ms. Watts.

I look up at Officer Anderson, hoping he really can read my mind this time: "You only had to deliver me to the correct door, and you screwed that up?"

"Please sit down, Miss Taylor."

What bothers me is that this lady is addressing me as if we've already met. The assertiveness in her voice sets my nerves on edge. Officer Anderson takes a moment to remove my cuffs and then motions for me to sit down.

"John, thank you so much for escorting Miss Taylor to my office. How is Deborah?" she asks, her face open and kind.

I sit down in the only chair left and start to fume. Great, so Mrs. What's-Her- Name is going to exchange polite chit-chat with Mr. Officer while I sit here growing older by the second. I start drumming my fingers impolitely on the arm of the out-of-date chair. I hope my tapping makes the stupid arm fall right off.

Everyone pretends not to notice. I decide to focus on something positive for a change, and so I smile to myself, because there is no Christmas music in this office. Crossing my arms in front of my chest and sagging down into my uncomfortable chair, I set my face in the best bored look I can muster and wait.

"Miss Taylor, my name is Ms. Ann, and I am your new case worker. I have reviewed your file, and it seems that we have not found a home that suits you as of yet. Is that correct?" New Lady says matter-of-factly.

She has her head tilted sideways, trying to make eye contact with me while she talks. In my attempt to hurry along the obvious, I nod my head in agreement.

"Is there any particular reason that you felt you needed to leave the Roberts' residence?" she continues.

Why bother? I shake my head no and wait for a lecture.

Adin you are supposed to call your case worker if there is a problem. My job is to make sure that you are doing okay, and I can't do my job if you don't talk to me...blah, blah, blah.

"Did you want to be moved to the Juvenile Detention Center?" She asks just as casually as the previous question.

I hate adults who try to manipulate me. Does she really expect me to say yes?

Yes, Ms. Ann, I would love to be locked down in a room with twenty other girls from whom I will have to withstand regular beatings from until another new girl shows up.

I shake my head no.

"All right then, I have another family who understands your circumstances and has an open room."

Before she continues, she hands me a picture of a couple—my new foster parents.

"This is David and Joan Baldwin. They own a home on Market Street, which is within walking distance to Central High where you will be attending high school." She pauses and then adds, "They have been foster parents for a better part of eight years. Any questions?"

I shake my head no again. The longer I've been in the foster system the more I've come to realize that the details that I used to think were important don't even really matter. I learned quickly that just because a family can take great care of a dog doesn't necessarily mean I'm going to get the same treatment.

"All right then, Miss Taylor, I hope that you appreciate what a blessing the Baldwin family can be to you. This will be your last opportunity to stay in a home rather than in a facility until you are eighteen. Once you get settled, you will be meeting with me every three months for updates."

Great, just great. Making sure boredom oozes from every pore, I nod my head in agreement while my stomach begins to nervously twist in knots.

Joan

"Thanks, Marge, I'll be there by 5:30."

I can't believe we are going to be getting another teen so soon. Matt just left for college in the fall, and I assumed that it would take a while for the state to place another kid in our home.

I close the cell phone that now lies static against my ear.

Marge Ann never ceases to amaze me; I wonder sometimes if she sleeps. She is such a saint with these kids. Marge brought Matt to us four years ago. Has it already been four years? Yes, he came to us right after Halloween. I will have to remember to call him at his dorm on my way to Marge's office, to see how he made out with finals.

Marge had said the girl's name is Adin…., Adin Taylor. She's sixteen years old and has been on the streets for a couple of months. Adin has been in and out of the system since she was in junior high, and as of yet, no foster home has stuck. There have been no complaints from her concerning her homes and none from any of the previous foster parents. Yet, she has run from every home in which they've placed her.

Her leaving doesn't make any sense. Dave and I were taught in fostering classes that system teens typically want to stay put until they hit eighteen when they can legally age-out. Adin hasn't followed the norm, and this makes me question what the foster system has missed.

Marge said that Adin's biological mother is alive but signed a no-contact waiver. Years ago, the Philadelphia Police Department found Adin asleep in an alley.

Lord, you know what Adin has been through. Father, please help me to help her. Lord, give me patience and wisdom for the days to come as I try to build a relationship with this girl. I pray that she will come to know you and find strength in dealing with her past. Lord, prepare Dave and me for what is to come and give us fortitude against all spiritual warfare that will take place as we stand in the gap for Adin. In Jesus's name I pray, Amen.

I pick up my phone to call Dave, letting him know that our dinner plans will be changing. We will be a trio once again. He will be so excited. Dave loves having a teen in our house. He doesn't know what to do when he is left alone.

I laugh to myself thinking about all the "stuff" he has in bins in the garage. Every time we've added to our family, Dave just dives right into to learning everything about his or her interests.

When Sara came to us eight years ago, she was curious about scuba diving. Dave called the YMCA and enrolled both of them in scuba lessons every Saturday. Matt loved baseball. There is a bin right when you walk out of the house into the garage that holds several mitts, balls, and cleats.

Once these kids move on into the next stage of their lives, Dave loses interest. Oh yes, he will be over the moon when he finds out we have a new guest.

CHAPTER 2

New Forms of Torture

<u>*Adin*</u>

I'm beginning to think that Ms. Ann is a very cunning woman. She's probably watching me on some TV monitor right now being tortured by all this Christmas music. I would rather be in a padded room with my arms tied down in front of my chest then have to withstand another verse of *Jingle Bells.*

I swear if that old man looks at me from the corner of his eye one more time, I'm going to karate chop that newspaper right out of his hands and then laugh manically while I shred it into tiny pieces of confetti.

I take a deep breath and start chewing my thumbnail.

What's crazy is that there has not been one other kid in this waiting room all day. Am I the only unwanted kid in the whole city of Philadelphia the day after Christmas? This is why I hate coming to this building: it's depressing. It's like being the runt puppy in a litter; although people stop by and look at you and state how adorable you are, they'd all still rather walk away.

Sometimes I feel like foster parents take one look at me and think to themselves, *"Well, she's okay looking enough, but definitely too much baggage."*

You get paid to let me sleep in your house! I'm self-sufficient; I can feed and clothe myself. What is your problem?

"Miss Taylor, I would like to walk you downstairs. Joan Baldwin is parked outside."

My head jolts up when Ms. Ann addresses me.

I never heard her enter the room. I could always hear Ms. Watts with her clicking heels. I might like Ms. Ann under different circumstances. She's got sincere eyes.

I applaud her for wearing jeans and a sweater instead of some professional suit. Ms. Watts always wore some business suit and too much perfume. Who was she dressing up for, little old me? I don't think so.

Her eyebrows are lifted when I meet her eyes, probably wondering if she should request a psychiatric evaluation since I still haven't gotten out of my seat. I jump up a little too quick all at once, grabbing my book bag. I swing it over both my shoulders and walk over to where she is standing.

Without another word, she turns, and we walk through the doors of the waiting room into a much bigger room where people are being directed from a welcome desk. We continue through this room to the front doors of the building. She starts to push open the door, stops, turns around, and puts her arm around me, enveloping me in a sideways hug.

What is this about? Is this an "I'm sorry" hug because the Baldwins are the last family that will take me in, or is this an "it's going to be okay" hug, that life will be getting better? Either way I don't want to be touched.

I shrug her arm off of me and look down at the ground. She just keeps on walking through the door, acting as if my reaction is normal. It's already getting dark outside; immediately, the cold air stings my face. I hug my body for warmth, rubbing my arms up and down to generate heat.

Ms. Ann is already greeting the woman from the picture I saw earlier. This lady is laughing at something Ms. Ann says before peering around her to take a look at me. I quickly glance down, pretending to inspect my worn sneakers as they approach me together.

"Adin Taylor, I would like for you to meet Joan Baldwin." Ms. Ann states calmly.

Joan reaches her hand out to shake mine. I leave my hand down at my side; however, I begrudgingly make eye contact, the only compromise I'm willing to make today.

Joan puts her hand down, her open smile staying intact. She looks at Mrs. Ann, and I hear her mention about going to some pizza joint to meet up with Dave, her husband, for dinner.

Ms. Ann turns to me and places a business card in my hand. "Call me if you need anything, Adin. I'm always available." Again, with those kind eyes.

I want to tell her no thanks, but without thinking I nod my head in agreement. The last twenty-four hours have left me exhausted. Self-pride is literally propelling me forward at this point. I don't get to lay down on the cold concrete side walk and cry for the injustices in my life; nope, been there, done that, and no one ever showed up.

I can remember when I was twelve, and Ms. Watts took me to meet a new foster family. It was this long drawn out process of meeting each member, walking through the home, and then checking in with me for a few days to make sure that I wasn't scared. Now, they just drop you at the curb and run.

Lifting my head, I notice that Mrs. Baldwin is waiting for me next to her car, her face scrunched in confusion. Did I just laugh out loud? Oops.

I wake-up to Mrs. Baldwin parallel parking in front of some brick building. Stretching my hands over my head, I take a look around.

"You must have been worn out; as soon as you laid your head back, you were gone. Don't worry, your snoring didn't bother me in the least." She ends with a mischievous smirk.

Mrs. Baldwin is teasing me? Okay.

Once we are in the restaurant, the blare of so many different televisions blocks out any other possible noise. The TV's are literally everywhere, and as I crank my head around, I see every kind of sport being played for the customers' viewing pleasure.

Men from all over the restaurant are busy yelling at televised referees as if their comments will make a difference. Despite such chaos, I notice a man's hand waving us over; time to meet David Baldwin.

As soon as we sit down, I find myself looking straight into his eyes, then quickly turn to look behind me. He's openly staring at something with this crazy grin on his face, which is kind of freaking me out. His expression is like a big, goofy kid. I turn back around to find that he is still openly staring… at me.

Joan laughs and tells him that he is scaring me. I wonder if she is aware that her husband is a weirdo.

Mr. Baldwin has an athletic build, so it doesn't surprise me that this is where we are eating. He's got brownish hair spiked up in the front like he's part of a boy band, complimented by large brown eyes. He's wearing a football jersey for a team that I couldn't care less about.

He puts his hand out to shake mine, but I leave it there, just like earlier with Joan. I don't play favorites. I cross my fingers under the table, hoping that they'll both catch on quickly that I'm not the kind of girl who shakes hands or hugs or touches people for that matter.

Undeterred by my rejection, he tries to make conversation, "I know that Marge already told you our names, but I like to introduce myself. I am David Baldwin, but I go by Dave, or Peanut- I'll let you decide."

He smiles really big after the whole "Peanut" comment, and pauses, probably to give me a chance to introduce myself, but I don't. Or maybe he thinks I'm going to laugh. Again, I don't.

Before the silence gets awkward, he continues, "I like this restaurant, they have the best pizza in town, and no matter what your favorite sport is, it's playing on a TV somewhere in here. The trick is to get seated in your sports area."

His arms extend out in the air, pointing out all of the TV's.

I've never been a sports person—my life has never included the extra-curricular. My mom was not the stay-at-home and invest in my life kind. Using the basketball game on the TV above as a ploy for interest, I hope my new roomies will take the hint.

I do not need the Baldwins to start prying. I don't have any answers for why my life is so messed up, and I don't feel like making any up tonight.

Out of the corner of my eye, I see Mr. Baldwin lie his hand over Mrs. Baldwin's while he is looking at the menu. How long have they been married? Probably not very long since he still holds hands with her. I can't even count how many men came through the revolving door of my mother's houses, but none of them ever held her hand; nope, they had other ways of using their hands, and none of them were ever so gentle.

My leg begins to shake under the table.

When is the waitress ever going to get here to break up these stupid thoughts?

I don't want to think about my mother. She doesn't even deserve the title. She was the incubator that carried me into this world. I would have been better off not knowing her at all.

Shaking my head, I try to dislodge such thoughts simply because I hate thinking about them; I just need to get over it. The continual drip of anger pooling in my stomach from today's activities begins to grow in Hulk-like form. I have to distract myself before I lose it.

I look up and around the room for a distraction; the memorabilia covering the walls will do in a pinch. I find Michael Jordan posters and old hockey jerseys. There is a signed football placed behind a glass dome. Right behind Mr. Baldwin's head is a bob sled and a pair of sneakers hung on the wall side by side. He wasn't lying, this place has it all.

Dave

She's not good with people, that's for sure. The way she looked behind her when I smiled at her, like she wasn't worthy of a smile. What happened to this girl? I check my rearview mirror before pulling out of my parking spot.

Joan and Adin have just left, and after walking them to their car, I found my way back to my own. What was in her book bag; she held it in a death grip all through dinner.

When I get home, I'm sure Joan will fill in the gaps. Looking down at the dash, I check the time: 7:30PM. I've still need to look over Coach Kay's basketball criteria for the Winter Tournament being held at the high school in a few days. I wouldn't have it any other way; it's why being the Athletic Director at the Central High School has worked out so well for me.

Usually I get bored after a few years of doing anything; it becomes too monotonous, no challenge, and I move on. However, with each season at Central High holding several sports to keep me occupied, there hasn't been a dull moment.

Right after the Boys' Basketball team has their tournament, I've got to get the Wrestling team in the gymnasium to set up their mats for their county tournament that we just happen to be hosting this year.

Maybe Adin will want to come with me tomorrow and check out her new school. If nothing else, it will allow us some time to talk. I'll get up and make her my famous pancakes, talk about her new school, and then invite her to tag along.

I feel the familiar jitters of excitement bubbling up at the awesomeness of getting another kid. *Thanks, God!*

CHAPTER 3

Hidden Agenda

Adin

Joan hasn't tried to talk to me at all on the drive towards her house. She has some religious music playing, lyrics about God and how laying down my sorrows would bring him joy. If God wants my sorrow, then I'd like to ask him a few questions first, like why did I have to get this life?

I'm guessing that Dave and Joan are the honk-if-you-love-Jesus kind of people. I'm okay with that as long as they're not expecting any conversions. I take a sideways glance at Joan while she hums along to yet another "Jesus" song.

Joan has brownish red hair that she has pulled up in a clip. She doesn't look like she's wearing much makeup, which is a thumbs-up in my book. My personal theory is that women who wear too much makeup are hiding something.

My mom was always applying another layer before she had "guests" over. Joan is dressed kind of preppy by my standards, wearing a peach sweater and khaki pants. The only jewelry I've seen thus far is her wedding band.

I look up as we pull into a driveway.

Home.

Nope, saying it to myself doesn't make it feel any more like the real thing. I can't wait for the day when I walk through a door and can say "Home" to myself, knowing that I'm not lying.

The second the car comes to a complete stop, I jump out. I hate those awkward gaps when you know someone should say something, but you have no idea what the right thing to say is. I will be playing the part of the mute, miserable teenager, so Joan shouldn't expect any heart-to-hearts.

I turn and look at the outside of my new shelter. It's a two story white house with black shutters. The shutters have a pine tree carved out of each one. The front door is red, and has a Christmas wreath hanging perfectly on the outside. The cuteness of it all receives an eye-roll from me.

I follow Joan in through the garage where there are a million bins with labels on the outsides of them. I'm guessing that someone in this house is a neat freak. Joan opens the door connecting the garage to the house, and we walk into the laundry room.

I follow her through the laundry room into the kitchen. There are two cookbooks left open on top of the island, which is in the middle of the room. We keep trucking it past the dining room where my eyes rest on a picture of Jesus hanging on a cross.

Is he looking at me?

I shake my head and keep following Joan until we are at the bottom of the staircase, which is located a few feet away from the front door.

"Your room is the first door on the right at the top of the stairs. The bathroom is the next door after it." She points up the staircase.

"I have already put some fresh towels and wash cloths up there for you. I was thinking that tomorrow we could go shopping and get you some school clothes and supplies." Joan smiles at me after the shopping offer.

"If you need anything, Dave's and my room is the last door on the left."

I anticipate her last word and answer with a faux over-the-top enthusiasm, "I'm a size six jeans and a medium top; whatever you pick out for me will be honkey-dory! You probably know what I need for school, so have at it!" I hold the double thumbs-up for a beat longer than necessary just so the obnoxiousness is not underscored on the catty spectrum.

I'd like to think I threw her with the paradox between my voice and my sneer. After all, these are the first words I've spoken to Joan since we've met. I'm looking forward to the reflection of shock in her eyes, but she just calmly smiles and shrugs her shoulders.

What a joy kill she's going to be.

I drag my feet across the carpet liner climbing up the stairs. I open what I assume is my bedroom door— this is definitely the biggest room I've ever had before, and all to myself? I slide my hand across the double bed pushed up against the wall, located to the left of the door, tingling at the softness of the navy blue down comforter.

A desk takes up most of the space against the far wall, sitting directly under a window that looks out the right side of the house. I separate the blinds, checking the possibility of a solid tree to use for escape if necessary.

No such luck. There are only a few pine trees that act as a boundary line between the Baldwins' and their neighbors, and none are close enough for me to use if circumstances warranted.

On the right wall is an armoire. It's the width of two of me, and I use my finger to trace the engraved spirals along the doors. Inside, I find a TV hooked up to a DVD player. I run my hand down the three drawers located under the entertainment section.

The walls are an off white color with no decor. It's as if the room offers me a clean slate. The Baldwins did a good job of cleaning out the personality of the previous tenant. I sit down on the edge of the bed and blink. Then, I blink again. I run my hand over the softness of the down comforter, wondering how long I can pull this gig off.

If the Baldwins are anything like the Roberts, it won't be my fault if I wind up in a facility until I'm eighteen.

My entire body stiffens at the thought of Mark Roberts, my last foster father. The Hulk inside of me grows faster, my breathing increasing and hands fisting. Rolling into a forced ball, I grab my book bag and pull the blanket over top myself.

Waking up, I spread my arms out wide and start to make my impression of a snow angel in the middle of my brand new bed. It is a wonderful feeling to sleep in a soft, comfy bed.

The warmth of the sun hits the left side of my face as it peeks in through the shades. The smell of coffee and pancake syrup wafts under my door from the downstairs and jump starts my stomach's growling hunger.

Now, how am I going to stall going downstairs?

My normal first day routine is to stay in my room all day. This is my way of subconsciously communicating that I don't need foster parents, and I don't want them to bother me. If only adults were smart enough to figure that simple gesture out.

This bed is pretty awesome; as good as those pancakes smell, I could cover my head with my nice smelling, soft blanket and go back to sleep. I try to cover my head up. Man, I can still smell the deliciousness.

I turn, rolling over to the edge of the bed farthest from my door. I roll back onto my stomach. This is so not working. I start rolling to the other side of the bed but accidentally roll right off the side.

Since I'm out of bed, I'll just get dressed. Opening up my backpack, I take out the only other shirt that I own, but notice that it kind of has a funk to it.

Wow, how long have I smelled like that?

Gross. Okay, I will just have to wear what I have on…again.

I grab my dirty shirt, and head downstairs, allowing my sense of smell to lead. Joan is sitting at the island already put together for the day. She is sipping a cup of coffee while looking through a J.C. Penny's leaflet.

Dave turns around, wearing his signature goofy grin. He walks around the island and puts his hand up for a high five. What am I a ten year old boy? No, no high five for you pal.

"Come on," he says to me in a voice that insinuates I hurt his feelings.

I give my head a firm shake no and sit down beside Joan, placing my shirt in my lap. Within seconds there is a plate put in front of me piled high with huge pancakes covered in butter and syrup.

"Would you like milk, orange juice, or coffee?" Dave asks.

"Orange juice," I reply through my first bite of food.

He chuckles at me, setting a tall glass of OJ next to my plate. Then he swipes my shirt, balls it up, and tosses it into the laundry room. Once it hits the basket in the doorway, he prances around in a self-victory cheer. It actually takes purposeful effort not to smile; what a goofball.

While eating, I simultaneously observe the kitchen. There are tall, mahogany cabinets that cover the back wall. To the right of the cabinets is a sliding glass door that I can only guess leads to a backyard. All of their appliances are stainless steel. The refrigerator has one of those buttons where you can get ice and water out of it.

These minute details help me to assess the kind of people that I am living with. I have been left in homes where I had to go outside to use the bathroom, and the state wonders why I run.

The Baldwins are foster parents because of their morals. The refrigerator isn't the giveaway in this family; no, it would be the vast amount of religious stuff that accessorizes this house.

Over the kitchen sink there is a small framed picture that states, "As for me and my house, we will serve the Lord." I'll let them tell the Lord that this statement won't be one hundred percent legit now that I've arrived.

Joan points to a girl's blouse in the J.C. Penny's teen section and asks me if I like it.

"Not really," I gurgle out, shoveling another fork-full of pancakes into my mouth.

"A little too girlie for you?" I'm not sure if she was asking me or not; I think it was rhetorical.

I keep my head down and eat prison style. As I'm stuffing in more pieces of buttery pancakes, Dave explains to me that he's the athletic director at my high school and how later today he is going to get some coach or other set-up for a basketball tournament.

"So do you?" Dave asks me.

What does he want? I look up at him puzzled.

"Do you want to go with me today and check out your new school?" he clarifies.

"No!" comes out a little too squeaky and fast. I smack my fork down loudly, even though there is still food left on my plate, and quickly push away from the island.

The pancakes were bait! I glare at them, shaking my head in disgust. I can't believe that I fell for this. There always has to be a hidden agenda.

What did this guy want me to do, go check out my new school for the day? With just him? I don't think so.

CHAPTER 4

Making Acquaintances

Joan

Impatient, my foot taps while I crane my neck around the ten or so other people in line in front of me at J.C. Penny's. I don't consider myself a weak woman, but I can feel the sweat trickling down my back and beads of perspiration forming across my hairline while I hold the mountain of clothing that I have picked out for Adin.

It is so much more exciting buying clothes for girls than boys. I just went shopping last week and bought Matt some winter polo's for college. The only fun part of shopping for him was getting the right shade of blue to match his eyes. He would have never thought of that, buying a shirt to bring out his eyes.

Matt was the first and, thus far, the only boy that Dave and I have taken into our family. He came to us in October of 2005. He was fourteen years old and in pretty bad shape. Matt's mom had died instantly in a car crash a few years prior.

His father had slipped into a bad depression following the accident, quitting his job and never leaving the house. He wouldn't even talk to Matt.

Social Services intervened when Matt's eighth grade teacher gave them a call concerning Matt's hygiene. When Social Services showed up to evaluate the home, Matt's dad never even got up off the couch.

After a few months in a group foster center, Matt was placed with us by Marge Ann. He was so skinny. I can remember the first time I looked into his eyes; it was the saddest moment of my life. I just wanted to hold him and let him know that love comes from all kinds of people, even foster parents.

I was determined to prove that love to him.

The lady in front of me drops a shirt out from the pile she is holding. She looks back at me, hoping for some help. I shrug my shoulders at her, smiling. I wrap my arms tighter around my own ample amount of clothing.

When we move up in line, she kicks it along with her. I can't help the laugh that escapes from my mouth. She turns sideways, grinning.

God, I hope that Adin cannot help but to love the clothes that I've gotten for her today. Father, I pray that you would give Dave and me wisdom on how to develop a relationship with this girl. This morning at breakfast it was so peaceful while we sat there and ate, but then she got so easily spooked when Dave wanted to spend time with her. Father, I pray for healing over Adin as she is in our care, healing from whatever made her flee the kitchen this morning. I pray that as she spends time in our home, she feels your presence so strongly. I pray that You would give her courage to deal with her past. Guide Dave and I as her guardians to love her through every bit of healing that will take place. I thank you for your daily blessings. In Jesus's name I pray, Amen.

I realize that I am next in line when I watch the woman in front of me dump everything in her arms down on the counter, and then bend down to pick up the remaining shirt wrapped around her foot. Another laugh bubbles past my lips; yet, this time she turns around and laughs with me.

Adin

I have spent the last two hours lying on my bed staring at the ceiling. I started counting after the first fifteen minutes but got bored when I got into the thousands. I walked around the room for a while before remembering that I had a TV.

Once I turned it on, I quickly realized it wasn't connected to a satellite or an antenna of any kind. It appears that the TV is here for the DVD player. There are no DVD's in my room.

Figures, the Baldwin's are clever in their torturous techniques, the kind of foster parents who understand what boredom does to a teenager. They don't worry about starving me out of my room. No, let's just tease her with the thought of being entertained.

I don't like to be left alone with my thoughts. I always try to stay moving because I don't want to think about my past. I read some quote once in a Snapple lid that I found on the streets that stated, "Don't look at the past. You're not going that way".

That's my motto: no looking back. That quote was put on this earth to explain, in some small way, that my past is where it belongs. I don't need to unravel it and try to make sense of it because it's behind me.

All of the sudden there is a noise coming from the direction of my window. I move the chair out from behind my desk and take a seat, resting my head on my hands to watch the distraction. So, there's a teen boy that lives next door—and since no one can hear my thoughts—a pretty hot one too!

Hot boy has white-blond hair, shaved close on the sides, but grown out on top. From here, he looks like he's probably a little taller than me. A sense of determination is set on his face, and I find myself drawn to his bright blue eyes.

He's stretching his right arm across his body while holding it with his left arm. I have this feeling that something is not right, and confirm my suspicion when I see his lips silently moving.

Is it odd that I feel relief when I realize he's wearing ear buds and probably just singing along to his favorite tunes instead of mentally impaired?

I suppress a giggle when he starts to hop up and down, shaking out his arms. People are so hilarious when they don't know they are being watched. When I lived out on the streets, I would sit on a bench for hours just watching people live their lives.

I lose my train of thought when I see the boy outside get into a fighting stance. I jump up from the desk and start looking everywhere that I couldn't see before. What in the world is getting ready to go down? I don't see anybody else. I look back over to him, finding him ducking his body to the right and left over and over again.

Is this guy for real?

He jogs down one end of his driveway and then sprints back up to the garage. The entire time he has this determined look on his face like he's actually racing someone. I am so confused by his behavior that I forget to sit back down.

After a few laps of running, he stops. He gets back into a fighting stance with his right foot in front of his left. He keeps bobbing tightly from left to right, and then he brings his right arm up in the air while simultaneously dropping to his left knee. Immediately, he rushes forward and to the left like he's holding something in between his legs, and his arms are wrapped around it with his head bent down.

What in the world is this guy on?

I had no idea that kids our age have imaginary friends. I stand there mesmerized while he repeats this menagerie of movements over and over, trying my best to figure out what he's doing, and why?

He stops, slowly turns around, and looks up—right into my eyes.

I run from the window and hide behind the side of my bed.

Crap!

Now hot-boy's imaginary friend secret is out.

I begin to laugh hysterically at myself.

I army crawl back to the desk, pull the chair back out, and slither up into it. I keep my head as far down as possible before I peek up over the windowsill.

He's gone.

Well, now what am I supposed to do for the rest of the day?

It's time to make an exit from this cage and find something to do. I crack my door a little, holding my breath, so I can hear better. Nothing. I open the door; my heart picking up pace at the loud creaking noise. Well, there won't be any sneaking out from this door, will there?

Of course the Baldwins gave me the squeaky door—their parenting tactics are beginning to impress me. I look up and down the hallway but observe nothing. I turn to shut my door and find a note taped to the outside of it.

Adin,

I went out shopping. Dave is at the High school setting up for a basketball game. My cell phone number is 678-0099. If you need anything just give me a call. There is plenty of food in the fridge for lunch, so help yourself. Dinner will be at 6pm.

~Joan

I crumple up the note into a little ball, angry for all the wrong reasons. I'm angry because she cares enough to leave me a note. She is not supposed to be so nice. I don't want to like these people. It would be easier if they were jerks; then I can have a legitimate reason to be bratty.

Despite such tension, I skip down the stairs to the kitchen with more freedom in my step knowing it's just me in the house. I open the refrigerator and whistle. There are yogurts and pudding snacks on one shelf, grapes and strawberries already picked in their separate containers on another shelf, and left over pizza in a Ziploc bag at eye level. I take the pizza out and toss it up on the island.

Thus begins the search for a plate. If I hadn't been so hungry this morning, I might have noticed where Dave got my plate from for my pancakes. I decide to start with the top cabinets all the way to the left.

First, I find all the serving bowls. Next cabinet is the glasses and coffee mugs. Bingo, next set of cabinets is the dinner plates. I grab one and serve myself up some pizza.

After I put it in the microwave, I go on a drink search. I peek into the laundry room to find an organized shelving unit with drinks. The top shelf is sodas, the middle shelf is different flavors of Gatorade, and the bottom shelf is bottled water.

Wow, I think that Joan has a problem with disorganization; I wonder what it will do to her psyche if I don't keep my room picked up? I might even cause a brain aneurysm if I rearrange her organized drink shelf.

Perhaps another time? I grab a blue Gatorade and head back to the kitchen to eat my pizza.

CHAPTER 5

Makeovers and Wrestling Mats

Dave

Reaching over Joan, I hit the snooze button on the radio alarm. It was Joan's idea to put my alarm on her side of the bed so that I would have to get up to turn it off. It's not fair that she knows my kinks so well.

I lay back down with the intention of sleeping for another few minutes only to hear Joan whisper, "You're not going back to sleep, are you?"

"No," I mutter as I flip my covers off and sit upright in bed.

I start to rub the sleep out of my eyes and am drawn back to the same thoughts I had as I lay in bed last night trying to fall asleep. What happened to Adin in her short sixteen years? What did her mother do to her?

When I had gotten home last night from setting up the wrestling match, Joan was busy in the dining room putting dinner on the table. I had really wanted to walk in and see her and Adin laughing over some silly girl thing, setting the table together like Joan and Sara, our first foster daughter, use to. I would go mad over their inside jokes, but I loved the light I saw in Sara's eyes.

Joan had been setting the table by herself; however, she seemed in a great mood. That's right, she went shopping, and not just any shopping, but shopping for a teenage girl.

"Good day at the office," I tease.

She looks up with a wry grin.

"Where's Adin?" I ask.

"She is still up in her room, but at least she came down and got something to eat while I was gone." Joan answers.

"You don't say Detective Baldwin. What clues led you to this conclusion?" I say in my best Sherlock Holmes voice.

"Well, first there was a Gatorade missing from the blue stack, and I just bought those yesterday. Then, the pizza was mysteriously gone from the refrigerator. All signs point to a teenager."

I grab Joan up in a tight hug, laughing. I love that we can still play games as long as we've been married.

"What do you think I did this morning that sent her running up the stairs?" I ask, talking into her hair.

"I don't know. Maybe it was an older guy who hurt her in the first place. Marge had said that Adin only lived with her mother, but that doesn't mean that her mother didn't have men in her life."

"Also, the other foster homes had fathers. One of those men could have tried something with her. But, to be fair, Adin never made any complaints against any of her foster parents. I really don't know honey, what do you think?" I can tell that Joan has been trying to figure Adin's behavior out just as much as I have. I sit down at the table and sigh.

"I scared her, that's for sure. I really wanted her to come to the school and see where she'll be next week. I don't think that it will be so overwhelming if she has a chance to check the place out first."

"But, I know for sure that she will not be coming with me. Do you think you could bring her by sometime next week? I could walk around with the two of you once you show up. She might find some kids that she gets along with at the wrestling tournament next Wednesday; all kinds of different kids from school will be there."

"I just need to figure out what she's into so that I can nurture that. You know, give her something that's hers. There has to be something besides her book bag that she cares about in this life, and we just have to be patient and figure that out. So, what's for dinner?"

I look up to see that Joan is still deep in thought. I am ready to move on. I know what I have to do to get the ball moving with Adin and there is really no point going over it any more. I wait until the crease eases on Joan's forehead before asking again.

"Cheese burgers, french fries, and baked beans," she answers.

I do love having a teen in the house. It changes up the dinner menu.

When I hear Adin walking down the stairs, I grab a portion of the newspaper out of the basket to appear occupied. I don't want there to be any awkward silence at the table since I can already tell she's not comfortable being around me alone.

She sits down at the table, putting one seat between us. She bites on her lip while staring down at her plate. Right on cue, Joan steps in and puts cheeseburgers on all three of our plates. The french fries and baked beans are already on the table for each of us to help ourselves.

After piling my plate, I pick up my fork to start on my baked beans when I realize that Adin's cheeseburger is missing. Is it that bad? Joan hasn't made cheeseburgers in a while, but are they so disgusting that Adin hid hers?

Out of my peripheral vision I look down at the ground, nothing. She ate it? That has to be a record! If I hadn't already promised myself that I was not interacting tonight, I would encourage her to race me.

I can't contain my grin as I continue to eat. Joan walks back into the dining room holding an armful of clothing. She also has a huge smile on her face. Adin looks up, completely surprised.

"Is that for me?" she whispers.

The stunned expression on her face feels like someone just sucker punched me in the gut. Didn't anyone ever buy her anything?

"Yes it is," Joan encourages, "and when you have some time, I would love it if you could try on everything and let me know what you like and what you don't. I am going to be running errands tomorrow, and I could return anything you need me to."

I can't help but move my eyes over to Adin to see how she responds, and her eyes appear glassy. Oh no, she's going to cry. Then, I'm going to cry.

She ascends from her chair in a clumsy rush, knocking her silverware against her plate. I grimace when I notice how hard she's biting her lip. She's going to wind up inadvertently piercing herself if she doesn't let up.

She slowly walks over to Joan, looking down at her feet the entire time. Joan happily piles everything into Adin's arms and steps back. They remind me of two athletes passing a baton. Women and their clothing, sheesh.

Adin turns around and jolts upstairs. Joan sits down looking like the cat who got the mouse. Usually, I am the one who connects with our foster kids first. I don't think that will be the case this time. This will be good for Joan.

When I got into bed last night, all I could see was Adin's stunned face when she accepted the clothes from Joan. What did her expression mean? I hope that Joan can get her over to the school soon so that I can see how she relates to other high schoolers.

"Quit worrying about Adin and get in the shower," I hear Joan say from under the covers.

"Get out of my head woman," I tease back and head for the bathroom.

While sprinting over to the wrestling coach, I see Joan walk in. Oh well, I guess Adin refused to come after all. I hand Coach Floyd the tape to wrap up his 155lb kid's knee before he hits the mat. I turn around, following the outside of the mats that are taped together, walk over to Joan, and give her a hug. She smiles up at me with a look of excitement on her face.

I turn my head in and look to Joan with an expression that asks, "What's going on?"

The energy coming off of her is pure exuberance, and it's got me curious. She grabs my hand and leads me back to the doors I watched her come in thru.

Joan purposely directs her eyes over to the vending machine where there is a girl bending down to get a soda. I turn around to Joan, putting my hands up as if to surrender, "I give up. What am I supposed to see?"

Joan huffs, crosses her arms over her chest, and looks up at me with glittering eyes.

What am I missing here?

I turn to look at the door, running into the girl from the vending machine. A sense of familiarity makes me look closer. Where do I know her from? I take a step back when the girl takes one look at me, and then immediately looks down at her feet.

That would be a mannerism from the teenage girl who lives in my home. This girl and the one I left at home this morning look nothing alike.

I turn to stare at Joan again, and she nods at me.

No way!

When I had met Adin at Pete's Pizza, she had long dark hair, almost black. Her face had been sickeningly pale, and there had been dark circles under her eyes. When I had introduced myself to her, there was pain evident in even her posture. This is not that girl.

Looking at Adin right now, her hair is cut into a short bob that has longer pieces in the front. Her hair is also a lighter shade, definitely not black, with chunks of blond mixed in. I tilt my head to the side, trying to get a better look at her face. She lifts her head when Joan says her name. She is breath-takingly beautiful.

"Nice," I say as I shake my head at her. I hold back the instinct to whistle, not sure if she'd take it the right way.

After fifteen years of marriage, I have learned that you must walk on eggshells when commenting on any new change in a woman. Also, never ever say she looks fine. Joan told me early on in our marriage that me saying she looks fine is equivalent to saying that she looks horrible but being polite about it.

Who knew that Joan could translate a man's language that I never knew existed.

I hug Joan to the side of me, now able to share her exuberance.

It took courage for Adin to come here today, and praise God that she has that. She will need that courage to face all that has held her back.

Father, I am overwhelmed with emotion as I stand here looking at one of your daughters. Adin Taylor is one of the strongest young women that I have ever met, and I just want to thank you for allowing her to be a part of our lives. God, I know that men scare her, and I pray that you would give me discernment in how to relate to her. I pray for Joan, that You will give her wisdom in ministering to Adin's needs. Thank you so much that Adin has let Joan in already. Thank you for the fun that they must have had today doing their girlie stuff. I pray that as Adin looks in the mirror, she will see the beauty that you have placed there. In Jesus's name I pray, Amen.

I feel Joan sigh beside me while we both continue to covertly glance at Adin without her feeling uncomfortable. I don't think anyone could miss the proud looks on our faces though, and I don't want them to.

Adin

Breathe, just breathe.

I've been saying this mantra in my head since I saw my reflection in the mirror this morning at the spa that Joan dragged me to. I do mean drag literally because she actually got behind me and pushed me through the door into the place.

The memory actually makes me smile and give Joan two bonus points for not allowing me to walk all over her.

I only had to sit in the waiting area for five minutes feeling sorry for myself before Tiffani came over and grabbed my hand, leading me to the shampoo chair. Tiffani is the coolest hairdresser that I've ever met, albeit the only, but that's beside the point. She's covered in tattoos, has a Monroe piercing, and boldly and flawlessly sashays around the salon in black leather pants paired with a hot pink t-shirt.

I purposely observed the rest of the salon, but there was no one else like her there. While she shampooed my hair, she kept up a steady stream of conversation, letting me know how she had gotten to know Joan when Sara lived with her.

Evidently, Sara was the Baldwin's first foster kid, and Tiffani and she are very close. As I was sitting in her chair, watching her cut off most of my hair, I wasn't worried about what I would look like; I was more captivated by her stories.

I wish that I had been Sara and had lived through crazy fun with Tiffani.

They loved borrowing Tiffani's dad's Jeep in the summer and driving to the Jersey shore to lie on the beach all day. They both loved to go to the local theater and watch movie after movie all Saturday long until the theater closed.

These memories were so real that when she turned me around and put her face down to mine, whispering in my ear that Sara healed, and she too had been a foster kid, I didn't hide my tears.

My heart opened to Tiffani in gratitude for being Sara's friend. For the first time I can remember, I allowed someone to get close to me.

So, when Joan asked me in the car afterwards if I would like to go to the high school and get some lunch at the wrestling tournament, I nodded my head in agreement. I crossed my fingers, hoping that maybe I could meet my Tiffani.

I continue to walk around the gymnasium in inconspicuous circles, trying to blend in to this new environment. It appears to have the stereo-typical high school cliques. I recognize the small co-ed groups sectioned here and there talking amongst themselves.

There are also boys walking around everywhere in ballet suits. I know that they really aren't ballet suits, but I have no idea what one should call a wrestling outfit. Every time another wrestler walks by me I have divert my eyes because their uniforms are so tight. Is that why this place is so crowded?

There are girls with bows and high ponytails sitting Indian style around the mats that cover the inner part of the whole gym; yeah,

I'm going to say those are the cheerleaders. Their conversation thus far revolves around make-up and what they each got for Christmas. Must be nice, is all I can think.

This new look may be a problem because it doesn't make me invisible. Usually, I can move freely among people, drawing no attention to myself. However, today, it seems that the girls are giving me curious looks, and the boys are smiling much bigger than necessary.

I can only assume that Tiffani is not only the coolest hairdresser that I've ever met but also the best.

I'm sure that the new clothes that Joan got for me add to this attention as well. There was so much stuff that she had bought me that I am still reeling. I chose tattered dark denim jeans with a black thermal long sleeved shirt. The shirt is cool because the end of the sleeves have holes for my thumbs, and the bottom doesn't just sit square on my hips, but bunches up on both sides.

Who knew that a solid black shirt could be so awesome?

I am still wearing my worn sneakers, but Joan said that she wanted me to pick out my own shoes after we left the tournament. Joan is an expert in weaseling into a girl's heart. I don't know if I can trust myself to not get too close her too.

One second I'm walking and thinking, and the next I'm watching myself, in slow motion (because isn't that always how these life experiences work), trip over the corner of a mat that was sticking out farther than the rest.

I fall forward, accidentally taking out the poor guy who was standing in front of me. The people around us start laughing. Embarrassed, I roll off the guy and try to stand up.

"I'm so sorry, I didn't see the mat…." I rush to explain, but then fall silent when I find myself staring into the bright blue eyes of a certain hot-boy who entertained me yesterday as I sat bored in my bedroom.

CHAPTER 6

First Day

<u>*Adin*</u>

I feel weird for having first day jitters. I don't want everyone at school to think I'm nervous, or worse—scared. I blow out a deep breath and stare at my reflection in the bathroom mirror.

After blow-drying my hair, I didn't need to do much else; Tiffany is a miracle worker. I wouldn't know how to maintain a style of any kind. I've never done it before. I bend my head down to look at the chunky blonde highlights. They are so on point.

Joan must have put make-up in the bathroom last night after I went to bed. She had taken me to some cosmetic lady in the mall over the weekend, but I pretended to be ignorant to the whole process.

Joan didn't make a big deal about it, just told the dressy lady that she would try to stop back later. She must have gone back and got me some stuff. It was all organized in a hot pink transparent bag. Leave it to Joan to get a bag that is not only cute but also functional.

I look at my face again in the mirror and can't help but to smile. I don't look half bad with my hair done and make-up on. I grab my new purple book bag off my bed, shut the bedroom door, and hop down the stairs.

Part of me wants to feel guilty for leaving my old book bag upstairs, shoved under the bed, but I have to be honest, it's my ratty get away bag, not my go-to-school nice new bag. I push the negativity aside for now and enter the kitchen.

I've probably gained ten pounds in the week and a half that I've lived here. Climbing into my chair at the island, I move toward my plate, which is already served with scrambled eggs, bacon, and toast.

Dave puts a tall glass of orange juice in front of me and grins one of his goofy grins. To his credit, he's backed off since I turned him down the day he asked me to go to the school with him alone. I still don't know how I feel about him, but the space between us makes life easier.

"I've got to get to the school early for a while, teacher's meetings over new stuff the education board put together for us. Adin, do you mind if Joan just gets you to school for the next few weeks?" His words come out rushed enough for me to know that Dave's a terrible liar.

Why hadn't I thought of this situation before?

"That's fine," I answer after a noticeable pause. My voice doesn't sound as indifferent as I was shooting for.

I put my fork down when my hand starts to shake. I tell myself it's all because of the jitters I've had all morning. Yeah, I'm a pretty bad liar too.

I get up and put my dishes in the sink, walking out to the living room. I flip on the TV, sit down on the couch, and try to look interested in the morning news.

What is wrong with me?

I ball my hands into fists and put them in my lap. I get so angry at my responses to stupid stuff, stuff like riding in a car with Dave Baldwin.

What's the big deal?

He's nice. He goes out of his way to make me breakfast. He noticed on Sunday that I was eyeing the funny papers, so he reached over and set them on the ottoman sitting between us. He doesn't yell at me for having my shoes on in the house, and, last night after dinner, he made me a bowl of ice cream. He hasn't flirted with me at all, and he doesn't stare at me when he shouldn't.

My heartbeat starts to return to normal. I close my eyes and lean back against the cushions, thankful that I can at least reason with myself.

Tears start to sting my eyes. I wish that I never had to get scared over everyday decisions like riding with mom or dad to school.

Okay, the pity party is over.

I stand up and turn the TV off when I notice Joan getting her purse off the wall hook by the front door.

She turns to me and asks, "Ready?"

As ready as I'm ever going to be.

"Yep," I respond, moving towards her when she opens the door for me.

Dave

Slamming on the brakes, I almost run a red light. Too deep in thought, I never even noticed the yellow light. I shake my head, impatient with myself for not concentrating on what is going on around me. Watching Adin's face fall this morning about undid me.

What jerk messed with her? What slime ball scared this young girl half crazy to even ride in a car with a man? I think I'm going to have to give Ms. Ann a call and ask her to start investigating those other foster homes. Adin is way too emotional for this to have happened a long time ago. I don't even want to dwell on how long this thing could have been going on. I feel sick to my stomach just imagining what might have taken place.

Lord, I am so angry right now I could hit someone. Father, why does this beautiful girl have to deal with such horrible consequences to someone else's mistake?

I pull over to the shoulder of the highway and rest my head against the steering wheel.

Father, I don't understand the magnitude of the cruelty in this world, but I know that regardless of what has already happened, you are very near and willing to heal Adin. Thank you for the hope that you provide in this sin-filled world. I pray conviction over whoever could have done this. I pray that whoever has done these things will be caught. I pray that they hurt over what they have done. Father, please give me wisdom in how to help her. I don't feel like Joan and I can just pay for therapy; this girl is just teetering towards trusting Joan. Protect over her, Lord, as we try to figure out what to do. In Jesus's name I pray, Amen.

I grab my cell phone out of the cup holder, going through my contact's list until I find Ms. Ann's name. I press send and wait as the phone rings.

Once I listen to her message explaining that she is not available, I wait for the beep.

"Hi, Mrs. Ann, this is Dave Baldwin. I really need to talk to you about a few things. Joan and I aren't having any problems with Adin."

I pause, thinking of the right way I want this to come across, "There is just some stuff that I've noticed that I think you should be made aware of. My phone is going to be turned off until three this afternoon, but after that you can call me. Thanks, bye."

CHAPTER 7

Librarians and Lunch Lines

Adin

Trying to look like I've got this whole school thing down is so much easier than I thought it would be. I've been sitting in the library all morning taking tests, so the school can determine where I stand academically since I've been in and out of school for the past year.

I could tell them to put me in eleventh grade, but past knowledge has led me to keep my mouth shut. Usually, the principal will take one look at my very thick file, raise his eyebrow, shake his head sadly, and give up on me.

Kudos to this school for at least taking the time to check me out. I'd have to say that receiving the royal treatment is probably due to the fact that Dave works here. I'll take advantage of the perks where they're offered.

I look up at the clock for the millionth time to see how much longer until the buzzer will go off, allowing me to go on to the next part in the test. So far, I've taken a comprehension test, a math test, and a geography map exam.

Thus far, this whole scenario has been way too easy. Maybe they're giving me the eighth grade test first to boost my ego. I don't know, but I am bored. The buzzer dings and the librarian rushes over to collect my answer sheet.

"You can go to the cafeteria now and get lunch. Do you know where that is?" she asks.

"Yep," I answer. It's my first day here, obviously I don't.

The last thing I need is this lady as my tour guide. I grab my book bag and walk through the double doors out into the hallway. A stampede of students rushes by me without so much as a glance. My guess is that they are all moving in the direction to the cafeteria.

Checking out the school as I meander behind the rush, I count three hallways and then turn a corner right in front of the principal's office. Walking by, I observe the principal talking on the phone while swiveling in his chair. I continue down the hallway and follow a group of boys through the gray door into the cafeteria.

The school must have sound proof walls surrounding this area because once I enter all that registers is a deafening buzz. There are three lunch lines. I find myself standing in a potato and soup line just entering into the cafeteria.

I put my hands in my pockets, keeping my head down as I move forward. The boys in front of me are debating how many bottle rockets it would take to catch someone's backyard on fire.

After I pay the lunch lady, I realize that I should have scoped out a lunch table in line instead of listening to the boys argue their pyro addictions. I stand a little too long by the cashier as I look for an empty table.

Maybe I can just go back to the library. I head for the door when some short, bald guy stops me from exiting.

"Food stays in the cafeteria. You know the rules." His whole body language dismisses me before he's done talking.

No, really I don't.

Turning around, I find myself looking up into hot-boy's familiar eyes. Man, not this guy again.

"Sorry," I mumble sarcastically, stepping sideways to get around him.

He moves sideways in the same direction. I shake my head and bob to the other side at the exact time that he does the same thing.

"You go first," he offers, extending his right arm to indicate which direction I should move.

Hmm, I like the sound of this guy's voice. Up close he doesn't have any outward signs of brain damage. If I hadn't already experienced firsthand this guy and his imaginary friend, I might have a different opinion of him.

I nod my head in agreement and walk to the left of him where I see a group of guys standing up to leave a table. I quickly take a seat and start eating.

In a school this size, it's a pretty big coincidence that I would run into him again. I'm pretty sure Dave said there were some 500 students attending Central High during one of his many informative discussions with Joan and me over dinner.

I didn't even have time to be embarrassed at the wrestling tournament when I fell over him. Dave and Joan magically appeared, apologized to this boy named Chase, and ushered me away. Curiosity almost had me asking questions about this guy, but pride slammed the door on that option immediately. I don't get to know people; I don't do attachments—self-preservation and all. He seemed normal enough today, so my assumption could be wrong. If so, then what was he doing in his driveway?

CHAPTER 8

Advanced Placement

Adin

"Can you believe that her parents bought her a brand new Aviator for Christmas? She thinks that makes her so much better than everyone else." This is the wonderful conversation I get to overhear while waiting for Joan to pick me up after school.

And she keeps going, "If my parents bought me everything I asked for, I'd be a stuck up know it all just like her." The red head puffing on the cigarette babbles on.

The conversation is nothing if not entertaining. So and so is such and such and blah, blah, blah. Girls can be so catty. If you have anything they want, then they are programmed to talk you down in an effort to make themselves feel better about who they are

Yay to female unity.

This is yet another reason why I don't have any friends; you confide any information to them, and they eventually use it against you. I would love to get in this girl's face and call her bluff about being jealous over this Aviator.

Then I would ask her how she would feel finding out that

everyone she thought were her friends were really standing out in front of the school talking about her behind her back.

"That's right sweetheart," I would say, "you thought they cared about you, but you were wrong."

I don't know why I find so much satisfaction in knowing that other kids struggle, but I do. I suppose that I feel they deserve to have some kind of unhappiness in their lives, no matter how shallow.

No, what I would really like to do is trade my past for one of theirs. Let's see how they manage then.

I uncross my arms and push off of the side of the building when I see Joan's old Civic pull along the circle in front of the school. I hope she doesn't get out of her car and start acting all motherly. I don't need to be coddled; this isn't my first day of kindergarten. I don't even remember going to kindergarten.

It's mind numbing: the black holes from my childhood.

The first memory I have of school is when I showed up for the first grade late into the school year. I remember my mom complaining about some lady who had called and said that if she didn't get me in school, she would lose her housing allowance. She was furious, and somehow the whole situation was, of course, my fault.

A bus had picked me up at the opposite end of the street where our trailer rested. I had waited out there for an hour because my mom couldn't remember my pick-up time.

I was so excited for anything to do that would be away from her. I remember getting off the bus, looking up at this big brick building, and being overwhelmed with joy at the possibilities that awaited me inside.

That was where the wonder ended.

After I got through the entrance, a teacher took me to my class, and, immediately, I found out how cruel other kids could be. How was I to know that my appearance would cause the other kids to ostracize me?

I was completely unprepared for how mean and judgmental not only the kids, but also my teacher, would be. I was only six and had yet to understand the caste system of elementary school.

I slam the door on the car too hard when I get in, my angry retaliation to the memories that have now surfaced, gritting my teeth against the hurt that hits too close. Joan looks concerned but doesn't say anything.

Closing my eyes, I think about the Biology test that I took right before the end of the school day. There were all these anatomy questions and, to my surprise, I knew most of them. I had to give myself a pat on the back for what my memory does hold onto.

Two years ago I stayed with a foster family where the dad was a doctor. He had his own personal library, and I spent all of my time in there. They had four other foster kids who were mostly indifferent as long as I stayed out of their way.

They didn't like sharing their resources with the new kid. It worked out that none of them were interested in Mr. Doctor's library.

Almost all of his books had to do with medicine or the human body. He had a ton of medical journal magazines, and I just kept reading until it started making sense. It's weird, but, today when I took the anatomy section of my test, it was like second nature. I felt proud, like maybe I'm not an idiot after all.

Joan

Putting my toothbrush in the cup beside the sink, I turn off the bathroom light. I sit down on the edge of the bed and pull my feet out of my house slippers. I just have this overwhelming need to get down on my knees and pray for Adin.

I don't know what happened today at school, but she was very upset when she got into the car. I really want for her to have a good experience at school. If not at Central High, then we'll look into school choice. Lost in my thoughts, I feel Dave's hand on my shoulder.

"It's going to be okay, Joan. Adin is so much stronger than either of us understand." He rests his chin on my shoulder and kisses my cheek. "You worrying does not help."

He has always known my weak points. Worrying over situations I can't control has always been a bad habit. I wish my worrying did change life. It would mean that for right now Adin would be happy.

"What are you thinking about?" Dave asks.

"I think we need to pray," I answer.

"All right," he agrees.

I hear him get up from his side of the bed beside me and walk around to my side. I get off the bed and bend down on my knees beside him. Feeling the Lord's presence so near, I began to cry.

"You pray," I whisper. My heart beats faster as I feel the Lord's presence wrapping his arms around me.

Dave's deep voice clears my thoughts and I concentrate on his prayer, "*Father, we are incapable of knowing right now what has been done to Adin. We want to be there for this broken girl. We don't know where to start. We don't want to ask a bunch of questions and scare her. We would love to reach out and hold her, but she isn't very receptive to touch right now.*

We pray that if we can't be those people who love on her then you will send someone into her life that she will let in. We pray for your presence to surround her. Even though she may not understand what is so different about her life here in our home, looking back one day, she will understand the power of prayer that took place.

God, please be with my Joan as she is overcome with compassion for Adin. Your word tells us in Matthew not to worry about tomorrow because tomorrow will worry about itself.

I pray that you will guide Joan and me in how to get Adin to trust us. Also, that you would give Ms. Ann wisdom in questioning the other foster homes. I pray that no more children are hurt in these homes like Adin.

I pray that you would equip Ms. Ann with all the resources necessary to put an end to the abuse that foster kids like Adin have had to endure. Thank you for who you are in our lives. In Jesus's name we pray, Amen."

I allow Dave to hold me tight while I marvel at the closeness we share with our Creator.

"I left a message for Ms. Ann this morning on my way to school. She called me back on my drive home," Dave starts.

"I told her that we have some concerns about Adin's past foster homes. She asked me if Adin had confided anything to us, and I admitted that she hasn't as of yet. However, I did tell Marge about her unusual behavior anytime I try to get near her." Dave stops and looks into my eyes before continuing.

"She agreed that it isn't normal and that she would check into the last few homes she's stayed at and make some unannounced visits."

I nod my head in agreement and take a deep breath; I'm glad that we are at least doing something about the situation.

When Dave and I looked into doing foster care eight years ago, I was astonished at the workload that the caseworkers are left to deal with. I truly believe that what Marge Ann does is more of a ministry than a job.

Thank God she is Adin's caseworker.

Adin

The loud ring startles me, signaling the end of the class period. I blink my eyes a few times before standing up. Mr. Torthers holds out his hand for me to turn over my Geometry quiz.

I think that I actually fell asleep with my eyes open. At least I hope I did, or I might be getting a call down to the office later.

I shrug into my book bag and follow the rest of the students out of the room. It's been a week since I've been at Central High, and I'm still not one hundred percent sure how I obtained the schedule they gave me.

The school had called the Baldwin's house right after I got home on the day I took the exams in the library. When Joan hung up the phone, she looked at me with a smug grin, explaining that the principal had wanted her to accompany me to school in the morning.

Joan's reaction to the phone call caught me completely off guard; I thought that she wanted me here. I tried to pretend like I didn't care as I jogged up the stairs to my bedroom.

Once I had gotten upstairs though, I had worried all night that this school was going to be like all the others. The principal would call me in and ab-lib his way through a speech about the necessity of being in school consistently, then he would hand me a schedule that he felt would be best for my caliber of person.

I thought that I had done really well on the exams; they had seemed easy enough. There is no way I could have done well if the principal is already asking for one of my guardians to have a conference.

I fumed in my room all night, even refusing to go downstairs for dinner.

The next morning Dave, Joan, and I collectively reported to Principal Cravet's office for the meeting. I feigned that I could care less, bobbing my head to an imaginary beat.

When the Principal entered the office, Dave shook his hand and Joan gave him a hug. They talked about some referendum topic that had just been voted on and then he opened up my file.

I shook my head in disgust just looking at that file. In a sad way, that file is the only record I have of my life. I don't have a baby book or a photo album of myself growing up. Nope, I have a very thick school file noting every school that I've ever been transferred to.

The irony pressed heavily on my heart.

"Adin, I am very impressed with your test scores!" Principal Cravet began.

When I heard the word *impressed* my head popped up.

"Oh, yes, young lady, don't look so surprised, you did marvelous! I would recommend that you take a few of our Junior AP classes, but because you are coming to us so late in the year, I can't do that."

"There are requirements for some of the AP classes that you have to adhere to before the classes began, and the date of your arrival doesn't allow us that option. But, I do have a little good news, you can still take the Biology AP course."

"What's an AP course?" I asked.

"An AP course is Advanced Placement, which allows you to receive college credit in a high school classroom. It's a way for you to enter college ahead of the game." He begins to explain.

"Now, as long as you do well in all of your classes this year, then you will be able to take the Senior AP courses next year. There are two classes that you will need to choose from this list as your electives." He handed me a sheet of paper with a list of classes.

I read down the list: culinary arts, calligraphy, debate, economical studies, fitness, and so on. I continued scanning the paper, but my mind was still trying to make sense of my test scores.

Principal Cravet cleared his throat, a clear indication that I needed to hurry up.

"Um, I don't know, uh, I guess calligraphy and fitness." I really just blabbered out the two that my eyes hit first on the long list.

I looked up to observe Dave beaming, then, turning to my left, I saw Joan with a giddy grin on her face as well.

"Did you know about this yesterday when they called?" I asked her.

She nodded her head no, rushing to explain "No, no, no. Mrs. Bailey, the secretary, didn't tell me anything other than Principal Cravet had already reviewed your exams and wanted to know if Dave and I could meet with him in the morning. I just had a feeling that you would do really well, that's all."

I felt bad after she explained, guilty for the assumptions that I had made the night before. I had wanted to apologize right then, but old habits die hard.

I remained quiet. It was becoming increasingly harder to be hateful to Joan.

CHAPTER 9

Hot-Boy and Home Visits

Adin

Entering the doorway, I walk into Calligraphy class and take my assigned seat. I never would have thought that I could enjoy a class like this.

My first day in Calligraphy Mrs. Hollander had said that I came at a perfect time for a new student because they were learning a new style of Calligraphy that day. She had sat with me for the first two days, showing me how to hold my calligraphy pen correctly and giving me pointers as I practiced.

I liked the way she corrected me. She didn't yell at me or belittle me for my mistakes. She would just wait until I got it right and then praise me. I found myself wanting to do a good job just to hear her voice.

Today, Mrs. Hollander is going to give us a project that we will be working on for the next five weeks using this new writing style.

"Quiet down everybody. Now, listen up because today you are getting the instructions for your third quarter grade." Mrs. Hollander begins.

She holds up a piece of poster board and continues, "You will partner up with someone who will draw your silhouette on this piece of poster board. Then, you will use your rulers and lightly draw your writing lines onto the board."

"Please remember to draw them lightly because you have to erase them once you have penned your words. The words you will pen are going to be a list of your characteristics."

"I don't care if you ask your friends or consult a dictionary; you will fill this entire poster board with character traits about yourself. After you have finished penning your personal characteristics, you will color in your silhouette with a colored pencil."

She smiles at the class's groans. "That's enough, I need you to be listening. Right now, I want you to take out a piece of paper and try to write out fifty individual words that you would use to describe yourself."

This is the first time I've ever felt dislike towards Mrs. Hollander. I don't know fifty words to describe myself, and I'm positive that neither does anyone else. After forty-five minutes, I sit frustrated staring at a blank piece of paper. Every word that crosses through my mind seems hypocritical for one reason or another.

Mrs. Hollander had written several words on her white board to help us out. Once I looked each of them up in the dictionary, not one of them felt wholly me. She had come over to me at one point, gently put her hand on my shoulder, telling me not to think too much into it.

She had smiled, her kind smile that makes her eyes get all crinkly at the sides, and said that she felt I had more than enough words to describe my specialness. That comment did boost my ego a little, but still left me wordless. Putting *special* on my poster is just not going to happen. What a miserable class. I gather my books and head for the door.

Junior Literature is next with Mrs. Hyde. I have no evidence to back up my theory, but I would bet money that she is also the Drama teacher. She dresses very colorful with wild zebra prints and crazy geometric shapes.

I walk right past my Literature class door, not paying attention to where I'm going. I turn around to go in but am stopped by an arm that mysteriously pops out, barricading the entrance.

"You're Adin, right?" random guy states.

I nod my head yes, tilting my head just so to demonstrate that I'm not real impressed with what he's doing.

He laughs at my response and continues, "Ouch, someone didn't get her Red Bull today. My mom always told me that the girls who act hard to get are the ones who want you to chase them."

What an idiot. Who opens with a line about something their mom says?

"Really, well, does your mom know me?" I ask matter-of-factly, continuing right on, sarcasm dripping from each word, "Look, I just want to get to my seat, preferably before the bell rings."

He lowers his arm for me to pass.

"If you wanted to talk to me, you could've tried acting like a normal human being and just introduced yourself. By the way, I don't play hard to get because I'm not available. If I wanted you to like me, you already would." My last three words punctuated with harshness before I put my book bag down beside my desk.

I cringe when I notice him ease himself down into the desk behind me. Leaning forward, he whispers, "My name is Keith Lewis, nice to make your acquaintance." He enunciates the 'c' in the last word like a snake hissing, and for some reason this pings around in my head like a loose pinball.

To distract myself from the overeager stalker sitting behind me, I scan the classroom. My eyes stop when I catch sight of hot-boy's white-blond hair. It's Chase, my next door neighbor who plays with an imaginary friend, and who I have a habit of literally knocking down on every occasion that we are in the same orbit of one other.

I stare at him. He sits in the next row over, two seats up. I'm close enough to observe that his hair curls at the ends.

As if he knows what I'm thinking, he turns his head slightly and smiles. He must know that I'm checking him out.

My eyes shut for a brief second, allowing myself to remember our first face-to-face contact, the one when I tripped over the wrestling mat, literally taking him down with me. He acted as my human-cushion from the floor. When I stood up, I had been mortified, unable to even apologize.

"Adin, besides your natural ability to talk a man down, are you also great at memorizing twenty-five vocab words for literature sentences," comes a whisper from creepy- Keith behind me.

Burned!

I scrunch my head down and began to copy the words that Mrs. Hyde penned on the white board at the front of the classroom.

Joan

"Marge, thank you so much for stopping by. Please come in. Here, let me take your coat." I take Marge Ann's coat and hang it on the peg beside the front door.

Marge Ann had called Dave earlier in the day, making sure that this evening would be an okay time to come by.

"Can I get you something to drink?" I ask.

"No thank you," she answers. "I keep a bottle of water with me wherever I go. Is Adin home from school?"

"Yes, she's up in her bedroom," I point up the stairs. "Did you want me to get her?"

"No, not yet. I would like to discuss some things with you and Dave first. Is Dave here?" she asks, looking around the living room.

I nod my head yes. "He just went upstairs to change out of his work clothes. He gets all sweaty after school, running around to all the different sports, acting like he can still participate," I admit jokingly.

"Oh really," she says while raising her eyebrows, clearly amused.

Just then Dave comes rushing down the stairs. He probably heard Marge come in and didn't want her to start without him.

"Ms. Ann, how are you doing?" Dave hugs her while asking.

"When are you going to start calling me Marge? You make me feel so old," smiling up at him, she returns.

"I know, I know, I'm sorry but it truly is out of respect for you," Dave admits.

She grabs Dave's face in her hands and gives him a soft pat. Then she and Dave sit down on the sofa, and I take the loveseat diagonally from them.

Dave and I lean in as she begins, "I went to one of Adin's previous foster homes yesterday. When Adin lived there, they had other foster children in the home. I asked them specifically about Adin."

"At first, they had no idea who I was talking about. The foster dad could only remember she liked to read his books. I asked him if Adin had any trouble being around him alone, and he admitted that the situation never occurred. Due to his work schedule, he usually got home after the kids were in bed."

"On the rare occasion that he was home at the same time as Adin, she never hung around the family. They felt that this might have been why she ran off, just that she never clicked with them."

I have a premonition that this foster father was not the man who had done these horrible things to Adin.

"Do you think you should ask Adin about this family and see how she responds?" Dave asks.

"That might be a good idea," admits Marge, "but she could also be on to us and get angry. Do you feel at this point she is capable of running from you? Have you two formed any kind of a bond with her that would make her want to stay if she feels threatened?"

I look over to Dave and shrug, not really knowing. "I hope so," is all I can say.

I only know that I want Adin to be able to heal and ignoring the situation is not doing that.

"Go ahead and get her then," says Marge.

I stand and walk up the stairs. I take a breath to calm myself before knocking on Adin's door. Immediately, I hear the music turn down. Dave had brought home some popular CD's from Target the night we had the conference with Principal Cravet. The door opens and Adin's face pops out.

"What's up?" she asks.

"Ms. Ann just stopped by for a minute, and I thought it would be nice for you to say hello. Do you mind just coming downstairs for a little bit?"

She rolls her eyes and comes out. Following me down the stairs, I can smell the perfume that I bought for her. I am impressed at how much better she looks now in comparison to when she first came home with us. She literally smelled like a garbage can upon our first meeting, not that I cared then, but it says something for her that she cares enough about herself to stay cleaned up when she has the opportunity.

"Adin, is that you? My goodness child, you look amazing!" Marge gushes.

Adin returns the comment with an uncomfortable smile. She sits down on the loveseat beside me. I would love to put my arm around her and give her a hug, but I don't want to push anything yet. I try to give her a convincing smile when she glances my way.

"I was just telling Dave and Joan that I visited one of your old foster families. Do you remember the Fritas?"

Adin nods her head yes but stays quiet. For once I wish she was an over talkative teenager like most girls her age.

"Good, I had to check in on one of their kids today because I'm his caseworker too. Mr. Frita was just coming in from work when I was leaving around 5:30. He told me that him getting home at that time is considered an early day for him. Is that what it was like when you lived there?"

Again, Adin nods her head yes. I wish I knew what is inside her mind right now. Adin is very good at hiding her thoughts; if I didn't know this already, I do now. She's acting as if she were nodding yes to a waitress over an order, like what we are talking about has no significance. I can feel my nerves start to get the better of me, my mouth going dry.

"Oh, did that ever bother you?" Marge persists.

This time Adin nods her head no, eyes still lowered to the floor.

"I'm only asking because I want to make sure this little boy is being taken care, you understand? What kind of family would you say the Fritas are?"

Adin sighs, clearly annoyed at the task of actually having to speak.

Dave and I lean in a little closer when she finally states, "I guess they are fine. There was always plenty of food, and I had a bed and clothes, so I would put them at a six on a scale of one to ten."

"That's okay, a six. Were there any negative aspects to this family that I should be aware of?" Marge continues.

Adin lays her head back against the cushions and stares at the ceiling. She blows air out of her mouth playing with her hair and then says, "Uh, I don't know. I guess there were a lot of kids staying there when I was, so the new kid needs to be aware of the typical dominance stuff. You know, no one likes to divide up the goods any more than they have to, and the Fritas never did anything about the way the other kids treated me. I don't really know if they ever saw it. I mean, they were both gone all the time."

"Hmm, okay, thanks Adin. I thought that Mrs. Frita didn't work. Did she ever tell you where she goes every day?" Marge asks.

Adin shakes her head no as she continues to blow her hair up when it falls on her face.

"One last question, did anyone in the house ever do anything that made you uncomfortable. Did anyone ever invade your personal space?"

Once the words are out of Marge's mouth the room goes still. Adin's entire body transforms from careless teen to rigid tension; she is no longer interested in entertaining herself with her hair. I think I see her eyes dart around, but I can't be sure.

Slowly, she sits upright, looks Marge right in the eyes and replies, "No, why?" Her voice sounds different, quieter.

"I'm just making sure the home is a safe place for this boy, and it's just a standard question." Marge counters calmly.

"Why hasn't anyone ever asked me that question before? In all the years that I've been a foster kid, no case worker has ever asked me that question. What makes you ask me now?" The anger in Adin's voice overwhelms the words coming out of her mouth, almost like they are trying to escape from between the prison of her teeth.

There is a tension between Marge and Adin that leaves me at a loss as to what will happen next. I can feel my heart beat behind my eyes. I turn my gaze towards Dave, but his eyes are fixed intensely upon Adin.

"I don't know why you haven't heard this question in the past, dear, but I am asking you now. Unfortunately, there is scum that leaks into the foster system, and the kids have to pay for those mistakes. I am of the opinion to be very careful where I place my kids. Is there a reason why this question makes you so upset?" Marge continues.

Adin pounces off the loveseat in one move, clenching her fists, and then booms, "Yeah, I got a problem with your questions. Like how it is that such *scum* is permitted to *leak* into the system? And, why weren't these questions asked before I had to live in some of my other homes?"

"You people will take anyone who puts in an application to be a foster parent just so you don't have to be responsible for watching us anymore. Kids get dropped off at any place and are left to deal. And here's the kicker, you have no idea how that feels."

"I bet this little boy that you are supposedly looking after is just another name on a long list that you get to feel better about checking off tonight when you go to bed in your nice house because you dropped in one day."

With that Adin rushes to the front door, flings it open, and sprints out across the side yard.

"Adin, wait!" I sputter, but she's already gone. I start to follow her, but Dave stops me.

"Joan, give her a few minutes. She has to know that we respect her space," he reasons.

"But she's hurt, and I don't want her to hurt anymore," I argue.

"God knows all of this," Dave reassures. He wraps me in a comforting hug.

"I don't think the Fritas hurt her, but I do know that someone in the system has. I'm sorry that she is so upset right now, but it is good that we were able to get an authentic reaction out of her." Marge explains while getting up from the chair.

"We understand," Dave replies for the both of us.

Marge collects her coat and purse and then opens the front door. "Thank you both for reflecting Jesus to a hurting young girl. God bless you."

Adin

The Hulk inside my stomach grows at a rapid rate. I run as fast as I can around to the side of the house where I begin kicking anything: pine cones, the flowers planted next to the house, the little gnome with the green hat.

I actually can see red. I only thought that was some dramatic way that other people described their anger. Not anymore. I blow out a breath and punch the air.

That's right jerk, take it.

I growl and kick up a pile of leaves. When I finally bend over to catch my breath, I try not to vomit. The Hulk wants out, and the ferocity of his anger churns inside my stomach, the acid a burning trail rising in my throat.

Why does Marge Ann have to be my case worker?

Life has never been fair to me, and I learned a long time ago to suck it up and just accept what is. But it's like rubbing salt in an open wound for her to start poking around. Only this time, the sting is too much.

I'm not this strong.

Where were the adults when I was naive? Where were they when I felt humiliated and ashamed and blamed myself? The hot tears roll down my cheeks. I collapse to my knees and start punching the ground over and over in hopes of releasing the pain caged inside of my chest.

I hate my life. I hate it. Why am I even here?

I grab at the dirt, relishing how easily it falls apart in my hands. I look up to the sky and shake my head screaming a few choice words at Dave's and Joan's God.

"Some God you are, sitting up there seeing it all and watching me cry. I bet your laughing, aren't you? Screw you!" I contemplate adding a hand gesture, but stop, knowing subconsciously that somewhere I have an audience.

I see Chase Harper sitting on his front porch. Great, now the head case thinks I'm the one with a problem. We can start a club.

In an effort to put myself back together, I stand up and start brushing the dirt and leaves off of my pants. I shake a few scattered leaves out of my hair.

Biting my lower lip, I look over to him again, but he has his head down, resting on his hands. I bet I know what he thinks about me now. Without trying to, I recall the few interludes we've shared.

First, I got caught spying on him when he was fighting his imaginary friend outside my window. Then, he became my personal landing pad when I tripped at the wrestling tournament. Oh yeah, and the cafeteria incident when we danced around each other while I attempted to get to a seat. Finally, today, he watches his own private show of me freaking out. Obviously, this is going to be a wonderful start to a life-long commitment to steer clear of one another.

"Hey, are you going to be okay?" Chase's voice is just above a whisper.

My instinct is to ignore the sincerity overlaying his question, but I'm spent, and I just can't do this anymore.

When did he even start to walk over here? I've really got to work on my observation skills.

"Fine." The word comes out stiff and unbelieving.

I put my hands in my pockets and try to act cool. He stands there. As awkward as this whole situation makes me feel, he doesn't look phased at all.

"Really, I'm going to be okay. I just got a little upset over nothing really, and I'm better now." I babble on, trying my hardest to sound convincing, but then stop because I don't know why I feel the need to explain myself.

This is not me: the girl who babbles. Irritated with myself, I clench my teeth.

"Who is it that you hang out with every day in your driveway?"

I ask casually, grasping for anything to divert the conversation elsewhere.

"What?" His head tilts in confusion, his adorable half-smile intact; you know, the one I'm internally convincing myself doesn't exist.

"You know, your imaginary friend," I joke, putting my hands in a surrender pose. "No, really, you come out here almost every afternoon and box around with absolutely no one. What is that?" I'm genuinely curious to figure this part of his life out.

He starts laughing so hard that his body folds over. I can feel my face get hot with embarrassment.

I glare at him for a moment and then continue, "I'm not crazy. See," I point up to my window, "I saw you the other day out here, and you were acting like you were fighting someone, only there was no one else here." I say the last part really slow like I'm talking to a small child just to clarify my point.

"Which is it then, did you see me the other day, or do you watch me every time I'm out here?" His ornery quip temporarily shuts me up.

Man though, he's quick. I try to remember what I had just said, but I can't. I've got to stop letting my emotions get the better of me. I roll my eyes, trying to pretend I could care less by his comment.

"Quit trying to hide the fact that you're a little too old to be playing pretend." I retaliate.

He straightens up a little, smiling at me. My heart seems to register his smile before my brain does, because all of the sudden I zone in on his smile, and this tingly, pins and needles feeling radiates from my core out to my fingertips.

I like this guy? I really don't want to go there.

"Seriously, there is no imaginary friend. I'm just practicing." He continues when I give him a bewildered expression, "Do you remember coming to the high school wrestling tournament—remember tripping and taking me down with you?"

I nod my head yes.

"I wrestle. I come out here and practice my single-leg takedown in the driveway. It's called shadow wrestling." He shrugs like wrestling your shadow isn't weird.

I wonder if he is aware that he's speaking a foreign language to me.

"I have no idea what you're talking about. A single what?"

He clucks his tongue in thought, trying to find a way for me to understand. His eyes scan his driveway. He looks back to me with a frightening grin. Again, my heart involuntarily speeds up. Trying to normalize my erratic breathing, I decide that I would rather deal with the Hulk inside of me than this gushy-girlie junk any day.

"Come with me," he gestures over to his house. "That is if you're not too scared."

I talk to this guy for what, like two minutes, and he already knows I'm hardwired to respond to that. I follow amid two of the pine trees that act as a barrier dividing the property between his home and the Baldwin's. He stops when we reach the driveway and turns to face me.

"Just stand still, okay?" he says.

"Sure, where am I going to go?" I want to ask, but don't know if it will come out as smooth as I want it to. After hesitating, I try to passively shrug my shoulders.

He crouches into that fighting stance that I remember from the first time I watched him. Then, with a confident smirk, he drops down to his right knee, pushing into me, coming up with me over his shoulder.

As I hang there, over his shoulder, my heart goes crazy. Okay, so this isn't exactly how I would like for him to hold me but whatever.

I shake my head against my traitorous thoughts and ask, "What are you doing?"

"This is a single leg takedown, well, sort of, because usually I wouldn't hold a guy up in the air; I would grab his leg and push him to the mat. Does it make any more sense to you now?"

"I'll let you know when I'm on solid ground again." I answer.

"Sure," his voice sure and steady, "when you tell me what made you so upset."

Is this guy for real? I have never let anyone know anything remotely personal about me. No matter what my heart thinks about this guy, I'm not giving in now.

"I'm in a perfect position to give you a major wedgie if you don't release me." I counter.

"You're no joke huh? Well, fine then," he slowly lowers me to the ground with impressive strength, gently setting me on my feet.

I get a little flustered with the way he keeps looking at me. I can't think straight. We stand there for what feels like forever before he breaks the silence.

"How do you like Central High?"

"Not too bad, I guess. I mean school is school."

Blah! I really can't come up with anything better than that? I bite the inside of my lip trying to think of something clever.

"Yeah, so did you have to write vocab sentences in your last Literature class?" Chase asks.

It was an easy enough question, but I don't know how to respond. I don't want him to pity me when I tell him that I haven't been in a school for about six months.

I shrug my shoulders and answer, "Nope."

I really don't want our conversation to end; there is something about this guy that strikes me as different. A good different. I peer up at him with a hopeful expectation that he will have another question.

He is looking over my shoulder at something, so I turn, my eyes following the same direction as his. Dave and Joan are standing on the front porch spying on us. They would have to ruin this. I feel the anger start welling up inside me once again. I clench my fists in an effort to control it.

"Adult spying should be against the law," I say, stating the obvious.

He smirks at me, "Yeah, I got to get out of here anyways. Don't be such a stranger now that you know the truth about my invisible friend." Laughing, he waves before turning to jog up his front steps and, opening the door, into his house.

I watch his back until he's completely gone before turning around to face a reality that I want no part of.

Joan

Lord, thank you so much that Adin has become friends with Chase. He is a good young man, and I know that you can use him as a tool in helping Adin to recognize who You are. Thank you that he was outside today and able to talk to her after what happened with Marge. You are so amazing, and today I am reminded about how much you care about the details in our lives.

Please forgive me for worrying. I know that you are in control of all things, and I am overjoyed at this new friendship between Adin and Chase. I pray that you would give Chase a deep compassion for whatever Adin shares with him. I pray for a maturity in him to help Adin grow closer to you. In Jesus's name I pray, Amen.

When Dave and I had finally agreed to walk outside and check on Adin, I was pleasantly surprised to see her next door talking with Chase Harper. Chase is our youth pastor's son. Pastor Ben and his wife Kami have three children. Corbin is their oldest son, and also good friends with Matt, then there is Chase, and finally Carter.

When Matt first came to live with us, I found myself drawn to Kami for advice. She was such a Godsend when I was at a loss trying to figure out Matt's behavior. She recommended some great books and was a true friend who prayed alongside Dave and me for Chase to heal.

I smile when I note the blush on Adin's face when she waves good-bye to Chase. Chase is a good looking boy.

Chase is on the football team in the fall, wrestles in the winter, plays baseball in the spring, and then throughout the summer travels to wrestling tournaments. Dave had told me that Chase has high hopes of wrestling in college.

The closer Adin gets to us, the more I can see that she doesn't look as hostile anymore. Perhaps annoyed, but not as erratic and explosive as when she ran out the front door. I was afraid that when we finally approached her she would be a wreck. I just didn't know what kind of a wreck—would she be angry or scared? Right now, she seems as though her outburst with Marge had never taken place.

I can let this go right now, especially if it will make the situation easier. I'll just have to be patient and let God figure this out in His timing instead of trying to control the outcome.

God is really stretching me right now with letting go of control. Automatically, I am reminded of a verse from my devotions this morning in Philippians that spoke to me about how God will continue working on all of us. Oh my, but God is going to work on me in giving up control.

"Spying on me?" Adin says, walking up the steps onto the porch.

"Not at all, we were just worried about you," I start, my voice high, trying to defend myself, but realize that her usual sarcasm is lacking, and she sounds as if she might even be teasing.

"Should we be?" Dave teases back. "That Harper kid is one hot dude, huh?"

Adin's eyes pop out, shocked at Dave's comment.

"Who? Oh, you mean Chase. It's not like that. We have Literature together, and I never apologized to him for falling on him at that wrestling tournament." Her words come out much too rushed.

The fact that she is even explaining herself at all only makes her interest in him more obvious to me. Dave starts making kissing noises behind her when we follow her inside.

CHAPTER 10

The Power of Prayer

<u>*Dave*</u>

Sighing, I throw off the covers and sit up in bed. I focus my eyes to where Joan lay still asleep, her hands tucked up under the side of her face. Stretching my view around her, I find where the alarm clock sits comfortably: three thirty in the morning. I am not going to want to get out of bed when that thing goes off.

I know what this is. I remember how this burden feels, remember from Sara and then Matt. I'm not inconvenienced in any way, just resistant so early in the morning.

Okay, Lord, okay, I'm up.

I rub what little sleep I have out of my eyes and try to clear my mind. My elbows reflexively rest on my thighs as I hold my head in my hands. I love this part. I love how God throws his arm across my shoulders, and we walk back in time, sifting through the memories of life. I recall immediately the day that Joan and I decided we wanted to become foster parents.

We were sitting on the back porch swing at her parents' house watching the sunset. Joan had just taken yet another failed pregnancy test, and her eyes were still red and puffy from crying. I was so confused at why the Lord didn't bless us with a family. We had never considered that this would take much effort.

The sting was so near that I was actually still a little hurt and, as a result, angry with God. Joan and I had done our part, traveling from specialist to specialist trying this and that whether it made logical sense at all. I felt like a failure simply because I couldn't give my wife what she so desperately wanted, and I was deflated at the possibility of that changing.

We sat there quiet for a while before she started talking about some woman who had come into the church that morning to meet the Youth Pastor. At that time, Joan was the church secretary. The woman had explained to Joan that she and her husband were foster parents to a teenage boy, and they thought that involving him in a youth group would help with this new transition in his life.

I didn't understand at the time where Joan was going with this story but listened anyway. I figured that if dodging the elephant in the room would help, then, I was happy to oblige. She continued telling me how the woman gave her all kinds of details and such about the Pennsylvania foster system and how they were always looking for stable families to open up their homes to hurt kids.

Then, out of nowhere, Joan tells me that she had made a deal with God. If she got another negative pregnancy test, she was going to accept that it was not in His will for her to have kids. I was in full protest mode right away, feeling that somehow admitting that out loud seemed the same as admitting failure.

She had held up her hand to quiet me, and when I did finally shut my mouth, she said that she was going to call Social Services the next day and research what it entailed to become foster parents. I was speechless. I could not even comprehend the magnitude this decision would have on our lives.

Looking back on that day now, I can see God sitting between us on that porch swing with each of his arms securely wrapped around us, smiling so huge at this new twist in our lives. This is Joan's way of dealing with anything in life: she dreams bigger and moves forward.

I look over at her sleeping and feel my heart soften. I love my wife so much.

Two weeks later we were signed up for the necessary classes and background checks it took to become foster parents. We had all kinds of people in and out of our house to ensure its safety as well as meetings with a psychiatrist determining that, in fact, we are sane people. Who would have ever guessed?

Six months after Joan's initial research, we became licensed foster parents. It had gone so quickly that I couldn't believe this meant we would have a kid soon, and we did. I smile remembering how nervous Joan and I were when Marge Ann called us to ask if we would be interested in fostering a thirteen year-old girl.

A few days before Marge called us, Sara's mom had passed away from stage four breast cancer, a battle that she had been fighting for two years. Marge had explained that Sara could be put in a group home for a while if we weren't ready, but we had said no.

The next day Joan went out to the book store and bought what I'm sure was every book ever written on a child losing a parent. I love that about her too: her willingness to search the ends of the world for a solution. Of course she had argued that she wanted to be prepared to help Sara, but I knew that this is her way of caring.

Looking back, I can see God preparing us for this adventure of foster parenting through Sara. She was our first kid and was by far the easiest we've had. Her mom had been a great mom, loving Sara in every way imaginable. Sara's hurt came from watching such a wonderful woman die before her young eyes.

However, Sara did let Joan and I love on her from the beginning. She didn't push us away in rebellion but willingly let us put our arms around her and lift her up when the waves of life seemed to try to hold her down. I wipe away a tear as it streams down. Over time Sara accepted that the why to her mother's death would not be answered in this life.

After Sara had graduated at Central High, she went on to Wilmington, North Carolina, where she attended The University of

North Carolina. She majored in Marine Biology and currently works for a company in New Jersey that protects marine habitats.

It makes me want to roll with laughter remembering her the first time as she tried to get on her scuba gear at the YMCA. In typical Sara style, she pretended that my annoying teasing didn't exist. What an amazing girl.

After Sara moved out, our house remained empty until that October when Ms. Ann called again. This time she had a boy who was fourteen and in the ninth grade. His father couldn't shake a deep depression since his wife, the boy's mother, had passed away two years prior.

A drunk driver had hit her head on while she was driving up a steep incline; she never had a chance. Matt says he can remember the police officer standing at their front door telling his father that there was absolutely no time for her to have swerved out of the way because she was hit at the very top.

She had gone out to get milk from a gas station right around the corner from their house and never returned. Matt's dad sunk into a deep depression, forgetting all about his only son, whose life was ripped to shreds as well. There was much more emotional damage with Matt because of the length of time that Matt had endured the emotional abuse. He didn't know how to handle any physical contact for quite a while.

There were many nights that I cried out to God on behalf of that boy, pouring out my own hurt every time Matt flinched when I got near him. During the first year he lived with us, the only external progress anyone would have noticed would have been his weight gain. He must have put on fifty-five pounds, and only then did he look like a skinny teenager.

It was Matt who taught Joan and me the power of prayer. We lived on our knees that year. It was a humbling experience to see God work in that boy through circumstances and other people. We were overjoyed to be on the sidelines watching.

Another tear rolls down when I remember the first time Matt and I went out into the backyard and threw an old baseball around.

I had been watching him from the glass door in the kitchen. He just kept pounding the baseball into his mitt like he was waiting for me to join him. I ran out to the garage in lightning speed, spilling over two bins until I found my own mitt and tried to appear calm as I opened the back door.

"Mind if I play catch with you?" I had asked casually.

His face had gotten really serious, like he knew that he saying yes would be life altering. With a boldness that he had not shown before, he nodded his head strongly and tossed me the ball.

Every day after school from then on we talked baseball. He loved to dissect Nolan Ryan's pitching skills and thus began our love for the game. I sigh and grab my heart realizing how much I miss Matt now that he's away at college.

Lord, you have taken me so far. Sara and Matt taught me so much, and now I know you have another lesson for me through Adin. Sara taught me how to love despite my questions, and Matt taught me the power of prayer on a person's life.

So far I have been awed at the amount of strength Adin has. I know you have me up tonight to lift her up to you. I don't know what is about to take place, but I pray your hand is upon it. I pray that Adin will grow closer to you.

Thank you for bringing a boy like Chase Harper into her life, a boy who already knows who you are. I pray that you will give Chase wisdom as he and Adin become friends. Thank you for loving me enough to keep stretching me. Oh, and Lord, let me sleep like a ton of bricks for the rest of the night. In Jesus's name I pray, Amen.

CHAPTER 11

Weight Training Like a Pro

Adin

Turning to the left, I check out my profile in the bathroom mirror, brushing the front of my hair to one side and then the other to see which side compliments me best. Angling my head, I smile at my reflection.

Is this how I should tilt my head talking with Chase?

My heart does a back flip just thinking about him. In my mind, I can see him smiling at me. This is so weird. I have never liked a guy like this before. There have been plenty of guys that I thought were cute but none that made me act like this. Just thinking about him makes it hard to breathe.

I wipe my sweaty palms on the front of my jeans and apply some lip gloss. Puckering my lips to the mirror, I wish myself luck and head down the stairs to the kitchen. Dave is telling Joan about a wrestling match that he'll be running the score board for at the school tonight and not to save him a seat at dinner.

"Hey," I add to the conversation when they both glance towards me.

Once seated I wait for Dave to fill my plate with scrambled eggs and sausage. I take a long drink from my glass of orange juice, which is sitting at my spot waiting for me.

"I think I'm going to walk to school today," I say and then quickly fill my mouth with food.

Joan and Dave give each other a quick look before Joan turns to me, "Are you sure you know the way?"

After a big swallow, I reply, "I turn left out the driveway and walk for a really long time, and then the school will be on my left. I'm pretty sure I can handle it."

Joan smiles at my ever ready sarcasm and pats my shoulder. I don't want to let on that I'm walking in hopes of running into Chase. I wish I knew something to talk about with him. My stomach flutters nervously thinking about walking beside him. I could actually brush up next to him. Without thinking, I hop down from the island.

"Are you okay?" Dave asks, his eyebrows raised in concern.

"Yeah, why?" I rush in reply, nervously looping my hands together in front of my body.

"You didn't eat much of your breakfast." He points to the mostly full plate of food left at my spot.

"Oh, I'm not that hungry. Thanks though." The answer spilling from my mouth without thought.

Coming up with an excuse with mush for a brain isn't likely, so I grab my book bag off the floor and head for the front door. Once outside, I run my hands through my hair and try to look as if I'm not staring at Chase's house while I walk down my driveway.

Would he have already left? I should have thought this through better. I don't want to leave before him, but if he's already left, then I'd better start walking fast. How would I ask him what time he leaves for school? That would be a hilarious conversation starter! I wish I would have paid more attention to the clock in Joan's car when I saw him walking to school yesterday. It was then that I realized I could walk too, and you know, if we wound up connecting on our way, that would be awesome.

Slowly, I walk past his driveway, figuring that if he is indeed inside his house still, he would have time to look out his front window and see me passing. I continue to walk slowly down the sidewalk in the direction of the school, just in case he needs some time to catch up with me.

After five minutes, I look at my watch and decide it is time to change to plan B and walk faster. I must have missed him. Well, this is just great. I am an idiot, and I have no idea what I'm doing. Frustrated, I begin to power walk up a steep hill. I'm going to have pit stains by the time I get to school. That's going to be real attractive.

Once I reach the top of the incline, I notice other kids walking in the same direction. I hang back from the groups that are clearly together, not wanting to appear like I'm with any of them.

I shake my head in defeat and trudge on. When I walk through the front doors of the school, I take a look around but still don't see Chase. Walking to my locker, I overhear a group of girls laughing together loudly.

"Shut up!" I want to shout at them. Why does their happiness bother me so much? Oh yeah, that's right, because I'm not. After I get out my Geometry and AP Biology book, I slam my locker.

I slap my forehead, a little too hard, remembering that today I would be taking my fitness class for the first time. I can't believe that I voluntarily signed up to be tortured. Can this day possibly get any worse? I lightly run my fingertip across the tender area of my forehead and hope that I didn't bruise myself.

Originally, Principal Cravet was letting me hang out in the library during third period because I needed a physical from the school nurse before I could participate in fitness. I had shown up to Nurse Windsor on Friday not really understanding what a school physical would entail.

Thankfully, she just checked my temperature, height, weight, and blood pressure. Then she signed something in my ever growing file and told me everything checked out. I was asked to kindly leave a sample in the bathroom before returning to class.

After getting writer's cramp in Geometry from Mr. Torther's practice problems and then listening to a boring lesson on the anatomy of a baby pig in AP Biology, I find myself changing into the mandatory Central High gym clothes.

Step right up boys and girls and you too can wear this lovely gray t-shirt matched with black sports shorts.

Grinding my teeth, I walk out of the girl's locker room, down the hallway, past the boy's locker room, and turn left into the weight room. My face falls when the door closes behind me. I am met by a room full of boys.

Oh crap, what have I done?

The room goes silent. Twenty sets of male eyes look at me with expectation. What am I supposed to say? My eyes dart around the room looking for an escape. I feel a hand on my shoulder. An older gentleman clears his throat.

"Gentleman, this is Adin Taylor. She is new to the school and has dared to enter this man cave. Now, partner up with someone and grab your sheets." Everyone moves in the direction of a filing cabinet located in the back corner of the weight room.

With his hand on my shoulder, the teacher directs me to the back of the room where a desk hides in a corner. He takes a seat and starts pulling papers out of the bottom drawer.

"I can't remember a girl ever signing up for this class before. Did you take weight training in your last school?" he asks absentmindedly, while searching through his folders.

"I thought this class was fitness, you know, like gym." I answer.

He stops what he's doing to gift me with an annoyed countenance. "You didn't read the course description?"

"I really didn't have much time. I just assumed," I retaliate defensively. Some latent anger from my morning spills over into this moment.

This guy's facial expressions are getting on my nerves. I'm pretty sure his snorts of indignation can be heard outside the classroom. I don't like this situation any more than he does.

Just give me whatever it is you've got for me and leave me alone.

"Okay, well, it's done now. Fitness is gaining the knowledge of the different exercises you can do with free weights and also knowledge pertaining to the different machines we have here in the weight training center." He explains, pointing around the weight room.

He continues to gesture around the room with his free hand. "You will be quizzed at the end of every two weeks on different exercises for different parts of your body. For instance, a dumbbell curl will increase the strength in your bicep, dips work on your triceps. Do you understand?"

"Got it." I clip, merely wanting to get as far away from this guy as possible.

I don't deal well with people who talk down to me and right now this guy is teetering on a ten for my hate scale. If I could burn him with my eyes, he would be a community bon-fire right now. Turning sharply on my heel, I walk away.

I cross to the other side of the fitness room, figuring that whatever I try out today will have to be far away from him. With my hands on my hips, I size up the pull up bar that is in front of me. I never realized how daunting a steel bar attached to a wall can be.

There is a light tap on my shoulder. I swear if this teacher has another stupid comment to make, I will have to rip this bar off the wall and shove it down his throat. I turn slowly to ensure that he understands how annoyed I am by his presence, scowling just to be sure my mood isn't misunderstood.

I look up into the ocean blue eyes of Chase Harper. How does he do that? He's holding out his hand to me, and I glance down to see that it's full of papers. I use my eyes to question what he's doing, to which he responds.

"I think you forgot these on Mr. Roads desk."

"Not really," I retort at little too harsh, "that guy is a jerk." Chase puts his hand on his mouth in an effort to hide a smirk.

"Okay, well, these are yours. Basically, these papers explain the different weights that are in this weight room and how you can best use them depending on which body part you're working on." He sifts through the papers, so I lean in to see what he's got.

"This paper," he pulls out some spreadsheet, "is where you write down which exercise you perform. Next to the exercise, you write down the amount of weight you use."

He looks up at me to make sure that I understand what he's saying, forcing me to take a step backwards. I can barely hear him talking over the thundering in my ears. My lips have gone dry, and I try to lick over them quickly, not wanting him to see how nervous I've gotten.

"We can be partners for a few weeks until you get the hang of it," he offers.

I nod my head yes right away. "That would be great. Thanks."

Adin

I wake up and stretch out my entire body as long as I can. I keep my upper body turned to one side, while simultaneously moving my legs in the opposite direction, stretching out my back as much as possible. Who knew that weight training hurt so much? Definitely not me! I curl my toes up and down trying to get the ache out of my calves.

Chase has been having too much fun showing me the ropes in fitness class. Having him so close the last few weeks has also been emotionally exhausting. He is the only person that my sarcasm is lost on. I hear myself speak around him and feel stupid. He must think I'm socially awkward; everything I say around him comes out wrong.

I sit up and stretch my hands high over my head. I try to remember the other stretches that I covertly memorized off of the poster hanging just inside the weight room. I didn't want to seem like I cared at the time, but stretching out every morning makes moving any body part at all much easier.

Dave made a comment yesterday to Joan that I am getting cut. I'm guessing that's athletic lingo for getting bigger muscles. At least the guys in my class aren't so interested in watching me every time I touch a dumbbell anymore. It was embarrassing knowing the weirdness in the class was due to my presence.

Chase has been considerate enough to explain every exercise we have done in full detail, like it was just us passing the time with any conversation. He has no idea how helpful all the information is to me.

I have never lifted weights before, and this class would have to be the one that I've invested most of my brain power in trying to get right.

Crazy enough, Mr. Road's quizzes are oral. He just walks up to a person while they are training, and then asks a simple question like, "What is one possible move to work your lower back?" That was it. Quiz over.

Chase had watched me like a hawk when Mr. Road had approached me the first time, like this was also a test for him. He had given me a sideways grin when Mr. Road walked away shaking his head in amazement at my perfect, 100 percent reply. It felt good to know that I had made Chase proud.

It takes me longer to get dressed in the morning. The sheer pain of lifting my hands over my head still lingers. I decide to go out on a limb and wear the dress that Joan had hung in my closet a few weeks ago. Every day it hangs there mocking me, insinuating I am not brave enough to at least try it on.

After a few nights of feeling ridiculous over being made fun by a piece of fabric, I did try it on, and soon after was astonished at how well it fit. I think I've figured out Joan's day job: she's a personal shopper.

I spin around in a circle to see the bottom of the dress lift a little with the air blowing around it. It is a deep green silk dress that has short sleeves with creases around them. The scoop neck also has pleats that angle in towards the waist line. At the waist is another piece of green silk fabric that appears to be like a belt. Then the bottom of the dress just flows down.

It is modern enough to not seem too dressy to wear to school. I make the decision to be bold this morning. I have to know if Chase is at least interested in me. I even put on some of the iridescent green eye shadow that I had found in one of the multi-color compacts that I have from Joan's original make-up shopping spree.

Tiptoeing carefully down the stairs, I don't know what to expect when Joan and Dave will see me. On one hand, I want them to look at me with big smiles, gushing over my new look, but on the other, I don't want too big of deal made over me simply dressing it up a little.

At the bottom of the stairs, I debate whether or not to just head out the front door without saying anything. Just then Dave rounds the corner of the kitchen, catching a glimpse of me. I can tell by the way his eyes open big and then the grin on his face that my appearance is above par.

All of the sudden I feel self-conscious; this really isn't my style. I turn to run up the stairs and change but he's on to me and runs to block the stairs.

"Don't change. You look great." He directs me to the kitchen where Joan is sitting at the island sipping a cup of coffee.

"Joan, look at Adin," he commands excitedly.

Joan turns around quickly and her eyes light up, "You look amazing!" She jumps down from her barstool and gives me a tight hug. Holding on to me still, she pulls me back from her and checks me over.

"I'm so glad you decided to wear these ballet flats, they look great with this dress."

I nod my head in agreement, not wanting to give away that just a few minutes ago I was thinking the same thing.

"Look, I got to go. I'm going to be late for school," I mumble, pulling away from her.

"You're not getting away without eating something this morning," Dave argues.

Stepping into the kitchen, he pulls something out of the oven. I smell cinnamon mixed with apple. He baked muffins. Maybe Dave missed his calling for the culinary arts. I give him a pursed smile while he cuts one out of the muffin tin, and, placing it in a paper towel, hands it to me.

"Something warm to add to your walk this morning." He bows, almost falling over in his usual over-the-top theatrics.

"Uh, thanks," I say, a little uncomfortable at all the fuss that's been made over me.

I take this as my cue to leave, and let myself out the front door. Looking up to the sky, the sun is shining brilliantly overhead. I laugh to myself, reveling in the giddiness I feel, like I just might be a magnet for something good.

Keeping my eyes averted downward while I walk, I don't notice that someone is trailing me until I feel someone tug on my back pack. My first inclination is to run. My body tenses up and my throat constricts while I try to quickly formulate an exit plan.

"Sorry, I didn't mean to scare you," Chase hesitates.

"You didn't," I fumble, realizing that it's only the guy I've been trying to walk with for weeks.

Does he notice the dress?

Part of me wishes that he understands what a sacrifice I am making wearing this for him, hoping in some small way that it would make him look at me more.

I don't realize that my eyes are closed until I feel myself opening them to look at him. I laugh awkwardly and continue in the direction of the school. He keeps in step beside me, walking silently until we reach the bottom of the hill.

"You look really nice today," he says quietly.

There it is, the only opinion that my heart needs. I can feel myself lighten and lift with happiness at a job well done. Turning, I reward him with a huge, genuine smile.

He blushes a little and puts his hands in his pockets. It would be nice if he felt the electricity that runs between us every time we stand within a foot of one another. I laugh at the pained look on his face when we both start trudging up the hill.

"Your legs don't hurt, do they?" I question sarcastically.

He smiles with all his boyish charm and returns, "What do you think? You actually look like you're handling this pretty well. What's your secret?"

"Lots and lots and lots of stretching." I say, looking around, even though no one else is walking with us, and cup my hand next to my mouth to whisper towards him.

"Who knew?" he jokes in a serious tone.

Over the next few minutes we travel together quietly. I like the silence that we are capable of putting between us while we are near each other. We don't have to talk to enjoy each other's company.

I have a million questions to ask Chase, and one day at a time, I hope I live here long enough to learn more about him. He holds the door open for me as we both enter the school together. I notice a lot of heads turning when we walk down the hall.

At first I assume it is the sheer fact that we are together, but then, comprehending the look I see in too many of the boys' eyes, I begin to understand it is my appearance.

Why did I put myself in this situation?

Hyperventilation is not the way to blend in. My brain can only comprehend fear. My skin feels like someone is running lit matches all over it. A random guy whistles at me in passing, but his face is a blur—just like every other face spinning slowly near me. My breath starts coming in spurts. Chase's worried gaze holds mine.

"What's happening?" he whispers.

I'm going to cry, that's what's happening.

I'm an idiot. All I thought of was testing Chase's reaction to my new style. I never realized that I would get unwanted attention from anyone else.

"What do you mean," I finally speak, or squeak, but, thankfully, words do come out.

"You look really worried. What's going on?" He has such a reassuring voice, like no matter how big my problems are he is capable enough to protect me.

I give him a tight smile in an effort to appear okay.

"I just remembered I forgot to do my um, Biology homework, and I know I won't have enough time to get it done in homeroom. Sorry, didn't mean to freak you out or anything." I can tell by his eyes that he doesn't buy what I'm selling, but I don't care. It says a lot about his patience level that he doesn't push me any further.

He waits for me at my locker while I put away some books and get out my Geometry Binder. While my locker door offers a sense of privacy, I deep breathe to calm my nerves. I shut the locker slowly, feeling his arm brush against mine when he moves closer to me, letting a few guys pass by in the hallway.

"Way to go Harper," some jerk comments, raising his eyebrows up and down.

Chase smiles at them but doesn't say anything. I don't really know how to take his lack of a response until I see the calm look on his face.

I get it. He's letting it go so that they don't have anything to draw the situation out any more than it already has been. He's a really smart guy.

He walks me to homeroom and then slides into his own across the hallway. I stand in the doorway for a minute, wanting to remember what it feels like to not be scared around a boy.

CHAPTER 12

Where Two or More are Gathered

Joan

"This was such a good idea Kami. We haven't caught up in forever," I say, while sitting in Kami's kitchen, drinking a cup of caramel tea. She smiles at me, pouring cream into her own cup.

"I have missed our conversations," I realize and then continue, "What have you been up to?"

"I just got back Sunday night from taking the girls to a youth conference. I'm so glad that our church was able to fundraise enough money for all the girls who went. Three girls who just started coming to youth group made a decision to accept Jesus Saturday night." She has tears in her eyes relating the story back to me.

I cherish how transparent Kami is with her emotions. She genuinely feels each of the teens' pain.

"I wish that Adin was ready for something like that. Dave and I haven't urged her to start coming to church yet. We wanted to earn some of her trust before we ask anything of her."

We don't want her to feel that church is just another rule in our home. I admit though, that it is becoming harder to leave on Sunday morning knowing she is upstairs sleeping."

"I wish that we could open other people's ears to God's voice. You and I know that God has sovereignly placed her in Dave's and my household for her to have the opportunity to be in his presence. I just get confused sometimes in how I am supposed to do that. I find myself second guessing everything that concerns her."

I stop to collect my thoughts, leaning in to Kami, awaiting her insight. She continues to look down at her tea while stirring it slowly. She looks up at me with compassion in her eyes and nods her head in agreement.

"I know too well what you mean about hearing the voice of God for someone else. There are so many people like that in my life that I catch myself wishing God would yank away their free will. Each time, God reminds me that He doesn't want us to be robots. He wants us to want him on our own, without having to be made to do it."

"Chase came in the other night and told Ben and I that he wanted us to start praying for Adin. He didn't have any details for us when we asked if there was anything specific. He said just to pray for her to have an open heart to the work that God was doing in her life," Kami shares.

"I am relieved to know that she is spending time with Chase. I've been praying that he might be an open door to Adin wanting to come to church," I admit.

"Chase hasn't mentioned anything else about her, but you know how great boys communicate, especially teenage boys with their mothers," Kami says.

We both laugh, reminiscing over trying to decode Matt's and Corbin's mannerisms. On the whole, they were very good boys, but both had a streak of orneriness that got them into trouble occasionally.

They had loved to perform pranks: the more outrageous the better. I remind Kami of the Sunday morning following Halloween the boys' senior year of high school. Pastor Tim had looked so serious when he had given an apology to the congregation that morning for running late. Then, with a much straighter face than I could have ever mustered, he explained that he had awaken to a yard with thousands of plastic forks sticking out of the ground.

Immediately, Kami and I had turned around to evaluate Matt's and Corbin's expressions. They appeared innocent enough, but Kami turned Corbin's hands over to discover grass stains.

"Please pray for Dave and I, that God would give us wisdom in how to go about speaking to Adin about church. I sense that God wants me to start making this a priority."

"You know I will," Kami grabs my hand across the table, "I'm also going to ask Chase about what his thoughts are in inviting Adin to come to youth group. Maybe they've become close enough that she would come check it out simply because he invites her."

"That would be perfect. Thank you so much," I say, thanking God for the blessing of a good friend.

Adin

With my head down on my elbow, I continue to use my orange colored pencil to color my calligraphy poster. My "Characteristic" poster is due tomorrow, and it has taken me staying after school the last week to be near finishing.

Initially, I had decided to skip over figuring out words that best described me, and instead, concentrated on measuring and drawing the lines on my poster board. Once that was finished, I got the girl who sits next to me in class to draw my silhouette out while I stood completely still in front of the white board with a light shone on me.

After all that, I was left to sit and labor over the words. For a solid week, I would show up and spend the entire class digging through the dictionary, adding a word here and there.

Mrs. Hollander gave me my space until the week that the project was due, and then she asked me to meet her after school. I had shown up with a sheepish look but ever ready for her to be upset with me.

Amazingly enough, she had welcomed me with a hug and then proceeded to sit down beside me with a dictionary of her own. My heart got stuck in my throat when I allowed myself to understand her intentions. Over the following three days, we debated words. She felt that I was strong-willed, brilliant, vivacious, and even fierce.

Taking in her perspective, I felt that I was invisible, insignificant, and cowardly. Going over these characteristics would have to be the most transparent I've ever allowed myself to be with any person.

She didn't make too much out of my misgivings though, just erased my demeaning words from the paper and replaced them with more of her own. All of the sudden, I saw myself penning beautiful, original, honest, and competitive. I openly wiped the tears away from my eyes while I wrote, not trying to hide the change that was taking place in myself.

Once I got to the portion of the project where I started penning the words, she sat at her desk reading. It wasn't until today that I took time to notice what book she held: a Bible.

Mrs. Hollander believes in God. I glance at her quickly while coloring the last corner of my silhouette, wondering how it is that she can fall asleep sitting up.

I hold my hand over my mouth, quietly laughing, thinking of tiptoeing up beside her desk and loudly placing my poster in front of her.

Confusion collides with my prank, putting the brakes on my tip-toe act when I catch her lips moving. She's praying? I don't want to think too hard about it. What does it matter?

I can't make today fall into my black and white categories, and it's blowing my mind that I will have to accept a little gray. Otherwise, I have to dislike Mrs. Hollander, and I just can't do that.

I remember when my Mom took me into a church service over one holiday season. It was a really posh church located near a rich neighborhood uptown. We sat all the way in the back and watched a play about the birth of Jesus.

I envied all the boys and girls in their shiny costumes. I kept tugging on my mom's jacket, trying to get her attention to show her the angel costume. I knew right then that if anyone ever got me a beautiful, shiny angel costume, they would be my hero.

Annoyed with me, she just kept swatting my hand away. After

the show my mom dragged me up the aisle to the front pew. She shoved me in front of some tall man who was all dressed up with a bright red tie.

I don't remember his face exactly, but his black and white dress shoes were intriguing. I remember that there was a petite woman with a pinched face and two twin boys in matching suits that sat beside him. Nothing in my life prepared me for what my mother said next.

"Meet your daughter, Stewart Hughes." There was such an intense hate emanating from my mom; my body instinctually hunched in on itself for protection.

I don't know why, but I felt ashamed. Without hesitation, he looked over to the woman beside him, explaining that he didn't know what my mother was talking about, that quite obviously she had the wrong man and was just another crack whore from the streets.

It didn't help my mother any to fly into one of her drunken rants about needing money to support his kid, and if he didn't want his perfect family to know about us, then he should've stayed home with his family in the first place.

Everyone in the church was staring at her and, for that matter, me. I was scared and began to cry. This did not help the situation. My mother wrenched my arm so tightly, flinging me in front of her, shaking me to the point my jaw hurt, that my body lost all control, and I wet myself. There is not a word in the English language that can describe the humiliation radiating off of me in that moment. I bit my lip so hard, begging the universe to swallow me whole, that I never tasted the copper blood as it dripped below.

Not one person in that church saved me that night. They let her drag me out the same way we had entered. In my eight year old mind, I knew that if there were good people in the world, they were supposed to be in church.

For whatever reason, God seemed fit to not have any decency in the world available that night. My hatred and anger was kindled that Christmas. I did get one present that year: the beginnings of a Hulk-sized anger.

Dave

"I'll be right there to help you guys roll up the mats," I tell two of the junior varsity boys on the wrestling team. Coach Floyd always has the JV team clean up the wrestling room, his theory being that you work your way up to Varsity and receive certain privileges.

I laugh to myself, hearing some of the boys in the locker room rolling up their towels and belting each other with them. Pushing out of my seat, I plan on checking on the boys to make sure it doesn't get too rowdy.

My office sits in between the girl's and boy's locker rooms down a hall that runs parallel with the gym. After exiting my office, I make a quick left into the boy's locker room, eyeing up the possibilities. Some of the boy's see me coming and immediately jump out of the way. I notice Chase Harper pulling a shirt over his head.

"Hey, Chase, can I talk with you once you're done here?" I ask.

A few boys start making booing noises, using a tone insinuating Chase is in trouble. I put my hands up in surrender and walk backwards out the door.

After rolling up the mats in the gym, I return to my office to find Chase leaned up against the door. He gives me a small grin but stay's quiet.

"How's your season going?" I start, trying to ease the stress obvious on his face.

"Well enough," he starts, "I've only lost one match, and it was close. I'll see that guy at States though, and this time I'll be ready."

"Good for you," I encourage, clearly impressed with his confidence. "And how are you doing in your classes?"

"Same I guess; nothing too hard." He looks a little confused at my questions. He's a smart kid. I'm sure he knows I'm just being polite until I get to the point.

"I noticed you and Adin are friends?" I begin.

"Yes sir," he answers, standing up straighter.

I try not to smile too big.

"I'm glad. Your brother Corbin was Matt's best friend through high school, and I think it's great that you and Adin are friends too. I just want you to be careful with her; she's been through a lot the last few years. She really could use a good friend, if you know what I mean?"

I look up, making direct eye contact to see if he understands my point, and then noticing him nodding his head, I continue, "I guess I'm hoping that eventually she will talk to you about it, and maybe you can help her."

Again, I take a hard look at Chase, sizing him up to see if he's up to this kind of responsibility. There is compassion in his eyes, and I know God has purpose for their friendship.

"I think that I can trust you to be a shoulder for her when she is ready to deal with this, so I want to thank you for that now. Also, I was hoping that maybe you could invite her to youth group soon," I say, getting all of my points made in succession.

"I've been thinking about how to do that. My mom also mentioned that it would be a good idea; I just don't want to seem rehearsed. I'm praying for God's timing." It's clear that Chase has already put thought into this too.

"I appreciate that, Chase," I say, standing and putting my hand out to shake his.

"Do you mind if we pray?" I ask.

"Not at all; please do. Sir, just so you know, I've been praying for Adin too." Chase answers.

I put my hand on Chase's shoulder and close my eyes, *"Lord, Chase and I come together today on behalf of Adin. Father, you tell us that where two or more are gathered in your name that you will be there also. We want you here right now, Lord.*

We need your wisdom and guidance to get Adin from where she stands now: guarded, to being open to the possibility of entering your house. Father, we know you want her to know you, and accept you into her heart. We also know that you have placed us in her life as instruments for this purpose. Now we need you to show us the path to lead her there.

Thank you so much for her friendship with Chase. I pray that you would guide this amazing young man and speak through him to her. In Jesus's name we pray, Amen.

CHAPTER 13

Single-Leg Takedown

Adin

I close Mrs. Hollander's door behind me. The school seems eerie when the day is over. The hallways are too dark and the silence makes me think that I'm hearing noises that aren't there.

I walk slowly down the main hallway, brushing up against the side of the windows that look out into the courtyard. My heart rises and falls like a roller coaster when I pass through each misshaped shadow. I stop, placing my forehead against the cold glass of the courtyard window.

Why are some Christian people genuinely nice, and others are so completely fake? How can God create both?

I turn my hot cheek against the cool glass and close my eyes. I'm a pretty good person. Does this mean that I'm on God's side? I jerk instantly when I feel some one pick up a piece of hair framing my face.

"Anybody home?" Keith Lewis, a.k.a Random-Stalker guy from Literature class, asks me, standing much too close to my face.

I take a few steps back. "Excuse me?" I counter, using a flippant tone.

"Where were you just then? I've been watching you stand here for like five minutes. You seemed lost." He keeps rolling his eyes from my face to my chest. He doesn't really care about me so much as my body.

What a creep.

I don't like how he always seems to be watching me either.

"None of your business," I answer curtly, pushing away from the window to walk around him.

His smile gets bigger.

This guy is such an idiot. Does he actually think that I'm flirting right now? I wonder what idiot code is for "Get lost."?

He reaches through the distance that I've purposely placed between us and grabs both of my hands in his, pressing his body up against mine.

"Come on, don't be that way. You can make it my business and then I can make it all better." His voice muffled in my hair.

My teeth begin to clack against one another when I feel his hot breath burn across the top of my right ear.

My mind rings with alarm bells. He has just smashed my panic button. The back of my throat hurts from breathing in and out too quickly. My vision is dotted with black specks and my hands begin to shake. There is a coldness inside of me that is freezing up my brain. I feel his smile growing bigger when his cheek clenches against my skull. He presses in tighter to me, mistaking my hyperventilation for acceptance.

Without thinking, I twist my hands out of his, drop down to my left knee, and push into him the way Chase did out on his driveway. I use my shoulder to shove into his body, bringing my right arm up between his legs, leaving him dangling above my head. I take a much needed deep breath, and then drop him onto the marble floor and step back.

What was that!?

I catch him staring at me, mouth open wide in disbelief. Before I can figure out what just happened, I turn to run away but am stopped by the footsteps running towards me. Chase pulls me towards him, taking a defensive pose in front of me.

"What did you think you were doing, Lewis?" Chase demands, an anger in his voice that I would have never guessed he had in him.

"What do you think?" Keith jumps to his feet, his surprised expression now hidden.

"Adin doesn't like you. Stay away from her." Although his voice is hard as stone, his arms stay softly around me.

"Or what? Do you think you can fight me, huh?" Keith starts jumping around like he's in a boxing ring.

"Fighting me ain't like wrestling out there on your little mat, you gotta be a man to handle this." His chest puffs out, ready for a confrontation.

Chase looks Keith up and down in disgust, leading me away.

"That's right, run! You'd better run if you know what's good for you. I was just about done with her anyway." I hear Keith laughing more loudly than necessary as we make our way out the front doors of the school.

My teeth start chattering again; too soon, my entire body begins to vibrate. I take a few slow, deep breaths in an effort to calm down.

I do not want Chase to think I'm one of those dramatic girls that makes everything bigger than necessary. I peek at him from under my eyelashes, trying to gage his mood.

"Thanks." I say, wanting with every fiber of my being to just be a normal, average girl.

He stops walking, whipping his head around to look at me. He looks as if he wants to say something but stops. I notice the hesitation in his eyes before he speaks.

"Do you realize what you did back there?" he asks, the last word raising an octave.

"I'm pretty sure I stood there like a paralyzed moron until you came running in, saving the day. We were just together in there weren't we?" I raise my eyebrows in an effort to lighten the mood.

"Yes, we were," he continues, "and you just picked up a boy

over your head, who is at least twice the size of you. It was kind of amazing." A small smile forms on his face.

"It must have been an adrenaline thing. I didn't really know what I was doing." I try to explain.

"You've practiced doing a single leg takedown. Haven't you?" Chase asks.

"I don't know what you're talking about." I evade, really not wanting to admit to anything.

"Yes, you do." His statement is solid truth.

I don't want to lie to Chase.

I clear my throat, delaying the impossible; then, looking down at my feet, confess, "Yes, I have been practicing. I don't really know why I do it. One day I got down in that fighting stance that you do, and watching myself in the mirror, I mimicked what you did to me in the driveway."

My heart feels like it is going to beat out of my chest. I'm too embarrassed to look at him. His hand comes under my chin, lifting my face level with his own, and I hold my breath. I find myself staring into the clearest, most pure blue eyes in the universe.

He holds my gaze steadily, and after a short pause, says quietly, "You are amazing."

I could melt right this minute. He releases my chin gently, and we resume walking towards home. We reach his driveway first, slowing up for his departure, when he says, "I was wondering if you have plans on Friday night?"

Surprised at his question, I answer quickly, "Nothing, why?"

"I was wondering if you would want to come somewhere with me."

"Yeah, sure." I respond, excited that this is finally happening.

"Do you want to know where?" he asks cautiously.

"No, I don't really care. What time?" I ask.

"I'll come over and get you around 6:30. Would that be okay?"

"Great," I reply. I turn towards my driveway to go home. Once inside, I shut the door and jump up and down. I can't believe that Chase Harper just asked me out on a date!

CHAPTER 14

First Date

<u>*Adin*</u>

Dave and Joan are sitting downstairs in the living room watching television when Chase knocks on the door. I have been planted at the top of the stairs for the past 15 minutes, anxious for his arrival.

It didn't take me long to pick out something to wear because Joan is phenomenal at finding clothes to fit my style. Tonight I put on a pair of black dress pants with a hot pink turtleneck. The hot pink reminds me of the shirt Tiffani was wearing when I got my haircut; I'm hoping to channel some of her confidence.

Hearing the knock at the door, I rush downstairs to open it before Dave does. Dave, being quicker than I thought, is right behind me when I inch the door open. Chase looks down at me right away, startling at Dave's baritone voice coming from somewhere behind me.

"Hey, Chase, come on in!" Dave roars enthusiastically.

I suppress a moan, open the door the rest of the way, and motion him in to the direction of the living room. Joan stands up and shuts the TV off before grinning at Chase.

I've never had to deal with my "parents" checking out my date before. I use the back of my hand to cover a huge grin when Chase sticks his hand out to shake Dave's. I wonder how well he knows Dave and Joan, considering they are neighbors.

"You two have fun tonight," Joan beams. She snakes her arm around Dave's waist and starts moving him backwards. I catch on that she's trying to help me escape. I make quick eye contact with her, hoping she understands my gratitude.

Isn't she going to ask us where we are going? They don't even give me a curfew? I get the feeling something's not right, but shrug it off. I will not let my paranoia ruin this evening.

I turn and grab my black pea coat from the hallway nook. Chase takes it out of my hands and holds it open for me to put each arm in. My mouth hangs open for a moment, but not wanting him to stand there any longer than necessary, I quickly shove my arms through each hole.

I have never been on a date before. I don't know what to expect. Maybe I should have asked Joan the basics of how this whole thing works. Again, he catches me off guard when he opens the front door and steps aside to let me exit first. What is all this about? I quickly step through and wait for him to shut the door behind us.

"What are you doing?" My confusion obvious.

"I don't know what you're talking about," Chase answers.

"My coat. The door. What is all that?" I state the obvious, my thumb pointing back towards the house while we walk side-by-side to the truck.

He laughs gently then says, "You know, trying to be a gentleman."

"Oh." The word seems inadequate, but I can't think of a better reply.

When we finally make it to the blue Ford pick-up truck sitting in the driveway, he walks over to the passenger door and opens it up. I've begun to catch on as how to this whole gentleman behavior works. As I step up into the cab of the truck, Chase tells me about our transportation for the night.

"It's my dad's, but I beg to drive it whenever I get a chance. You know, mom needs milk I'm gone type of deal." There is no end to his charm.

I really like this guy. My cheeks already hurt from smiling too big and this whole date thing is just starting. At this rate, I'm going to have to spend all day tomorrow frowning to even out my face.

I slide into the passenger seat, trying to act like having a boy treat me so nicely is an everyday occurrence. Should I reach over and open his door for him? Not having much time to deliberate, I scoot over and pull the inside handle just as he reaches for the door. He looks up at me and smiles.

About ten minutes later, Chase pulls the truck into a parking lot. Where we are doesn't register until he turns the truck off. I look around cautiously, wondering if being here is just part of his humor that I'm getting to know.

We are parked on the side of a huge brick building. I could be wrong, and I really, really hope that I am, but it looks like a church to me. Who goes to a church for their first date?

Okay, no jumping to conclusions, down paranoia, down!

Turning my body towards Chase, I raise an eyebrow and stare at him. He is already staring at me. Suddenly, the whole situation is too weird, and I feel like I'm standing on the outside of someone's inside joke.

This is our date?

I jerk my head away from his searching eyes and stare out the passenger window.

My brain goes hyperactive, negatively tearing me apart with several theories.

Chase feels sorry for me and, after watching me scream out against God, decides that I need an exorcism.

Again, I ponder how well Dave and Joan know him. Humiliation sets in while my mind continues to construct more assumptions before any sort of logic and reason has a chance to defend Chase.

What if, after seeing Chase and I talk a few weeks ago, Dave pulled him aside at school and asked him to take me out as a favor. Chase probably got a free day out of school for showing up to church with me.

Traitorous tears begin to surface. My throat becomes clogged with all the self-deprecating thoughts running me over like a Mac truck. Too quickly, the Hulk inside of me bursts, and my anger boils over.

You can hear a pin drop in the hush cab. Sharply, I turn my entire body forward to focus on the inky night through the front windshield. Unfortunately, the light poles' glow allows for Chase's reflection to easily be seen, and he's just sitting there, a sense of calm covering his features.

There is a tornado going on in here! Why am I the only one being turned inside out? Why did I put myself in this situation?

Things like this never work out for girls like me.

What does he expect me to say?

Thank you for accepting me as your charity case. Is there any way you could possibly like me for real?

How pathetic. My anger spikes the more vulnerable my thoughts become.

I notice his hand slide over towards mine, lying there in between us on the seat. Floodgates open, and against my will, tears fall. Acid creeps up my throat, gagging me in between my sobs.

Chase's eyes take on a glassy look while he continues to hold my stare in the windshield. It's like looking at us through someone else's eyes—him sitting calmly beside a girl who is clearly losing her mind.

His hand is less than an inch from my own, and I find myself staring at it, as if taking his hand in mine is a possibility. Somehow these thoughts drench my anger in peace. I watch Chase bow his head, and I just know that we are both staring at the distance separating us.

Gently, purposefully, Chase places his hand on top of mine. A small gasp escapes me, feeling the warmth of his touch. There is such honesty in his hand sitting there on top of mine. This could be our whole date, and I would be a very happy girl. He radiates warmth, a heat that somehow quiets the noise inside my head.

Hearing Chase clear his throat, I hesitantly raise my eyes to rest on his. I realize for the first time that tears that have trailed down his cheeks too.

"Oh, no, what have I done? Did I hurt him? I take it all back," I plead inwardly, but another wave of peace snatches my thoughts.

After a few minutes, and some labored breathing, I begin to calm down. It's hard to remember what I was thinking about. I cast my eyes down, ashamed at yet another break down that Chase has had to witness.

"Adin, I am so sorry." Chase empathizes, his voice reflecting guilt.

"For what?" I question, clearing my throat, trying to sound as if I don't know what he's talking about.

"For upsetting you. I was not trying to do that. This is where I come on Friday nights. My parents are the Youth Pastors of this church, and every Friday night teens come here and hang out. We don't have to stay."

His sincerity shocks me. How can I not believe him?

"I'm okay. I'm sorry that I lose it sometimes. Really, it's no big deal. There was just some crazy church stuff that happened when I was a kid." I pull on the handle of my door to get out of the truck.

Chase pulls me back into the car with the hand he's still holding, stopping me from getting out. His face is so close to mine that my heart begins doing somersaults. Life freezes for just a moment.

"Adin, I don't want you to hide who you are from me. I don't care if you cry. I want you to cry if it means you're figuring stuff out. I don't really know if I can help. I doubt I've suffered one tenth of what you have."

He shakes his head sadly and continues, "I do know that God never wanted this pain for you."

He must see the apprehension in my eyes.

"Adin, truly, God loves you. He did not purposely put hurt in your life. God is the shelter in the storm, the rock to stand on when life doesn't make any sense."

He hugs me then, and whispering in my ear, keeps talking, "I want to help you. I want you to know that I am not going anywhere, and you can trust me."

I lay my cheek on his shoulder, rubbing it against the softness of his gray cotton shirt. Closing my eyes, I let myself enjoy being held in the arms of a boy that life probably won't let me keep.

Do I trust him? No one has ever put their hand out and genuinely meant it.

I know for certain that if he leaves me like everyone else, it will cut me like none before. I also know that if I decide to walk away from him now, when he is so willing to be here, it will be a regret I will never forgive myself for.

What should I do?

I see him lower his head and close his eyes, and it's like watching Mrs. Hollander on Wednesday praying at her desk.

Chase has never tried to pretend to be something that he's not, and he's not hiding what he believes in. I admire him. He is one of the good guys.

On the rare occasions that I've witnessed anyone praying, it has made me uncomfortable, even agitated. Chase isn't praying to be the center of attention. He's praying to God because he actually thinks God is listening. I feel sorry for him, but definitely not angry.

I realize that I do trust him, whether it's from his honesty or the number of times he's seen me go psycho and stuck around. I don't really know, but in my book all of it has to count for something.

"I'm not going anywhere as long as you aren't," I say into the silence.

His shoulders visibly relax. Releasing my hand, he quickly opens his door and jogs around to my side of the truck. The hand that he was holding feels different now that he is no longer holding it. I clasp it in my other one, rubbing them together. I look up into the calm, peaceful ocean of Chase's eyes when he opens my door.

"M'lady," he says in a faux British accent.

My heart skips a beat at his playfulness. I pause a second before taking his outreached hand, desperately trying to freeze this moment in time so that I have something special to hold onto later when this all ends.

Joan

My heart beats with excitement. I sprint up the stairs, taking the last two in one swoop, needing to tell Dave about my conversation with Kami, who called me as soon as Chase and Adin had left the church to head home.

"Dave! Dave!" I shout. I know he's in our room, but I want his full attention when I get there.

I hear him jump out of bed, clearly preparing himself for some kind of alarm.

"Whoa! What is going on?" he asks, astonished at my entrance.

"Adin went to church tonight with Chase! She had a good time! Kami invited her to come check out Youth on Wednesday night, and Adin told her yes! Oh, Dave, can you believe the work God is doing in her life?" Tears of joy roll freely down my face. I have never been so quickly attached to any one of our kids.

Sara had gone to church with us right from the start. Her mother had raised her in church, and even though she was upset with God, she knew she still needed Him.

Matt had to be reached by Dave first because his mother's death was the source of the emotional abuse. Once Dave was able to create a bond of trust with him, I was allowed to slowly find my place.

Today, I have a wonderful, deep relationship with both of those kids, but it was a long road. Adin is the first one out of all of them that I have fell so completely in love with so soon.

Dave hugs me tightly, lifting me up off the floor. I rest my face in between his neck and shoulder, breathing in the scent of my husband. Everything in the world is right for this second in time. I sigh, feeling a little worn at my adrenaline rush. Dave sets me down.

"Tell me everything," he says, sitting down on the edge of the bed.

"Kami said that when they arrived, she tried to stay back, giving Chase the opportunity to introduce Adin to everyone. When he brought her over to Kami, Kami said that she couldn't help but give her a hug. She said that she just reacted."

"Adin accepted the hug and told Kami that the youth room looked really cool with all the graffiti everywhere. For the rest of the night Chase stuck by her side, and they just hung out with the other teens. Kami agreed with me that Chase was smart to get her to go for the first time on a Friday night because it allowed her a chance to get comfortable with the surroundings."

"You know, on Friday's they just have a local Christian band come in and play and have stations of games going on. I think Kami said that there was a *Just Dance* contest tonight. She thinks that Chase and Adin like each other more than just friends. She told me that she will have to reenact their lovey-dovey eyes for me at church on Sunday."

I can't sit down; there is too much energy buzzing around inside when I think of Adin's progress tonight.

"That is awesome. We're going to need to pray for all of these new people that will be a part of Adin's life and that she will gain her own understanding of who God is," Dave reminds me.

His logic brings my euphoria down a notch. I nod in agreement. There is still much that must take place before Adin heals. Unable to contain myself, I push Dave off of the bed and tell him we have to start praying right this minute.

Together we bow our heads, and I pray aloud: "*Thank you so very much, Lord, for the progress made tonight. We pray for a hedge of protection around Adin as she becomes more open to being around Christian people. Thank you for Ben, Kami, and Chase Harper. Thank you for the reflection of you so clearly seen in their everyday lives. We pray that you would strengthen them and prepare them to help in Adin's recovery. We pray that you would make yourself so obvious in Adin's daily life that she is overwhelmed with the reality of your existence. Guide Dave and me in what we can do to help. We are yours, Lord. Thank you for the blessing of your ministry. In Jesus's name we pray, Amen.*"

CHAPTER 15

Romeo and Juliet

Adin

Waiting at the end of my driveway is Chase Harper. I look down, trying to hide my smile, which is much too big. He meets me with a small grin, like there's an inside secret that only we share. I can never tell him what that smile does to me.

"Where were you all those mornings that I waited for you?" I wince at how freely I just gave myself away.

His eyebrows raise, but keeping in step with me, replies, "If only I had known, I would have tried harder to be here."

"It's not fair how easy it is for you; how long have you been waiting?" I ask.

He stays quiet, a clear indication that he doesn't want to share this information. So, it's going to be like that is it? I wonder where his tickle spots are. I jump in front of him and lunge left and right as he tries to move around me, my hands up, fingers wiggling to indicate his punishment for withholding information.

"You're not bad," he starts. Then much too easily he grabs my wrists in one hand, and holding them together, comes up under me and throws me over his shoulder.

"Unbelievable!" I mutter, my hair falling into my eyes.

"What are you going to do now?" I can hear the smirk in his voice.

"Wouldn't you like to know," I huff. Instantly I grab the top of his jeans and pull upward, forcing him to drop me squarely on my feet. I stand there in mock surprise, my eyes big and mouth open in a type of fake shock.

"Why, Chase Harper, did you just let me go?" I flutter my eyelashes for the full effect. He attempts to give me a sinister look, but the smile on his lips proof that he's only playing with me.

"Tell me!" I really want to know if he suffered as much as I already have.

"Okay, but then you have to answer a question for me." He says, placing his hands behind his head, stopping right where we are.

"Fair enough," I reply, turning more of my body towards his.

"Okay," sheepishly, he confesses, "I was out there for about ten minutes. I almost left, thinking that I missed you." His head jolts up to see if I'm laughing at him.

"Awe." I croon wrapping my arm around his. Although I'm trying to be silly, my insides melt. My heart rate triple times. This has to mean that he sees me more than just a friend.

"My turn." He scowls, again the facial expression as fake as those Gucci purses the girls at school fling on their shoulders. "Why were you really practicing that single-leg takedown that I showed you?"

He would have to pick some ultra-personal question. I bite the inside of my lip trying to figure out how to explain my reasoning without coming across as a nut job.

I sigh, "Well, I guess I figured that it wouldn't hurt to know some self-defense. I'm not going to go into some dramatic retelling of my past, but if I had known how to protect myself before, it would have helped me."

I keep my head down, looking at my new boots. I feel him put his arm around my shoulders. His body warms my own. There is this foreign feeling coursing through me right this minute: happiness, and it feels great.

It'll never last; it never does.

Where did that come from? Why does my mind have to screw everything up; that could have been a perfectly good moment.

"You know, I could teach you some more stuff. If you want?" he offers.

"Really, like what?" I ask.

"There are all kinds of basic wrestling moves that you could learn that would help you protect yourself. I usually play baseball in the spring, but I'm not going to this year. I really want to wrestle in college, so I've decided focus on that. I have a mat in my garage, and I'm there every day after the school's wrestling practice doing my own thing. If you ever want to drop in, I'll teach you some wrestling moves."

Touched by his generosity, I lean my head against his shoulder and whisper, "Thanks."

This world just doesn't make guys like Chase very often, and I feel extremely lucky that some way, somehow, I've caught his eye.

Chase won't want you once he knows what you really are. You're broken.

I really hate myself right now. How do I make myself shut-up? I've got to distract myself from me.

"Mrs. Hyde is kind of going overboard with the whole *Romeo and Juliet* play in class, huh?" I ask, trying to distract myself.

Mrs. Hyde, in all her dramatic glory, has been single handedly reenacting Shakespeare's *Romeo and Juliet*. It's entertaining listening to her change voices from a young woman to a young man, but then to watch her throw her whole body into scenes, literally, is quite impressive.

Chase laughs, clearly agreeing with my analysis of the situation. Then he asks me, "What do you think about the play?"

"I love and hate it. I love that they were both brave enough to overcome what stood in their way to be together, but I hate that they both die in the end, like they failed. It takes hope away, you know?" I look up at him, waiting for his response.

"I don't know; I guess I see what you're saying. But I also see how they could have just waited, you know, let some time pass instead of running away and getting married behind their parents' back. Like maybe if they had just been more patient, they could have had their own happily ever after."

His explanation doesn't make any sense to me.

"So, you're blaming them?" I ask incredulously, not quite sure at the moment why his feelings towards a play from a high school Literature class is bothering me so much.

"In a way, I guess I am. I mean it's just a story. I think every person gets something different from it. Isn't that what great literature is supposed to be about, or so Mrs. Hyde says, right?" He tries to lighten the mood.

Our complete opposite responses bother me more than I'm willing to think about at this moment. I try to shake the feeling that both of us see the play differently because we see life differently. It's obvious that he believes in going about life playing by the rules, but the rules have never worked out for me.

CHAPTER 16

Closer to the Truth

Dave

Shock registers as I close my cell phone. Marge Ann had just called, wanting to discuss Adin's last foster parents before she moved in with us. Marge seemed concerned about her investigation into one particular family.

I'm sure there must be legalities she has to make sure are in place before she should confide in me, but this time Marge side-stepped them. The anxiety in her voice was so clear; I felt my entire body tense up when she asked if I had a moment.

Normally, I don't keep my cell phone on during work hours, but today I was waiting to hear back from Pastor Tim in reference to a men's bible study that we are putting together. When my cell phone started vibrating across my desk, I answered, expecting Tim's baritone voice.

I recovered quickly when Marge said hello. I had a feeling that something was wrong.

Marge had gone over to this family's home before lunch, knowing that three of the foster children were not yet school age. She said that one of the foster children is a girl, and based upon the behavior she observed, there is evidence enough to justify a further investigation.

She had apologized for not being able to give me further details but as a friend asked that I pray. My heart drops thinking that another girl could also suffer like Adin. I thanked Marge, letting her know that of course I would be in prayer.

Before the end of our call, she reminded me that Joan or I would need to bring Adin to her office for her mandatory check-in. After writing the date on my desk calendar, we said good-bye.

I feel light headed after our conversation. I stand up and blow out a long breath. Closing the door to my office, I get down on my knees and begin to pray.

"Lord, in the book of Matthew you say, 'Come to me, all you who are weary and burdened, and I will give you rest.' I am burdened. Adin is burdened, Lord. Both of us need your rest. Everyday my understanding of Adin's distance from you becomes clearer. There has been so much unfairness in her life. Lord, satan has used this abuse to destroy every connection Adin could have had with you. She has identified the actions of some jerk in correlation with you. Lord, your word promises that you are close to the broken hearted and save those who are crushed in spirit. Father, on Adin's behalf, I beg that you would draw close enough to hold her in your arms. Break through her rough exterior and guarded heart to make yourself known. Lord, challenge her to discover the truth. I don't know what to do; lead me. I am here, Lord, no matter how chaotic satan tries to make life. I am here. I believe that you will protect Joan and me. We claim Adin as yours. Your will be done! In Jesus's name I pray, Amen."

CHAPTER 17

Day to Day

Adin

Balancing my lunch tray with one hand and holding my fitness folder with the other, I make my way over to the lunch table. Over the last few weeks, I have forced myself to learn the other kids' names that sit at this table.

Chase had realized that my usual lunch experience was eating alone. Upon this discovery, he came up behind me, picked up my tray, and walked to his table. Annoyed, I followed him over, finding an empty seat with my tray sitting conveniently in front of it.

Looking around at the other kids sitting there, no one seemed to overtly care that I was becoming an addition to their group.

Today, being more confident to show up, I listen to their erratic conversations, sneak looks at Chase, and eat. Most of my lunch table go to the bi-weekly church events that have been added to my schedule.

I slide my fitness folder sideways in front of Chase. Over the last month, Mr. Roads took away our privileges of training with a partner. At first this had bummed me out, but over time, I realized that I got a lot more accomplished.

Our class's end-of-the-year project is to create a fitness plan enabling a person to drop body fat and inches while increasing their strength. We have to use our own bodies to reflect these changes.

Mr. Roads gave us folders with spreadsheets for each of us to write down our original height, weight, and measurements for each major body part. Also, we have to journal what we eat every day. At the end of each week, we have to turn in these sheets.

I can't help but to gloat to Chase in regard to my personal progress. In the last four weeks, I have decreased my body mass by three percent. My measurements around my biceps have increased, while my waist has decreased. I'm pretty proud of myself.

I created a goal and am now personally seeing myself to the finish line. I hear Chase whistle beside me, clearly impressed.

"Flex your bicep." He commands, trying his best to stay in a voice like that of Mr. Roads'.

I lift up my arm and tighten my muscle.

"Ouch," he pretends his fingertips are burned when he touches me. I roll my eyes but laugh with everyone else.

"You're all buff now, Adin." A girl named Lisa says excitedly.

"Yeah, I was always too scared to take fitness because I never knew any other girls who signed up. Next year I am totally taking that class." Another girl named Aubrey says matter-of-factly.

I'd like to confide in them that my taking the class was a total misunderstanding on my own part, but not quite sure how to do that, I decide to keep my mouth shut. Talking to girls my own age is still somewhat of an adjustment.

I look over to Chase, joking around with the boy sitting next to him. He has helped me out so much. I know that since I've been here I've gained confidence in being around other people because of the amount of time I spend with him.

Every day we walk to school together. After school, I go home and work on my homework, and around 4:30 I walk over and let myself into his garage.

By this time there is always loud music blaring and a sweaty Chase shadow wrestling across the huge mat on the garage floor. I really like when he doesn't see me come in right away, and I get to watch him, uninhibited, doing something that he loves.

He has me jump rope or do fifty jumping jacks to warm up my muscles. Every week he teaches me a new wrestling move. First, we worked on my stance, which is the general way that wrestlers stand across from another. Then, he had me perfect my single-leg takedown.

Right now, he is doing his best to show me how to keep wrist control. He says that if anyone tries to overpower me by holding my wrist, I'll be able to turn out of it and actually control their wrists.

No lie, it's extremely hard to concentrate when we practice wrist control. Chase stands directly behind me and puts each of his wrists on top of mine. The concept is that I have to keep turning mine out, away from my body. Then, I have to quickly grab his wrists, placing my own hands on top.

I've purposely leaned into him on occasion, just because I can. I can feel the rhythm of his heartbeat. This amazing guy is real. Chase always snaps me back to reality though, making me do whatever move we're working on over and over again.

On Wednesday and Friday nights, I've been going to Youth Group with Chase's family. The first Wednesday that I rode with them I was so nervous I felt sick to my stomach.

I figured they would assume that I was a bad influence for Chase, and I'd get those looks from the corner of their eyes—you know, the kind that insinuate they don't trust me.

Like Chase, the rest of his family surprised me. Mr. and Mrs. Harper tease each other mercilessly about which kind of music to listen to on the way to church. Their childlike play has such innocence that I find myself laughing with them. It's easy to be with them, and nothing in my life has ever been easy.

Chase's little brother Carter is annoying at all the right times. He occupies the entire back seat of the van, giving Chase and me no other choice but to sit in the bucket seats located in the middle. Once we get to church, Carter purposely walks in between us. I like it though because he's not fighting for Chase's attention, but mine.

Life at the Baldwin's has gotten easier too. Dave cooks breakfast every day. Joan is waiting for me at home after school. I sit at the kitchen table doing my homework, and she places a snack in front of me.

Once I'm done with my homework, she finds her way back into the dining room, sitting down beside me. She always asks me about my day, and I find myself telling her more and more.

Then, I go over to Chases for my personal training. When I get home, Dave is there and dinner is ready. I really appreciate our routine. I welcome it. I have never felt this calm in my life.

Up until now, I was perpetually looking over my shoulder, waiting for the bad luck that was never far behind. I wonder if I'm flying high because of all the people in my life who believe in God. One thing I know for sure, I definitely want to keep them close: they're my good luck charms.

CHAPTER 18

Foster Kid Appointments

<u>*Adin*</u>

I can't believe that it is already the end of March. I actually had to take off my winter coat when I got outside this morning to walk to school because I was too hot. Right on cue, there was Chase waiting for me at the end of the driveway. Has it always been this easy for me to smile?

I inhale deeply, smelling the spring air. Once I reach Chase, we turn in step to one another and begin the walk to school. It stays quiet except for the sound of our feet hitting the pavement.

"So, you're leaving school early today? Will you be at lunch?" Chase asks.

"I don't know. Joan is picking me up at 10:30. My caseworker is new, so I don't really know if she stays on schedule or what. It could be fifteen minutes or three hours. Social services kind of sucks like that." I explain.

"I hope that you don't have to sit and wait all day," Chase empathizes.

"Definitely," I agree, "but what's worse is the State building doesn't even have up-to-date magazines to look through or anything. I mean, shouldn't they have some money for some kind of entertainment? I swear, every time I'm there the only thing on the tiny TV mounted up to the ceiling is Wheel of Fortune. I think they record the same episode and run it all day long." I joke.

Chase laughs as we trudge up the hill. His laugh makes me laugh. I begin to lose my balance, but he is quick to steady me. Funny, I think to myself, I always feel safe when I'm with him.

When is he ever going to ask me to be his girlfriend? I find myself thinking about this question more and more. Wouldn't he have already asked me out on a real date if he is really into me?

I can't stop thinking about him. I wake up, and I think about rushing out the front door to walk to school with him. I get home from school and hurry to get my homework done just so I can anxiously wait for him to get done with wrestling practice, so I can go over to his house to work on wrestling moves with him.

I come home on Wednesday and Friday nights to eat dinner with Dave and Joan, and then watch the clock slowly tick by until I can go over to his house to ride to church with his family.

I keep waiting for him to pop that all important question: "Adin, will you be my girlfriend?"

I look over at him, imagining how he might look when he finally does ask. Isn't fantasy great? He glances over in my direction, and catching me staring at him, raises his eyebrows up and down. I punch his arm.

"Ouch," he rubs his arm and continues, "You know, those are deadly weapons now."

He opens the school door for me.

"No way, you deserved it," I counter in good humor.

"What did I do?" he asks innocently.

"Oh, please, whatever," I banter back, loving the flirtatiousness of what we have going on here.

I stop at my locker, quickly spin the lock, and pop it open. I put away some books and take out my Geometry book. I turn to wave at Chase right before he disappears into homeroom.

Adin

I shut the door to Joan's Honda Civic, waiting for her to hit the lock button on her key ring before walking beside her up the steps into One Park Building. This is one of the many State run buildings located in downtown Philadelphia.

Once Joan and I enter the main doors into the building, we are directed by a receptionist to the appropriate door. I don't even need to ask for directions; I've been coming here for almost half my life. Now that I think of it, that's pretty sad.

Not today. Today started good, so let's try to finish it that way.

We both continue to the right. I follow Joan through the ugly, olive green painted door covered with an aluminum sign stating the obvious: Foster Care.

Joan leads us in, walking to the far end of the room to sign me in on the clipboard for my appointment. I turn to my right to see which elderly patient the state hijacked from the geriatric wing of the hospital to man the door today.

I recognize the large man behind the desk as Officer Anderson. What? I cover my mouth with my hand and cough in an attempt to disguise my laugh. He looks up when he hears my rather strange cough, bending his head to the side, trying to place my face.

I turn away from him and walk over to the other side of the room, plopping myself down in a bright blue plastic chair. Joan makes her way over to me, picking the bright red plastic chair to my left. She looks around to find what I can only assume is some form of entertainment.

"There are none," I state matter-of-factly.

"None what?" She smiles and asks.

"Magazines. There are no magazines here. The Foster Care system enjoys torturing us with reruns of Wheel of Fortune on the midget sized television hanging from the rafters above." I point up to the far corner over Officer Anderson on the other side of the room to give her the exact location of the only source of entertainment offered by this lovely establishment.

"Right. I almost forgot." She rummages around in her purse, eventually pulling out a paperback book.

In the few months that I've lived with the Baldwins, I've come to realize that Joan is always prepared. She reminds me of Mary Poppins with that purse of hers. If we happen to get stranded on a deserted island with her purse, we'd probably be able to build a cruise ship and take the long way home.

I move my neck back and forth listening to it crack. I picked up that habit from Chase. I smile just thinking about him. Then I begin to crack each of my fingers. I twist my ankles back and forth, smiling to myself as I hear the clicking noises. I start to turn my upper body towards Joan in an effort to pop my back when I notice that a lot of people have stopped what they were doing to watch me.

"Sorry," I say loud enough for the room to hear.

I look over at Joan, but she is the only person not paying attention to all my joint dislocation. How long is this going to take? *I could start counting.* Nah, that was an old habit, and I've prided myself on all my new, clever habits.

It's almost as if I enjoy shedding off the little oddities that I brought with me to the Baldwin's family. I could go and toy with Officer Anderson. What did Ms. Ann say his wife's name was when I was here three months ago? I close my eyes to concentrate better while I try to remember.

I hear my name being called over the intercom. I guess Officer Anderson will have to wait. I stand up and look down at Joan. She peers up at me.

"Do you want me to come with you?" she asks.

"Nah, I got this. The new caseworker is just going to ask me how my new foster home is, and I'll tell her the truth. You know, how I'm locked in the basement most of the time and fed dog food. But don't worry, I'll tell them you're really nice when you shove the food under the door," I manage to get out this entire embellishment with a straight face.

To Joan's credit, she just waves her hand like what I just said is no big deal and returns, "Good idea. Sounds great. Tell Marge I said hi." With that, she returns to her book.

Her response reminds me what a joy kill she can be at times. However, when I look over her shoulder, I observe the look of mortification plastered all over the old lady's face who must have been listening in. I wink at her and lick my lips.

"Mmm, tastes just like bacon," I say, rubbing my stomach.

I make my way over to Officer Anderson, so he can buzz me into the back where Ms. Ann's office awaits me. Who will be escorting me to her door today?

CHAPTER 19

Reality Check

Adin

Some nice Latina lady leads me back to Ms. Ann's office. She gestures that I can take the seat outside of Ms. Ann's door.

"Ms. Ann's on a phone call right now," she explains, a slight accent interspersed throughout the sentence.

I want to believe the lady, but for all I know Ms. Ann could be out to lunch. That definitely would have been something that my old caseworker, Ms. Watts, would have done. There was something just not right about that woman. While I'm thinking about her, I realize that I haven't seen her since Ms. Ann became my new caseworker.

I lean forward in my seat, resting my elbows on top of my thighs, holding my head in my hands, taking the work atmosphere in around me. I see piles and piles of thick folders on everyone's desks. It's not like I'm eavesdropping or sneaking around because there aren't any cubicles that separate all of the desks from one another.

Unlike Ms. Ann's office, these desks are lined up beside one another, and everyone who is sitting behind them is on the telephone talking at once. I have no idea how they concentrate on their own conversations.

Again, my eyes are drawn back to the thick files. I start counting all of the files that are stacked up on their desks, beginning to feel nauseous when I get into the thirties. The realization that all those files represent kids' lives just like mine rips me in two.

Anger jolts me to my feet; the unfairness making me clench my fists. There's that Hulk-like anger; it's been awhile, but obviously the beast was merely hibernating.

What is wrong with people? I hate this building—it's quick to remind me how ugly the world is.

What about the Baldwins?

Huh? What about them?

For every file on that desk, there is also the possibility of a loving home. Those files can also represent hope.

Is that Chase in my head? When did I start accepting Chase's reasoning—even more so, repeating it? I shake my head as if to shake the voice away. Deep down I know that my change in perception is about more than hanging out with Chase. The whole *hope* concept comes from the messages that I keep hearing at church.

I don't need to be thinking about God stuff right now. As a result of attending all of these church outings with Chase, I listen to Pastor Ben talk about God quite often, and he has this way of making all the confusion go away.

It has become so much harder to keep the God questions I have at arm's length when Pastor Ben brings every single one of them up during Youth Group. Ms. Ann interrupts my thoughts when she opens her office door. Finally.

"Good morning, Adin! Please come in and take a seat." She opens her office door the rest of the way and moves to the side to let me enter. I begin to roll my eyes, expecting the familiar smell of cigarettes and old mothballs, but am taken aback when the smell of cinnamon registers. I see the candle lit on her desk. The cinnamon gives her office more of a cozy, comfortable smell.

I sit down and wait for her to get seated behind her desk. I look around, expecting to find my huge file opened in the center of her desk, but don't see it anywhere. I shift my eyes to the right and the left, but still can't locate it. Okay, what is going on?

Every single time I had gone to my counseling sessions with Ms. Watts she had to dig for my file and then review it for like twenty minutes while I sat there growing more and more bitter at the fact that she had no clue who I was and why I was in her office. I would think, "I see you every three months lady, get a clue." I give Ms. Ann a *now what* look, making my eyes all big, while she sits across from me quietly and just watches.

"What?" I say exasperated.

"You," she states confidently.

Rather confused, I respond, "Okay, what about me?"

"I am very proud of you," she responds, her kind smile sitting comfortably on her face.

An involuntary blush settles on my face. I'm not really use to having someone be proud of me.

"Why?" I ask, my curiosity relentless.

"For one, you are here. I am proud of you that you kept our appointment. It says a lot about a young lady when she keeps her word. Two, you look great. You look content. I am so proud that you are allowing yourself to be happy."

She says everything with such sincerity that I can't get angry with her. All I can do is nod my head yes. My eyes get drawn to a framed quote sitting on her desk. I read it silently inside my head: 1Sameul 16:7 "The Lord does not look at the things man looks at. Man looks at the outward appearances, but the Lord looks at the heart."

Oh, so Ms. Ann is a Christian too. Okay, so Mrs. Hollander, Chase, Pastor Ben and Kami, Dave and Joan, and, now, Ms. Ann are all Christians. So were all those people in that church that just stood there and watched my mom throw a fit. Isn't that just like this God of theirs!

Okay, God, so now you care? Now you want to be a part of my life? If you are looking at my heart, do you see how many times I've had to keep it together while people invaded it and ripped it to shreds? Were you even there? Why didn't you save me then, huh?

Tears fill my eyes. I straighten in my chair to concentrate on Ms. Ann's face. I block out all other thoughts and focus on her eyes.

"What were you thinking about just then?" She asks quietly. Her perception is annoying.

"Nothing I'm going to share." I quip. Snotty Adin has reappeared, and I'm going to use her as body armor.

"Adin, I only want to help you," Ms. Ann responds softly—firm words wrapped in too much kindness.

Do I really want to tell her?

Before I know what I'm doing, I find myself answering, "I was reading the God plaque on your desk."

I point to the framed quote. "And I was wondering what God thought about my heart."

"And what did you come up with?" She asks, her eyes searching my own.

"Shouldn't you have a piece of paper and a pen to write down everything we talk about?" I ask, trying to deflect.

"Answer my question, Adin, and then I will answer yours," she counters.

She's good. I still don't know why I'm telling her anything, but that's exactly what I find myself doing.

"Okay, I was thinking that God would had to have seen how many times my heart got hurt, and if he is real and could see all that, why did he let it happen?" I look at my hands, trying to put my thoughts into words correctly but then peer up into Ms. Ann's eyes when I come to my question. I want her to give me the answer. I really need to know the truth.

"And what conclusion did you come to?" she asks.

She doesn't know either.

Figures.

"I don't know." My eyebrows furrow in exasperation.

"That's why I asked you." I can't believe I thought she could help me with this. Irritation causes my insides to itch—a place I can never seem to scratch just right and get rid of for good.

After a moment of silence, Ms. Ann leans towards me, "Do you really want to know?"

Don't play with me lady.

"Yeah, I really want to know." I tilt my chin up. She had better not be messing with me.

"I think that God cried every time someone tore at your heart. People were not created to hurt each other. God created us to love one another. However, there are people in this world that choose to ignore God. They create their own set of rules, and, many times, these rules are self-serving and allow them to hurt others without much thought to anyone besides themselves."

"I also believe that God is bigger than anyone's mistakes, and that He can take anyone's pain and suffering and turn it into a victory. God is the ultimate healer, and He can take any messed up, torn heart and piece it back together stronger and more powerful than it ever was before." Ms. Ann holds my gaze the entire time she speaks. There is a conviction that I can hear in her voice when she talks about God.

I really want to believe like she does. It would make my life so much easier. Tears begin to roll freely down my face. They aren't the kind of tears that hurt to cry but rather the kind that push the hurt out.

If Ms. Ann is correct, that would mean that God didn't hurt me. God didn't create my mother to hate me. He didn't want me to be dumped in one foster family after another. It would have to mean that the only person in my life that has ever wanted me and loved me is God.

Could that be possible?

A lump forms in my throat at this thought. Ms. Ann's arms wrap around me in a tight hug. I cry so hard my shoulders shake, but she never lets go. I cry until snot rolls out of my nose and my throat is scratchy.

She pulls out a tissue from the box on the corner of her desk and hands it to me. I blow my nose. She hands me more to dry my face.

"I think we are done today, Miss Adin. Thank you so much for coming in to see me. If you have anything else that you ever want to talk to me about, I want you to call my cell phone. Do you still have the business card I gave you when you and I first met?"

Her face is so close to mine that her voice is almost a whisper. Looking at the path of tears running from her eyes to her chin, I can tell that today meant something to her as well. She really cares about me.

I shake my head yes.

"Thank you," I whisper back.

Joan

Rinsing another glass, I put it in the dishwasher.

Lord, thank you so much for your hand in Adin's life. I am honored to be a part of the healing that you are bringing into her life. She is so beautiful and strong. God, I just don't know how she has dealt with so much in her young life.

I pray over my relationship with Adin. My favorite part of each day is when she comes home from school and shares the events of her day with me.

The difference you have made in her life over the last few months is just remarkable. She came here flighty and bitter, but no one who meets her today would be able to see that. You are an awesome God!

Chase has been great in getting her involved in the Youth Group, but I would really like to be the one to invite her to Sunday morning service. I don't want to push too hard, so please give me discernment. I want her to know all of your love, Lord, but in your time, not mine. I love you Father. In Jesus's name I pray, Amen.

"Gotcha!" Dave pounces up behind me, wrapping me in a huge bear hug. I laugh at his boyish antics.

"You sure did!" I respond, covering his hands with my own. We stand there together for a while before I notice Adin in my peripheral vision.

I remain quiet, giving her the courtesy of observation. I notice her biting her lower lip, a habit I've seen many times when she does her homework. I lean back into Dave a little further.

Eventually I see her grab a school notebook off of the island and turn to go upstairs. When she reaches the top, I hear her making kissing noises. Dave starts laughing immediately.

CHAPTER 20

Too Good to Stay Good

Adin

It's raining outside today, adding to my gloomy mood. And not just sprinkles of droplets; no, it's like the sky is on super soaker mode. Rain means I can't walk to school with Chase. It means that Joan has to take me. I don't actually get to see Chase in school until third period when we have Fitness together, then again at lunch, and for the last time during sixth period Literature class.

Even though wrestling practice is over, I still don't get to see him right after school because he and a few friends wrestle together for summer tournaments. Ugh, the downside of crushing on a jock.

Thankfully, the sun peeks through darkened clouds by the end of the school day. I make the decision to look for the positive despite not getting exactly what I want: more time with Chase. For instance, walking home solo gives me free time to think. Slowly, I've made a circle of friends. Occasionally I'll walk part of the way home with Aubrey. She sits at my lunch table, and I see her every week at Youth Group.

Aubrey is really pretty, with shiny red hair and big green eyes.

There is a dusting of freckles across her nose and cheeks. She only wears a little bit of eye shadow and clear lip gloss.

She dances ballet every evening after school except for Youth night. I'm pretty sure I overheard her telling another girl at our lunch table that her dream would be to go to Julliard when she graduates. I've never heard her say anything mean about anyone else. If anything, she's always encouraging people, and she has a laugh that I'm completely jealous of—the kind where she throws her entire body into it, her head bent back, mouth gaping open. I call it a belly laugh; those are my favorite kind.

I'm a little angry with myself for judging her so quickly, just because she is pretty. When I lived out on the streets it always seemed to be the *pretty* people that would cover their noses and mouths when they would walk by me. Homeless people have feelings too, you know?

There were even times when people would notice me huddled inside of a store front out in the cold. Yeah, they just crossed over to the other side of the street, so they wouldn't have to be near me. Did they think that I couldn't see them? Did it even register with them that I stayed out in that cold until I literally couldn't feel the cold anymore?

Aubrey has never looked at me like that. She understood my need for space the first few weeks that I sat at the lunch table, but, eventually, she began to nudge me during conversations and laugh, bringing me into the group without me having to talk.

Next, I'm drawn back to when Joan asked me on the drive to school this morning if I might be interested in attending the Easter Service at church this Sunday with her and Dave. She tried to ask the question as though it was just another topic that we usually talk about, but I could tell it was really important to her.

"Well, why not?" I asked myself.

I had said "sure" as passively as she had tried to ask.

I had to fight the urge to bust out laughing at her huge smile. I just made her day. It felt good to be able to do that for her.

Mrs. Hollander asked me if I'd be interested in staying after school today to help her clean up remnants from our latest art project. It only took thirty minutes, and I got to hang out with my favorite teacher. I also figured it would make my walk home easier since the rain stopped somewhere after lunchtime. The extra time would allow the sun to dry up more of the puddles.

Dave

Whistling as I lock up the gym, I grab my keys from the lock and head out the side doors of the high school towards the faculty parking lot. The boys varsity baseball team just may take division this year. There are plenty of seniors on the team, with an equal amount of athletic juniors. Coach Fentworth won't be having any problems filling positions.

The girls tennis team is also looking great. Coach Howe has been building the team for the past three years, and this year they are a powerhouse. Every single position from first singles down to second doubles have been playing indoor tennis this winter. These girls want the first place trophy more than any other team I've seen in a long while.

I enjoy watching the teenagers rising up to challenges and dedicating themselves toward a goal. I believe that the responsibility they take on when staying committed to such activities as their sports will stay with them, creating good habits, which they can take with them when they leave high school and go out into the world.

As soon as I get into the car, I turn on my cell phone. Immediately, it rings with missed calls. What happened today? I flip through my missed calls and see a missed called from Ms. Ann around ten this morning, then four missed calls from Joan right before the end of the school day.

I don't have a good feeling about this. I turn the key in the ignition and quickly put my car in reverse.

Lord, please let everything be okay. I'm feeling anxious about all of these missed calls. You are in control, Lord, always. Even if I don't understand. Please clear my mind and allow me to focus on your truths no matter what awaits me when I call Joan. Thank you, Lord, for staying beside me through everything. In Jesus's name I pray, Amen.

I hold down the number one on my cell phone, speed dialing Joan. She picks up the phone, and I her voice cracks when she says, "Dave!"

"Joan, yes honey, what is it?" I answer as calmly as I can make myself.

"Where have you been? I've tried calling you all afternoon. Oh, Dave, I don't know what's happening. Did Ms. Ann talk to you this morning?"

"Slow down, Joan, I don't know what you're talking about. I didn't have my cell phone on me. I left it in the car all day. I didn't listen to my message from Ms. Ann when I noticed how many missed calls I had from you. I am clueless right now, so, honey, please calm down and tell me what's going on." I try to keep my voice even, creating the environment that everything will be fine, and I am in control. I need to be the calm one right now because I can tell that Joan is emotionally spent.

"Okay, okay," she says, taking a few deep breaths. "I wasn't at home at all today. I went with Mrs. Peggy today to Newark to pick up some decorations for the Easter Service at church. I had left my phone in the car when Mrs. Peggy and I went into the flower shop. When I came out, I had a missed call from Ms. Ann."

I hear her moving around while she retells me everything. I know it is important for her to share with me all the details of the entire situation, so I try to be patient as I turn the car into our driveway.

"The message from Ms. Ann said that she had finished her investigation with one of Adin's previous foster family's last week and would need to speak with Adin. She said that she would try to stop by the house this evening because there was reason to speak with Adin right away. Ms. Ann sounded agitated, which I've never heard in her voice before."

"I didn't really think that there was anything to worry about, especially with how well Adin has been doing lately, so I let it go to the back of my mind while I continued to shop with Mrs. Peggy. As the afternoon wore on, I kept feeling like Adin shouldn't walk home today. When I prayed to God about it, I just knew I would feel better if she got a ride home."

"I knew that I wouldn't be home in time to pick her up myself, so I tried to contact you to see if she and Chase could ride with you, or if she could ride with Chase. I called the school and your cell phone, but no one could find you, and you never answered your cell phone. I even tried to get a hold of Kami, but she wasn't answering her home or cell phone either. I was so anxious all the way home. When I got home, I kept telling myself that I would feel better when I walked in the door and could set my eyes on Adin. Dave, she's not here!"

Joan sounded more and more panicked the closer she neared to end of her last sentence. Right then, I walked into our bedroom and threw down my phone. She ran into my arms, and I held her while she sobbed loudly. My wife's entire body is shaking, and it scares me. Joan has become so attuned to Adin that I don't doubt God was trying to let us know something. I rub on her back.

"What are we going to do?" she whispers.

"First, we are going to go back up to the high school and make sure that she didn't stay after school for anything. For all we know, she could have decided to go watch Chase wrestle. We will start there." I hold Joan tightly and speak in a firm voice.

Truly, my gut is telling me that something is very wrong, but I can't tell that to Joan right now. She won't be able to handle it. I watch while Joan grabs her raincoat from our closet and pulls her purse over her arm. Then she stomps past me out of our room, down the stairs, and out the front door.

I love that all I have to do it put a game plan in front of Joan and she is on point. I get down on my knees, head leaning against the floor, and began to pray from the depths of my worry.

Lord, something is terribly wrong right now. I don't know what has happened to Adin, but there are warning bells going off all inside of me.

Father, I cannot protect her wherever she is right this second, but you can. You are the only Rock she can stand on, and I pray you would send her your wisdom for whatever situation she is facing right now. I would love for this entire predicament to be a complete misunderstanding, but you have taught me to listen to your steady voice within me, and it is telling me that there is danger.

I don't know what you want me to do, but, Lord, please lead my steps to her. When I can be near her again, fill me with your words and your heart for the need. Lord, please calm my Joan. Fill her with your love and peace as we go through this. She loves that girl to the core, and I pray that you can sustain her with your peace. In Jesus's name I pray, Amen.

As I raise up off my knees, I hear the front door open again, and Joan yells up the stairs, "Well, come on already!"

She is not one to be patient when something needs to get done. I open the door and dash down the stairs with much more peace than before.

Joan

Lord, where is she? Please, you know that my patience is terrible! I can't do this, Lord! I love that girl too much to lose her. You know this. I'm sorry, Lord. You know every part of me!

Immediately, I am comforted by a verse that comes to my mind. I embrace God's nearness remembering Joshua 1:9: "Be strong and courageous. Don't be terrified; don't be discouraged for the Lord your God will be with you wherever you go."

Thank you, Lord, I needed that reminder right now. Keep me in your hands. Bless me with your patience. Please be with Adin; let her be okay. I love you, Lord.

Dave and I have been driving around everywhere near our neighborhood the last few hours. We had gone back up to Central High, and while he checked the hallways and classrooms, I had run to the gym and asked all the boys milling around if they had seen Adin. As soon as Chase heard, he was concerned. He left wrestling practice to join Dave and me in our search.

I pick up my cell phone yet again and hit send. I have been trying to contact Marge Ann since I had the bad feeling this afternoon. Each time, I get her voice mail. Nothing about today makes any sense. It has never taken Marge this long to get back to me.

I turn around to see anxiousness illustrated all over Chase's face. Poor boy. He really cares for her too. I reach over and pat his hand, the one that is white-knuckle gripping the back of my seat.

"I just don't know where she would have gone." Chase starts, more talking to himself out loud than anything else, "She has never gone anywhere after school before. The only other person at school that she even talks to is Aubrey, and they've never gotten together outside of school." There is a look of intense concentration on his face as he tries to wrap his own mind around Adin's disappearance.

There is an understood agreement within the car that nothing about today is adding up. I can feel the anxiety within myself rising when I notice the light posts outside turning on. It's getting dark. I cannot imagine Adin out there on the streets in the cold night. I know that she lived on the streets for a long time before coming to our home, but it still doesn't make it okay to me.

Something bad must have happened for her to not come home. I recall Marge saying that Adin fled every foster home she's ever been in before without complaint from herself or the foster families, but this is different. I know that this is different because there has been a heart change within this beautiful young woman.

"Dave, should we call the police?" I think, for the first time, to ask.

"I already did while I was in the school. They can't do anything until she has been missing for 24 hours. I didn't mention it because I'm angry about the whole conversation. We should go back home, Joan. I know that you've been calling the home line, but maybe she's upset and not answering."

Dave makes a left turn at Maple Street to cut across a few back roads towards home. I lean my head against the passenger window and look out at the street, willing her to be home when we get there.

CHAPTER 21

Pain is Weakness Leaving the Body

Adin

My hands shake uncontrollably while I try to get a good enough grip on the knob to turn on the water in the upstairs bathroom. I've been telling myself over and over to not look in the mirror—kind of like the whole don't look down when you're afraid of heights.

I take a deep breath and beg myself to focus on the easy tasks at hand, like getting a washcloth out of the closet, then soak it in water, and ring it out. Turning my back to the mirror, I gingerly pat my face. White hot pain jolts my eyes open. Momentarily, the shock causes my hands to still.

A sob catches in my throat. My mind involuntarily takes me back to this afternoon. Since my race back home this afternoon, my mind has housed an internal battle of purposely forgetting and remembering.

I will not think about it right now. Clenching my teeth in an effort to focus, I command my mind to shut off. My heart continues to race despite the safety of being home.

When I put the wash cloth back under the faucet, the water turns red. Instinctively, I look up and catch my reflection. It's too much all at once. I fall to my knees in the bathroom, wanting to cover my face, any mannerism to hide away. I can't though—because it hurts too much.

I give in and scream. I wail loudly, relinquishing the misery that has followed me my entire life.

Why me? What black spell was put on me in the womb? Why do I even exist? I'm done! Do you hear me, God! I'm done! Screw you! You're loving and giving? Yeah right! Where were you tonight?

You left me to myself yet again. Pastor Ben told me just this week at youth group that you would fight for me! We were reading in the book of Jeremiah, and the one thing that had stuck out to me and gave me hope is a total lie! Pastor Ben explained that people who fight against me will not overcome me because you are with me and will rescue me. Where was the rescue? I'm pretty sure that, as per usual, I came through for myself.

My emotional outburst induces a throbbing in my right eye, the one so swollen I can't see out of it at all. Switching gears, I store this hysterical eruption to the back of my mind and decide to concentrate on more important issues. I've got to get downstairs to get some ice on this eye before Joan and Dave get home and then come up with a plausible excuse for my appearance.

What am I going to tell them!?

Feeling more determined, I get up, catching sight of my right hand as I turn off the bathroom light. My knuckles are all completely bruised. Even though the pain is excruciating, I'm proud of this mark. Right there, on my own hand, is the proof that the jerk didn't get away without a little something as well.

My attempt at turning off the light elicits a pinch across the top of my right hand, giving me no choice but to turn and use my left hand. Tip-toeing slowly downstairs, I hold my breath. I hadn't heard anyone come in while I was upstairs, but I was also in the middle of a screaming episode. I edge through the dark house into the kitchen.

It's amazing how easy it is to remember your own home. I freeze.

I bend down, sobbing all over again. I've called this place "home" several times within the last five minutes, and it was real. This is my home? My entire body gets all prickly, and not being too sure about what this feeling is, I hug myself tightly. As a result, a sharp stab shoots through my entire right arm, beginning at my hand. Good thing I'm not too big on hugging.

Pain is weakness leaving the body. I can hear Dave saying that right now. Despite my circumstances, I smile when I think of Dave. This night has been a roller coaster of emotion, and I am ready to exit the ride.

I continue to the fridge, open the freezer, take out a piece of ice, and hold it over my right eye. Crap, it stings. I've caught glimpses of a few boxing matches on TV. How in the world do those boxers allow anyone to rub on their jacked-up eyes?

I take a deep breath, causing more pain to radiate from my ribs. Maybe I should have taken a better look in the mirror, just to assess the damage.

The headlights coming up the driveway cause me to brace myself against the island. What do I do? Think, Adin.

My heart thunders in my ears, picking up pace once again. My mind goes immediately blank. I could run upstairs and buy myself some time, but they'll just come in and swarm me with questions.

I run to the kitchen light and flip it on, flinching at the ache in my hand. Does Dave know how long knuckles stay bruised?

Not right now, Adin. Focus.

I look around for my book bag, but then remember I left it in the bathroom. I grab one of Joan's many notebooks, which just so happens to be sitting on the counter next to the back door. She always has notebooks lying around so she can make more lists. I rip out a sheet of paper and jump up to the island.

Adrenaline courses through my body, barricading any physical discomfort. I hear Joan's and Dave's worried voices when they open the front door. My eyes water when I hear Chase's baritone voice intermixed with theirs. Their anticipation is like an electric current running between us when the three of them hurriedly make their way to the kitchen.

I put my name at the top of my paper, and quickly write down half of a math formula from class today. I let out a painful gasp when Joan hugs me tightly from behind. Immediately, she stiffens and slowly turns me around. I keep my head down, knowing all of their eyes must be resting on me.

"Hey guys," I say, eyes still down, hoping that they don't hear the strain in my voice.

"Adin, look at me." The concern in Chase's voice evident. A traitorous tear rolls down my good eye when I look up into his face. I've never seen anger on Chase's face before, but jaw-locked, bulged-eyed, red-faced Chase—I'm going to say this is his really, really mad face.

"Oh, honey, who did this to you?" Tears roll down Joan's devastated face.

Dave's eyes look like they, too, are going to pop right out of his head. As if this isn't enough, we all turn towards the front door when we hear someone knocking. Dave shifts to answer the door, while Chase and Joan move closer to me, taking on a protective stance.

"I don't really know," I explain. Man, I've got to get my poker face on right now. "I didn't get a good look at his face, but I did get a good punch in! Look." I lift up my right hand for them both to inspect my purple knuckles. Of course, this would have to be the moment that Ms. Ann takes to join our group. Tonight of all nights my case worker would have to drop by.

God, you can't just give me a break ever, can you?

"Adin Taylor, what happened to you this afternoon?" Ms. Ann firmly questions me. I sit there stumped for a moment, a little thrown off by her no nonsense tone of voice. I dart my good eye back and forth from each one of them as they all push in a little closer, awaiting my explanation.

"Umm, well, I was walking home from school, and when I hit the bottom of the hill, I felt like something was wrong." I decide to keep everything as close as possible to the truth, so it won't be hard to remember later.

"I didn't know why I kept feeling like something was wrong, so I figured I could just walk faster to try to get home sooner. I began to hear footsteps behind me. I focused on the sound to see how close they were without having to look back, but I couldn't make it out. I panicked and began to run. Only, I didn't run home; I took the first street to my right and just started sprinting. I ran for as long as I could and then jumped a fence into a construction site."

"I hid between two dumpsters for a really long time to try to calm myself down. When it started to get dark out, I made up my mind to try to find my way back home because I hadn't seen or heard anything. It took me a while to figure out which direction was home. When I got close to the main road, this big guy in a black ski mask jumped out from behind a tree and punched me in the face."

I point to my right eye and move my face around so each of them can get a good look at it. "He tried to grab my book bag, but I guess old habits die hard, and I wouldn't let him take it." I try to make my face look a little sheepish. This would be the point where my amazing acting abilities have to come in handy.

"He went to punch me again, but I did the single-leg take down that Chase taught me and put him on his butt." I can't help the laugh that comes out despite the seriousness of the situation. The look on the jerk's face was priceless.

"When I turned to run, he grabbed my ankle and brought me down to the ground. He rolled on top of me and punched me in the side. He tried holding my wrist down, but Chase also taught me how to gain wrist control, so when I got my wrist free, I punched him as hard as I could in the face. He rolled back, and that's when I jumped up and ran all the way home."

I grimace in pain. I take a moment to look each one of them in the eyes, hoping this direct eye contact will the seal the deal. I almost want to curl my fingers around each other for good luck.

Dave clears his throat, approaches me, and carefully puts his hand under my chin, lifting my face to take a good look at it.

"Good thing you put ice on that right away; you're definitely going to have a shiner." He rummages around in the freezer and pulls out a bag of peas.

"Here, put this on your eye." I take the bag of peas from him in compliance.

"Thanks." I respond, simultaneously reminding myself to breathe normal. It is a priority that everyone in this room buys my story.

I'm finding it hard to make eye contact with Chase, because I know out of everyone here, he can read me best. I just need to stay calm, so everyone else can too.

Ms. Ann nods her head and bites down on her bottom lip. She's not buying what I'm selling. Oh well, that's the best I can do tonight, given what's already happened. In any case, this is all their getting. Ever.

I tilt my head to side as if to say, "Go on. Try me." Ms. Ann closes her eyes and rubs her temples.

"I had come here tonight to discuss a situation with you, Adin, but I can see this is not the best time." She looks over to where Joan and Dave are standing.

"I'm so sorry I didn't return your calls from earlier today. I was in and out of conference meetings the entire time," she explains.

"That's fine, Marge. Don't worry about it. We were actually getting concerned about your whereabouts as well," Dave admits.

Joan walks over to Dave, and he wraps her up in one of his bear hugs. They sure do like hugging a lot. Finally, I allow myself a peek at Chase. He looks like a wreck. His reaction to my story makes me feel terrible. I really am protecting him though.

"Chase, I'm so sorry for making you worry about me. I'm okay though, thanks to all those wrestling moves you taught me." I want for him to hear the sincerity in my voice.

He holds my gaze, but doesn't respond. At least he's calmed down since he saw my face, but I don't like the confusion I find registered in his eyes. It makes me feel like he isn't going to make this an easy situation to let go.

"Dave, do you think we should take her to the Emergency Room?" Joan asks.

"Couldn't hurt," Dave replies. "We should also contact the police and file a report against whoever attacked her. Adin, I don't think you should be walking to school anymore."

I groan inwardly. *No, no, no.* I look forward to walking to school with Chase every single day. I can feel myself pouting like a four year old. I look up to Chase with a pleading look. He has to fix this.

Chase clears his throat. "Mr. Baldwin, sir. I could ask my parents to drive the truck to school. No one uses it during the day since my dad has the church van, and mom has her own car."

Dave raises his eyebrows and nods his head, "Thanks, Chase, that would be great. As long as your parents are okay with it, we are. Tell them we'll split the gas. Adin, Joan will pick you up from school every day since Chase has wrestling practice. I never want this to happen to you again!" He walks over to me and gifts me with a loose hug.

This is the first time that I've allowed Dave to get within any type of touching range to me. It doesn't feel wrong though, so I leave that to think over later.

"Don't worry, it won't," I reply, without realizing how I phrase my answer.

Everyone looks at me in confusion. I quickly attempt damage control, "I mean, I'm sure it won't. It's not as if I didn't get my own punch in there. The lunatic probably won't be messing with anyone for a long time." I smile confidently, giving the impression that I actually believe what I'm saying.

CHAPTER 22

After the Attack

Adin

It's been a few days since *the incident*, and almost everything in my life has gotten back to normal…almost. Chase just cannot let it go. I've allowed Joan to mother me a bit more than necessary, and Dave has hugged me a few more times. I'll sacrifice some of my rules to get back the peaceful relationship we had.

Chase, however, is still brooding. First, he just knew it was Keith Lewis, my Literature class stalker. Chase assumed that Keith still wasn't over the snub that happened months ago. I reminded Chase that I know Keith's build and voice, and the person who did this to me was not anything like Keith, which is when Chase turned into a detective.

He has had a ton of detail questions. It was a little heady, trying to remember all of the tiny miniscule parts and keep them in order. The big picture that I crafted was no problem; however, the millions of nanosecond type facts have blurred together.

His questioning puts me in a bad mood. I'd like nothing better than to just forget about the entire ordeal. Every time I remind Chase of this fact, he shakes his head stubbornly and says that it should have never happened, and he is going to make sure that whoever did this to me can never do it again.

The most horrible part is that he thinks he has to try and make me understand how this guy could be out there, doing the same thing to another young girl. He has no idea how close to the truth he's actually getting. I've lived my whole life having to protect myself, and just because I've made some changes since I've moved in with the Baldwins, doesn't mean I'm a completely different person.

Instead of looking forward to our time together, I've begun to dread it. This is not the Chase that I love to flirt and goof off with. This intense Chase is a bit too much for me right now. So, I've had to back away and give excuses instead of hanging around. I figure that when he calms down, and can let it all go, then we can pick up exactly where we left off.

It's much harder than it sounds though. It's only been three days and not going over to his house after he gets home from wrestling is near impossible. I've had to really focus. A few times I've literally caught myself just walking in the direction of his house without even thinking about it. My mind will be elsewhere, and so my heart leads. It's so frustrating.

All of this runs through my mind as I open the passenger door to his truck. Even though I've been avoiding him, he still picks me up for school in the morning. The first thing I notice are the big black circles under his eyes. There is too much guilt if I look at him for very long, so I opt to check out my Dr. Marten Mary Janes instead.

For the first time ever, I'm thankful that the ride to school is short. Once Chase parks the truck in the student parking lot, I reach for my door handle. He reaches over to me, lying his hand on my shoulder. I know he wants me to turn and look him in the eye, but I don't want to.

My heart begins its normal tirade anytime he gets this close. I want to put my hand over his and intertwine our fingers.

Get it together, Adin. This isn't the time.

I take my time raising my head. Tilting my head and raising my eyebrows, I question him.

He grimaces and then asks, "Adin, I miss you. What is going on?"

The pain in his voice pierces my heart. I cannot possibly explain everything to him; it's too dangerous, but I have to do something. He closes his eyes, defeated, when I don't answer right away.

"I miss you too. I'm just really sick and tired of all the fuss from my run in with the ski mask guy. I know that what happened was horrible, but hey, that's my usual luck." There is too much anger in my voice for my excuse to come off as simple as I want him to hear it. I try again.

"Anyways," I continue, "I don't want to talk about it anymore. Chase, when you've lived through some of things that I have, you just try to be grateful for what is good in your life. You don't constantly try to figure out all the bad. Can you try to see it my way?"

I hold my breath. I am being honest. This would be the closest thing I have to a life philosophy. I just hope that Chase can accept it. I watch as his eyes soften with understanding.

Thank God. Thank who? Oh, never mind; not right now!

"So, you're not avoiding me because you don't want to be around me? You are avoiding me because I keep bringing up what happened? You don't want to talk about it anymore? I don't understand how you can just let it go, but you're right, I haven't lived your life."

He slides across the bench seat until he is right next to me. I swallow hard, never breaking eye contact. His arms come around me, holding me. I close my eyes, lost in the security of his embrace.

"When we couldn't find you the other day, I was so lost. I wouldn't even allow myself to imagine what could've been happening to you. Initially, I was angry with God, but then I realized how stupid that was. God didn't want some jerk to hurt you any more than I did. God gave me peace and strength as I prayed for you."

When he looks up into my eyes, there are tears in his. My heart rises in my chest with love for this tender boy. The lump in my throat keeps me from responding.

How do you tell a guy that isn't even your boyfriend that you love him? You don't, and that makes it worse. If he loves me so much, and can't imagine his life without me in it, then why hasn't he asked me out yet? Ugh, it's all too much. I nod my head up and down to let him know that I heard him and rest my forehead against his.

What does he mean that God was angry too? I thought God controlled everything. I thought that if anybody could've stopped what took place, it would have been God. None of this makes any sense.

My breath comes out in shallow puffs at the nearness of him. He continues to stare right into my eyes, just like he can see all of me—every single secret that I've hidden down deep. It's a bit intimidating, allowing him this much access to me, but if I am honest with myself, I let my guard down around him a long time ago.

Joan

"Okay, Marge. I appreciate everything you're doing. We'll see you next Wednesday at 11AM. Bye." My voice thick with emotion when I say goodbye and close my cell phone. I have that terrible gut feeling, just like the day Adin went missing.

Has it already been five days? That day alone took forever to get through, or to be more precise, each minute she was missing felt like an hour in itself.

I am so grateful that when we got home she was here waiting for us. I didn't think to ask the obvious questions until later, after my original shock wore off. There she was, sitting at the island in the kitchen, working on math homework, as if her black eye was nothing out of the ordinary.

The recap of her event made perfect sense initially, but after I was able to step back and analyze the situation, it didn't fit. If she was chased to the point of hiding for a few hours, and the attacker was still waiting for her, then why didn't he follow her home? Once she got inside of the house, why didn't she call for help? Why was the front door left unlocked?

It has taken me every bit of self-control to remain quiet about that day. I have prayed over and over for God's discernment, and right now, he is telling me to keep my mouth closed and my ears open.

I know that this is why Adin has been so open about Chase. She is at her wits end with Chase's prying. I'll just remain her sounding board until God nudges me otherwise.

My phone has been ringing off the hook today. I smile, remembering my conversation with Matt this morning. I miss my son.

He is right in the middle of his second semester as a freshman at the University of Delaware. He is attending there on a full athletic scholarship for baseball.

I can still remember the way his eyes glittered in triumph when he came running through the front door, waving his acceptance letter in the air, then picking me up in a Matt-style hug.

This morning's call was a pleasant surprise. He was just calling to check in. His schedule has been hectic since baseball season started. He has been traveling everywhere for his Division I games. Dave makes sure to tape every game we can find on TV.

Matt could tell that something was bothering me, so I decided to tell him about Adin's attack. He listened quietly, and I could just imagine his face bunching up as the events unfolded. He is a fix-it kind of guy, and I knew that he would have advice.

After a pause, he agreed that I should remain quiet and let Adin come to me. He also concurred that her story didn't add up, but he encouraged me to stay calm because it must be something important to her if she felt that she had to hide information. His insight into the situation eased my worrying, and I inwardly thanked God for Matt's wisdom.

He continued to point out the positive aspects of that day's disaster. Mainly, Adin came home. She could have run away at whatever happened to her, but she came back to us, which means that she must feel safe in our family.

His encouragement allowed me to finally sigh with relief. I thanked Matt for his positive perception and let him know that I would be praying for him as well. After I finished my stereotypical mom lecture of doing his laundry and staying on top of his studies, I let him know I loved him and said goodbye.

Marge also voiced that Adin's story didn't make sense. She had been at Adin's previous foster parents for most of the evening before coming to our house. Marge said that the entire evening she was there, the foster father never came home even though she had scheduled the appointment for him and his wife both.

She had already been planning on stopping by the night that Adin was attacked to ask Adin some questions, but in lieu of the night's events, she decided to wait.

I have to be careful when I permit my mind to think about this particular foster father, because my imagination has formed an opinion of its own with him taking the lead role of the villain.

When we had taken her to the Emergency Room, she had turned pasty white. It had never occurred to me that the hospital would scare her. Her hands wouldn't quit shaking, and her eyes kept darting around. I stayed as close to her as I could the entire time we were there, praying for God's peace and comfort.

When the nurse called us to the back and led us to our private examining room, I thought Adin was going to make a run for it. Her eyes had a very distinct look of defensiveness. I just couldn't figure it out. I had tried to remain calm for her, but her mannerisms were erratic.

At the time, I just chalked it up to shock. Looking back now, I'm not so sure. Again, when the nurse had asked her to change out of her clothes and into a hospital gown, through clenched teeth Adin firmly retorted, "No."

The nurse had given Dave and me a questionable look, and when I had directed my own confused eyes towards Adin, she had her arms wrapped tightly around herself, eyes averted towards the ground.

I did not want Adin reverting back to isolating herself, so I had crossed the room and put my arms around her, politely telling the nurse, "No thank you. The gown will not be necessary."

Adin seemed to relax, allowing me to take charge. She asked me to stay with her during the entire exam. In fact, she never once looked at the doctor but rather held eye-contact with me instead.

During the x-rays, she also asked me to remain with her. My

heart had wanted to burst. She wanted me around her! She wanted me to stay!

Lord, there has been so much difficulty that has taken place this week. I am exhausted. Thank you for holding my family close and keeping Adin safe. Thank you for being our Savior.

I don't know what has happened to Adin to give her such an adverse reaction to hospitals, but you do. Lord, thank you for letting me be there with her. I pray that you can use me to help Adin see the goodness in this world.

I feel like she has seen much more evil in her short life than anyone should. I know satan has been on her heals, but I also know that you have already conquered this adversary. Thank you for your victory that I can stand firm on every single day.

I am reminded of Galatians 5:6, where your word says, 'The only thing that counts is faith expressing itself through love.' I love Adin so, so much, Lord. Thank you for sending her to my home. Thank you for giving me the privilege of being part of her life.

I have faith that you are going to open her eyes to your salvation. I pray for Pastor Tim, that this Sunday you would anoint his message. I pray that you use him as a vessel to not only reach Adin but anyone in our service who doesn't already have a personal relationship with you. Please, open their ears and hearts to your voice. Allow our church to unify and glorify you. In Jesus's name I pray, Amen.

CHAPTER 23

Perfect Pink Dresses and Pews

Adin

I have never seen so many people all dressed up in one place before. I scan the crowd for Chase. People are either darting here and there saying, "Excuse me" every five seconds, or they are standing in groups with their pastel dresses or neck ties smiling and talking.

I run my fingers down the side of my own new dress that Joan had surprised me with at breakfast this morning. More correctly, she had three dresses laid out on the island when I came downstairs. At first my stomach protested because I'm use to Dave having breakfast on the island in front of my chair, so the dresses were more of an annoyance. Then, I rubbed the sleep out of my eyes and saw how gorgeous all three of them were.

I held up my hands in acquiesce of surrender and told Joan there was no way I would be able to choose, so she would have to do it for me. She made me go to the downstairs bathroom and try each dress on and then attempt to sashay around the kitchen for her.

Dave acted the stereotypical dad, smiling a toothy-grin every time I would exit the restroom to twirl for Joan. He even put his hand over his heart when I modeled in *the* dress, the one we all decided was perfect for Easter service. I'm astonished and grateful that I finally had a normal father-daughter moment.

Joan's eyes lit up when I exited the bathroom in the strawberry pink, silk dress. I blushed at her and Dave's reactions. It is beautiful, and I feel extraordinary wearing it.

The dress is sleeveless with a sweetheart neckline accessorized with little ruffles. There is a triangle shaped embroidery that is floral on the bodice. I love that the dress has an empire waist, so when I twirl the bottom flows up just a little. Then, she handed me a set of strappy silver heals, and the ensemble was complete.

Once I ran upstairs and saw how gorgeous the dress was on me, I decided to put my hair in hot rollers. I took my time doing my make-up, making sure to cover up my black eye. I literally bounced down the stairs. I was greeted by a camera flash and one of Dave's toothy smiles. I couldn't even pretend to be mad. I was riding the beauty high.

Dave ushered Joan and I into the car and kept going on and on about having the best two looking girls at church this Sunday. The sun was shining brightly in the car window, and all I could think was that this must be what it feels like to be a part of a family.

I sense Chase staring at me from somewhere, the goose bumps racing from my shoulders to my wrists. Slowly, I look around for those brilliant blue eyes but end up backing right into him. I don't know how I know it's him, I just do.

Catching a whiff of his cologne, the familiarity sets my heart racing. He grabs my hand and whirls me around. Our eyes connect and the world around me has paused. My lips curve into a special smile that only he can trigger. The thousands of butterflies in my stomach release a euphoric sensation that I have become addicted to in his presence.

He leans his face down to my ear, tickling it when he whispers, "You look amazing!"

I want to say something back, but I can't. I'm lost in the uncharted territory of caring about someone more than myself. He begins to laugh, and then Aubrey rushes up and grabs me on both sides of my arms, "Oh my goodness, Adin, I love this dress!"

She envelopes me in a girly hug as more people from our Youth Group create a circle with us. Chase hasn't let go of my hand, and it's all I can think about. He rubs his thumb back and forth lightly over my knuckles, causing everything but this sensation to fade in a blur behind what I can feel.

All the girls are giggling about something, and feeling a little self-conscious, I tune into their conversation. All of them are congratulating some girl whose name I don't remember for accepting Jesus into her life Friday night. I didn't know such a decision warranted a celebration.

"You okay?" Chase asks me.

"Yeah, I'm great. Why?" I ask, still watching the group of girls.

"You were just biting your lip," He points out.

Trumped, I fume. When did I become so easy to read?

Chase leads me out of the foyer and in through a set of doors that are already opened. As we pass through, an older man dressed in a gray suit hands me a piece of paper. I look at Chase tentatively, but watching him take one, I follow suit.

We enter the sanctuary, the vastness overwhelming me. The sun shines brilliantly through all of the stained glass windows, and the colors overlap miniature rainbows over everything. There is a cacophony of noise while everyone simultaneously visits with the people around them. Unease accelerates my heart, and instinctively, I begin to back up, bumping into Chase.

He releases his hand from mine, gently placing it on the lower part of my back, directing me forward. This would be the time to run, to flee before anyone can pass judgment, before anyone here might remember the story of the eight-year old girl and her embarrassing past. My heart races at the memory of that Christmas program so long ago. I wonder if a story like that would've been passed over to the people at this church.

As we head down the aisle towards the front, I remember making this walk before, following the most magical play I had ever witnessed and look what happened then. I scan all of the people milling about; I don't know why I expect to notice a friend of some kind. Really, Chase is my closest friend, and he is standing right behind me.

Robotically, I continue forward not really thinking of any destination, just inching forward as Chase's hand guides me. I let out a sigh of relief when he delivers me to a pew far enough from the front that I won't be making any eye contact with the Pastor. I just don't feel much like looking into the man's eyes while he talks about Jesus dying on a cross or whatever else this whole Easter Holiday is about anyway.

I scoot over towards Joan, making room for Chase to sit beside me when I realize that he has already stepped back one pew and is sitting behind us. I sigh in frustration. He's not even directly behind me, but rather all the way down at the other end of his pew. I'm right smack in the middle of mine.

Can anything in my life just be easy? No, because then it wouldn't be consistent. I grind my teeth together, resentful at the uneasiness that continues to inch up my throat.

All at once, people start quieting down; an older couple politely wave at Joan and Dave, sitting down in the same pew as us. Sweat trickles down my back in a game of follow-the-leader. My chest rises and falls a little faster as I scan the packed-full church. Gulping, I try to formulate an escape route, but there's not very much leg room to get around the people squishing me up against Joan.

As soon as Joan looks over at me, I straighten up in my seat like everything is fine. I remind myself that this service really isn't a big deal; I've been attending Youth Group for weeks now. I don't need Chase sitting beside me, holding my hand, to get through this.

In all reality, I was hoping that would've been the case; it was kind of a daydream that I've been nurturing for a while, so the letdown of him being a pew behind is messing with my beauty high a bit, but, again, I never let myself get my hopes up too high because the result is barely ever what I wanted in the first place.

I raise my chin up, clench my trembling hands, and force my

jerking knee to still as if to tell this church that though this is not where I want to be, I can handle it...all by myself.

So, bring it on God, because it's not as if you've ever made my life simple, and yet, here I am.

There is a fire that ignites inside while I taunt God to try and mess with me today, because no matter what, I will win.

Anger begins to ignite. I figured I'd walk in, sit down next to Chase, concentrate on his hand being so very close to mine, tune out the endless droning of the Pastor, bow my head when I was supposed to, make a timely exit, all the time smiling as best I could to make Joan and Dave believe that I was actually paying attention and appreciated their invitation.

Then, I would never come back again. At least not to the big church. Youth group is okay.

As usual, I came into this entire fiasco with a game plan in check. What I didn't prepare for was my own self being the traitor. Being angry at all this drama going on inside myself, I miss the importance of everyone around me standing. *Whoops, already drawing attention to myself!*

Joan eyes me sideways as she continues to sing. I want so badly to turn around and see Chase, but not right this second while I know he has to be embarrassed just watching me sit in ignorance while everyone else is on point with synchronized standing and what not. Why don't churches hand out instruction manuals for how this whole Sunday morning thing works?

I stand up slowly, trying to put on the guise that I meant to be sitting for so long, run my hand over the hymnals placed in front of me, finally resting on the last one. I pick it up and flip through the pages until I land on the same page as the older lady beside me. The way she has her hymnal thrust open in her hand as she sings, her eyes closed, seems a bit stupid to me, but whatever. Due to her weird behavior, I'm able to appear as if I know what's going on.

I can't help but stare at her though. She has her hymnal lying open in one hand, eyes shut in a relaxed way—almost like she is seeing something, and her right hand is held up high in the air as if she is in my history class waiting to be called on with the right answer.

I tilt my head trying to figure out what this old lady is actually doing when I notice another arm thrust high in the air, coming from the very front. How could I not? It's covered in some pretty familiar tattoos.

CHAPTER 24

Making Sense of Things

Dave

Lord, I am overcome with love for you right now. Pastor Tim was amazing this morning: once again painting a picture of a day so long ago in time when your son, your only son, willingly laid down his life for the sin that still runs so rampant in this world today.

I'm quite sure you must have been wringing your hands—at least I would have been. Matt is the closest thing I have to my own son; and Lord, because you already know my heart, I'm sure that you know I would have begged to take his place.

I could not have watched him raised up on that cross, his hands and feet pierced with nails. I am beyond grateful for your love, the kind of love that gave up your only son, the perfect lamb, for a world full of sinners.

Thank you, Father, for all of your children that chose to recommit their lives today or accepted you for the first time into their hearts. I must admit, I am a bit deflated that Adin didn't make her way up to the altar.

I just want it so badly for her; I have the picture of it all in my mind. But, in your timing Lord, definitely not mine. It breaks my heart to think of her without your comfort and love. She has never known true love because she has never known you.

She was rather thoughtful all throughout the service. I pray that she trusts someone enough to talk to them about her questions. Please prepare whomever that might be with your words, Lord, with your wisdom and discernment.

Lord, thank you for the progress that has already taken place within Adin. I never know what to expect, simply because it is in your capable hands. I am so very humbled at just being allowed to be part of the process. It is truly beyond words to be a front row audience to your miracles. I am honored.

Pastor Tim really touched me today when he spoke about Romans 8:17: 'If we share in the Lord's sufferings, then we may share in his glory.' Father, may I never complain about my sufferings. I desire to stand in glory with you throughout this life and into eternity. I love you, Father. In Jesus's name I pray, Amen.

I lift my eyes when Pastor Tim finishes his own prayer over our congregation and immediately swing my head to the right, searching Adin's countenance. She is biting on her lower lip, standing on her tiptoes, trying to see something going on in the front of the church.

Mr. Tapper is standing in front of her, and I chuckle, thinking that if she wants to see anything around him, she will need the assistance of a ladder. Her annoyance makes me only want to laugh harder, so I cover my mouth with my left hand and hold my stomach with the other, desperately trying to act as if I don't see her.

Taking a few deep breaths, I calm myself. When I look over again, she's given up on that mission. I observe her discrete glances behind us at Chase. However, when I look back at Chase, he is sitting down in his pew, head dropped down in his hands praying.

Good for you son, I coax.

I'm quite sure his prayers include Adin as well, and my heart wants to explode at the goodness of God. Adin is lifted up in prayer from so many: Joan, Pastor Ben and Kami, Chase, Pastor Tim, Ms. Ann, and myself. God is so faithful.

I'm starting to become as impatient as Joan wanting God to fix it all up right now in a nice, neat little bow. *Sorry, God.* The journey to this point is what will keep Adin strong among so much doubt in this world.

Help me to not get in your way, Father. I only want to be in your will as to when and how she accepts you.

People are filing out of their pews and into the foyer to say their goodbyes. Mr. And Mrs. Whaley have made their way out the end of our pew, but Adin just stands there fiddling with a bracelet around her wrist. She looks rather thoughtful.

I sit down and motion for Joan to do the same. I don't want to rush Adin if she is thinking about anything that Pastor Tim spoke about this morning. I want to give her the freedom to do so.

I take out my Bible and begin to look up a few verses that he covered this morning; this way if she feels guilty in any way for holding us up, she'll see that I'm occupied as well.

Once Mr. Tapper moves out of his pew, I watch her head snap up and lock on Tiffani Isley, the Pastor's daughter. The look in her eyes seems to be one of recognition, and I wonder if she and Tiffani have already met.

"Joan," I hear Adin say.

"Hmmm," Joan responds, her head down reading over today's church program.

"Isn't that Tiffani from the salon where you took me to get my hair cut?" She whispers, as Tiffani and her parents make their way to the other side of the sanctuary to a side exit.

Joan lifts her head, scanning the church, finally resting her gaze where Adin is pointing out to the right.

"Oh, yes it is. That's right, I forgot it was Tiffani who cut your hair. Pastor Tim is her father."

I give Joan a bewildered glance when I watch Adin's jaw drop in shock

Adin.

It's taking me longer than usual to get ready today. I feel like I've got glue in my brain, trying to make sense of Tiffani being the Pastor's daughter. It's been this way for three days, like I walk around in a zombie-like-state, trying to make sense of something that just doesn't fit.

Joan and Dave have given me plenty of space, and I'm grateful for their intuitiveness. Chase has been extra quiet, and I'm hoping it's just because he's busy thinking about the first big spring wrestling tournament that he has coming up.

I place my hands over my face, rubbing it roughly up and down, trying to rub out the inconsistencies that still remain. Tiffani is the coolest, most stand-outish person that I've ever met; for her to be a Christian is over-the-top.

I never realized that God was okay with people like her, or more precisely, people like me. It shakes the very foundation of why I've justified giving God the cold shoulder whenever something sneaks its way in that makes some sense. Monroe pierced, sleeve tattooed Tiffani and God hanging out–that is just insane.

It would mean that God isn't the hypocrite, but everyone else is. Because really, everyone else is cliquish. Like if you don't agree with their circle of values, then you're not one of them. However, the constant thought among all these cliques is that Christians are hypocrites because they don't accept everyone for who they are, and if you try to be the real you, then you would never be good enough for God.

I always thought that being a Christian meant that I could never be me; that somehow, allowing him to come in would just make me ashamed of what I am and guilty over my past. Where did I get that? I sit down on the edge of my bed and concentrate. Where have my own beliefs come from?

I see my mother's face, puffing on the last bit of a cigarette. I look down at my hands and realize that I must be young, eight or nine at the most. I'm looking up at her again, her eyes closed even though I know that when they open they won't be clear, they won't even be white around her pupils.

Whatever my mom is on, it makes her eyes yellow. She smells like sweat; her hair is matted down on her head, giving the appearance that she just got out of the shower, but I already know that's impossible. We don't have any running water here.

Looking around the one room 'home' that we share, there isn't even a sink in here. There is a dirty mattress pushed up against the farthest corner of the room, but there isn't a blanket anywhere in sight.

There is one window looking out into a back alley, but it's covered with so much grime that I couldn't make out anything more than a blur, even if it was right smack up against the window.

The walls have stains everywhere, and as a child, I constantly wonder how they got onto the ceiling. I stay on the mattress, my knees up to my chin, head down. I can hear my mother talking to herself. She does this sometimes, has full blown conversations with no one at all.

I've tried talking to her when she's like this, but I can tell that I just get on her nerves. I've learned that it's safer staying hidden in the shadows cast all over this room.

Sometimes she leaves me here, and after a few sleeps, I hear her letting herself in, laughing at things that I can't comprehend. She usually brings back a paper bag from some fast food joint, and I gobble it down.

I haven't been in school for a while, but that thought no longer bothers me, because I can't hide the tears when all the other kids make fun of my clothes and my hair, and it breaks me when I just watch the teachers avert their eyes because they don't know what to do with me.

I sit in this room all day, and I wonder who made me, and why? I don't think most kids live this way, or I wouldn't be made fun of so much.

Whenever I do find the courage to poke my head out our door, I don't see or hear any other kids running around. I do hear lots of screaming women, but I don't understand their slurred words.

If this is all there is to a life, then I don't think I want to stay. When

I had gone to that magical play last year and the snow was falling, the characters on stage had talked a lot about someone called God.

The only thing I remember is one of the angels saying over and over, 'Glory to God in the highest, peace on earth, and goodwill to all men.' I don't know what glory is, but I do understand peace.

Peace would mean comfort, right? My child-like mind tries to understand such a word. Wouldn't peace mean love? I don't have any of those things, so maybe God doesn't love everyone, and I'm on the hate list.

I shiver at the coldness that builds inside my innocent heart. My teeth begin to chatter, burdened with the reality of how unloved I really am.

A waterfall of tears crashes down my face, awakening me from my memories. That was real. I've never allowed myself to look back; it's been my shield against all the long ago pain that I pushed down.

It hurts so much; how can I even have a heart inside when it is so broken? There must be a million jagged fragments barely held together by sheer will. That's probably why Chase hasn't asked me to be his girlfriend, because he can see what I can't. He can see the sharp splinters of my heart ready to pierce him too.

Slipping down from the edge of my bed, I hide my face in my knees just like I remember doing as a child. Another memory begins to surface, but I push it down, hard. Emotional pain floods my entire body, a pain that won't let me forget the quiet loneliness of my childhood.

This is why God is a jerk. These memories won't let me forget how often I was left on my own. If there is a real God who cares, then I would never have had to live this life. Never!

Sobs rack my entire body. My lungs ache from the pressure that suffocates me. I have to force myself to breathe. I have to let this out; I'm the one who invited it in. The fight within me stirs. I have never before allowed myself to be this weak. I'm spent; it is all I can do to lie down on the floor.

Joan knocks on my door, letting me know breakfast has been on the table for a few minutes. I tell her that I don't feel good. I can see her feet under my door just standing there, and if I scooted forward a couple of inches, I could reach out and touch her.

A preposterous thought forms in my mind watching her stand there: that maybe if I reached out and touched her, I would heal with her goodness, and it could be an anchor of love in the middle of this storm called my life where the waves of loneliness daily threaten to drown me. I shake my head, exhausted, not really wanting to explore where that thought came from.

"Adin, honey, why don't you lie down and rest for a few hours. We aren't supposed to meet Ms. Ann until 11. I'll come up around 10 and see how you feel. Do you want anything to drink?" Joan's voice sounds worried and motherly.

"No thank you," I whisper under the door.

I hear Joan sigh at the door, like she has her own thoughts that she is wrestling with. I continue to watch her feet stand there. I can't take my eyes off them, even though the tears are still finding their way down from my eyes. I don't want to sniffle and alarm her, so I just let all of it go, blurring my vision and clogging my nose.

"All right, honey. I'll be back up in a little while. You rest." Finally, she turns from the door and walks downstairs.

CHAPTER 25

Past and Present Collide

<u>*Adin*</u>

Sitting sideways in the car, I keep my eyes focused on what is out the window, watching all of the spring scenery passing us by. Focusing on the new buds trying to burst forth from mostly bare trees and bright green foliage in spurts along the highway occupies every thought because I push any and every other deviation out. I don't want Joan to question the puffiness of my eyes or the red splotches covering my face because I'm really trying not to take my rage out on her.

I know that she saw it all when I came out of my room, but I had just shrugged my shoulders, telling her it must be the cold I'm getting.

She had made mention that we might need to stop at the doctor's office because I could be getting the flu. The frown of concern on her face pricked my already softened heart. Normally, I have it encased in an armor so thickly covered with obnoxious sarcasm that concern would never have a chance, but today is different and, if I have to be honest, the way I feel towards Joan is different too.

Today, memory lane was a walk that I naively thought I could endure. I was so very wrong. My shoulder's slump down, outwardly symbolizing the defeat that took place in my mind.

When Joan parallel parks in front of One Park Building, I don't even have the will to wonder at this meeting. I had just met with Ms. Ann in March; it's only the end of April. I'm not supposed to have another counseling session until at least June.

Whatever. I'm probably seeing her because of the attack. I just sigh. My pain never seems to be because of my choices, but that doesn't seem to make any difference at all.

We walk quietly into the building and over to the ugly green door. Joan opens it and gestures for me to go ahead thru. I walk on, never bothering to take a look at the guard; it really doesn't even matter.

I sit down in the bright blue plastic chair located in the furthest corner of the room, right beside an ancient water fountain making a loud humming noise. Maybe it can drown out my thoughts.

I rest my elbows on my knees and slip my head down into them. I yearn for blackness. I don't want to think about anything. I hear Joan fold down into the chair across from me. I can tell she wants to talk, but she doesn't. She has some major self-control. It's a good thing too, because anything could set me off right now.

The past is lying much too close to the present, and the friction of them meeting has left me raw. I don't even know what I'm going to tell Ms. Ann; perhaps she will buy the whole "flu" charade. Probably not. That woman has a radar to the truth like she was born with GPS directions. It can be frustrating.

Why did I allow Joan to bring me here today of all days, when I am literally falling apart? I stand up, mumbling towards Joan that I've got to use the restroom. Once inside, I slam the stall door back, barely making it to the toilet before throwing up.

If this is what remembering does to me, I promise myself I will never do it again. My entire body temperature has skyrocketed, and I feel like I'm in the desert. I stand up, awkwardly stumbling out of the stall, walking out to look in the mirror. Chalk-white skin with red swollen eye-lids does not look good, that's for sure. It does validate some kind of sickness though; flu story it is.

I turn on the water and splash some onto my face. The coolness has a mild calming effect. Looking down to the hand that is turning off the water, I notice the light traces of a bruise. I can't help but smile. That punch was pretty amazing.

I have no idea where the confidence came from either because the last time I was in his presence fear locked away my voice. That day was different though, it was as if I wasn't scared of him anymore. What changed?

I'm still thinking about this when Joan enters the bathroom to let me know that my name just came over the intercom, the frown of worry still obvious on her face. She is holding her arms tight in a self-hugging kind of way, and I get this weird premonition that she is fighting an urge to reach out and hold me.

I don't want to think about Joan's kindness right now, so I just walk around her without saying a word and take myself over to the door to be buzzed into the back. A wrinkly hand pushes the button, and I am greeted by yet another unfamiliar face.

I place my hands in my pockets in a blasé kind of way and, keeping my head down, follow the petite woman in front of me. I don't care to look around today.

She gestures with her hand for me to take a seat outside of an office, and I oblige. I'm hoping I'm not going to be left out here for very long, just in case I need to dry heave again.

I look up to see if I can make out a door with a bathroom symbol close by when I notice Mrs. Roberts, my last foster mother, sitting down the hallway with her arms across her chest. In a dead panic, my eyes sweep the area for Mark, her husband. Adrenaline rushes through my veins; I jump up, dizzy at the sudden change in altitude, ready to flee.

Ms. Ann's door jars open, and I find myself looking down into the prettiest brown eyes of a little girl. She looks like she has been crying, but is lovingly holding on to the side of Ms. Ann's dress.

"Adin, I'm so glad you could come and see me today." Ms. Ann wears a tight smile. “I just need to get Jessica back. I won’t be but a few minutes. Why don’t you go ahead in my office and take a seat.”

I nod my head to indicate that I heard her but make no move to enter her office. I stand to the side for them to exit and then observe the pair as they continue walking together. Ms. Ann pauses to bend down to little Jessica’s height while the little girl talks into her ear.

Mrs. Roberts walks over and envelopes Jessica into a hug. She peers down at Jessica with a fake smile reflecting that everything is okay. Yeah, I’ve seen that smile a few times. While I’m watching them converse, I catch Jessica looking at me.

She might be ten, her head only coming slightly above Ms. Ann’s waist. She has long brown hair that is french-braided back into pigtails. She is wearing a plain pastel pink t-shirt and blue jeans with pink and purple flowers embroidered all over the bottom hem. Her white and pink sneakers look fairly new. She is holding Mrs. Roberts’s hand while watching me, tuning out their conversation.

Mrs. Ann follows her gaze and then grips Mrs. Roberts arm in a friendly goodbye, turning around towards me. I see Mrs. Roberts look of recognition as she follows Ms. Ann’s gaze in my direction. Once Ms. Ann reaches me, she extends her hand towards her office, and, touching my elbow, guides me in before shutting her door.

“Adin, thank you so much for coming in today. I know you don’t feel good. Joan called me earlier this morning to let me know that you might not be make it here. I appreciate you trying.” Her voice sounds weary.

I nod my head, letting her know that I’m listening. Looking down at her desk, I notice a tape recorder sitting closer to me than to her.

When she sees my confusion, she explains, “One of my kids and I had a talk that I thought you might want to hear.” Her voice cracks on the word ‘talk’.

My head slowly comes up to where our eyes meet. I lift my eyebrows to let her know I don’t understand what she means.

“No, Adin, you don’t know this child. However, I think you might be of some help to her.” She interlaces her fingers and rests them on top of her desk, never once breaking eye contact, and then presses the play button.

Joan

If I thought Adin looked pale when we went into see Ms. Ann, she is ghostly now. I drum my fingers nervously on the steering wheel while Adin sits back in her seat, eyes closed. Her fingers have had a death grip on her legs since she got into the car.

Lord, I just don't understand what has happened. Does she need therapy from the attack? Father, none of her behavior is making sense. I'm trying so hard to remain calm and open to letting her work through this.

This is the hardest moment in my life, sitting back and being patient while my daughter fights a war all by herself. I can see it in her eyes, the turmoil that lies inside her soul. I am feeling a bit worthless here, God. Please, do something!

A song by Casting Crowns comes over the radio. I love listening to the local Christian radio station. The testimonies and Godly advice are priceless. Casting Crowns' *I Will Praise You in This Storm* comes blaring through the speakers. I can feel God's peace come over me and don't try to wipe away the tears that have made their way down my face.

God washes away my fears. I sing along with the lyrics: "I was sure by now, God, that you would have reached down and wiped our tears away, stepped in and saved the day, but once again I say amen, and it's still raining."

I watch Adin open her eyes as the lyrics make some kind of impact. I also notice her watching the tears that I have freely released. She is biting her lip again, and I am thankful that she is considering the goodness of our Savior.

I continue to sing, "As the thunder rolls, I barely hear you whisper through the rain, 'I'm with you' and as your mercy falls, I raise my hands and praise the God who gives and takes away."

I am so immersed in the song that I don't realize Adin has shut it off until I'm singing the chorus all by myself, but I decide to continue through it anyways, "And I'll praise you in this storm, and I will lift my hands, for you are who you are no matter where I am. And every tear I've cried, you hold in your hand, you never left my side, and though my heart is torn, I will praise you in this storm."

I pull into the driveway and hit the automatic lock button on the doors before Adin can rush out of the car. I sit silently praying to God.

Lord, I need to say something. I know that you allowed that particular song to come over the radio in this moment for a specific reason. You are not a God of coincidences but a God of detail.

I know she heard every lyric, and she is overwhelmed. I cannot let her run from you when what you are saying is so obvious. I am angry right now too.

I am angry at the evil that satan has surrounded her with. I am angry at the sickness of a man who has violated her. I am angry that she also had to go through a needless attack while in my care. But so are you.

Thank you for being my Rock, my shelter in the storm. Thank you that I don't have to have all the answers to be in your will. Lord, from the depths of me: help. Help Adin. Open her heart. Lord, don't let her hate me for what I have to say today. In Jesus's name I pray, Amen.

Prayer takes away my nervousness, and I set the keys down in the cup holder. I shift my body towards hers, observing her obvious anger. It is almost as if steam is emanating from her very being. Her jaw is taunt as she grits her teeth together, and I can tell she is just waiting to unleash some of her pent up anger.

I can be that punching bag today, every day if it helps her to deal with her past. I focus my eyes on hers and notice that there is fear there, like a caged animal. Her labored breathing confirms that her anger is close to erupting. She just looks at me, daring me to break her restraint. She wants this fight. I give it to her.

"Adin, we need to talk." I begin.

"NO! WE DON'T!" she yells. Her chest heaves from producing such volume.

As calmly as I can I return, "Yes, sweetheart, we do." I put up my hand to silence her, knowing she is getting ready to let loose. *Not yet. Lord, please let me get this out.*

"I know that you are angry about your life; you have every right to be. I know that something terrible has happened to you besides your mother walking out on you. That would be more than enough for any person to have to deal with, without some person violating you."

"I know that you have not confided any of this to me, but I have been watching you, and I care so much about you. Adin, I love you. I know how to love because I have a Savior, Jesus Christ, who showed me true love. He loves each of us enough to lay down his life that we may share in eternity despite our imperfections and bad choices."

"I know that a lot of people's bad choices have overflowed into your life. But, I also want you to see that God has put his arms out to you despite their sin. He has given you the ability to assess people for who they are. He has never let you go hungry or thirsty."

"You are here today because God wills it. You are in my home because He loves you beyond the capability of anyone else. He wants you to know him, but He will never force you. He wants you to love him of your own accord."

"He will not invade your personal space because He respects you. He will not make you do the right thing because He gave you your own mind. He will not choose any path for you, Adin, because He desires for you to desire him."

"I know you heard those lyrics that were just on the radio and they made you furious, but they are true. No one person's life is ever perfect. To you, it might seem that way because there has been so much hardship in yours, but there is hardship elsewhere as well."

"Please take the time to research God; you are too smart of a young woman to make a decision simply based on what you see. Also, know that it is a glorious peace to walk with a God who understands every aspect about you and loves it all. That I know well." I am crying as I finish up, and I have no idea how much she heard and how much her anger kept out.

I hit the unlock button and watch her scramble out of the car, sprinting up to the front step and, I can only guess, up the stairs to her bedroom. I look over to Ben and Kami's house to see Chase sitting on his front step praying, his Bible lay out beside him.

Thank you, Lord, that Adin is being lifted up in prayer. Thank you for the heart of Chase Harper. I pray that you give him wisdom when he talks with Adin. Thank you that she feels like she can open up to him.

This is a nasty storm we are all going through, but I praise you that change is taking place. I will continue to praise you in this storm because I know that your will is perfect and you never fail. I love you so much. In Jesus's name I pray, Amen.

CHAPTER 26

Teddy-Bear Hugs

<u>*Adin*</u>

I would like nothing better than to pretend that the last few weeks just didn't happen. The attack didn't exist. I never went to church and saw Tiffani. I never went to Ms. Ann's office and had to listen to that recording. I definitely never had the conversation with Joan.

I want to take it all back, hit rewind, and choose a different path. I would like to cut it out and paste it onto someone else's life. Let someone else deal with all the drama for a change.

I can't remember what it's like to genuinely smile or belly laugh. The last time I laughed was my runway model experience in the kitchen before church almost a week ago. My heart aches at the lack of happiness inside. I feel horrible. I'm not sleeping, I can't eat, and all I can think about is God, or rather the lack of God in my life.

How does telling God that I might believe in him change anything? Waving that white flag in defeat is the last thing that I haven't done yet. It's like we've been battling over this moment forever, and now that it's here, I don't want to go down without a fight.

It just wouldn't be me, and me not being true to myself is just not an option. I've always had me.

I haven't gone to school since Wednesday, telling Joan yesterday that I still didn't feel very good. I haven't accepted any of Chase's phone calls, just telling Joan to let him know that I don't feel well enough to talk.

He stopped by yesterday right after school to drop off my make-up work. I was surprised because he is supposed to have wrestling practice right after school, but when Joan asked why he didn't go, I heard him tell her that he missed me and was hoping to see me.

Hurting him is like hurting myself. He definitely doesn't deserve to be hurt, but, selfishly, it is nice to have someone sharing in my pain.

Joan knocks on my door this morning to check my status, and I can tell she is dumbfounded when I open the door and say, "Good morning, I was just heading down." I'm hoping that she will take my lead and pretend that Wednesday never happened.

I smirk a bit, finally getting that startled look that I've been aiming for since the first day I came here. She's been a tough case, but the victory falls flat as I realize that I no longer want to frustrate her.

I hop down the stairs as carefree as I can muster, grabbing a muffin from the island before Dave can turn around from the stove scrambling eggs. I head for the front door before remembering that I don't have a ride to school.

I never let Chase know that I was coming back today. Oh well, I'd rather chance walking then riding with Joan or Dave. What they don't know won't kill them.

Trying to act natural, I grab my book bag from the peg on the wall behind the front door and dash outside. Walking as quickly as I can down the driveway, I look over, and in between the pine trees separating our houses, I see Chase leaned up against his Dad's truck.

My heart goes full throttle just seeing him. I wish he would run to me and grab me close, erasing the last week, and then ask me to be his girlfriend. Oh, the stuff that dreams are made from.

I loop my thumbs through my book bag straps on my shoulders and make my way over to the truck. When I go around to the passenger side, he meets me there, surprising me by pulling me close and crushing me in an air tight hug.

It's exactly what I need. I rest my head on his shoulder, bringing my hands around his torso. I cling to him just as tightly as he is holding me.

Man, I missed him so much. I can feel myself tearing up, but I don't want to be the one to break this; it's too perfect. I'm taken aback when I feel another set of arms come around from behind me. Then, the tears fall.

It's Carter, Chase's little brother. He's got his face smooshed into my back while he teddy bear hugs me as forcefully as he can. I let go of Chase to reciprocate Carter's hug.

"Thanks, Carter," I say. "I missed you too."

"You have no idea how boring it is to ride to church when you're not there. Please don't make me do it again, Adin. I've been praying for you every night since Mrs. Joan told my mom that you were sick. I hope you're all better now. I told Jesus to make you even better than before, so that I don't ever have to ride to church without you again."

I'm startled at his honesty, how freely he can talk about how much he missed me. None of it sounded phony or cheesy, really just genuine. I'm speechless. All I can do is hug him tighter.

Then he runs to the end of the driveway where his mom is waiting in her car to take him to school. She waves at me with a big smile, her cell phone pressed up to one ear. I wave back.

Chase opens my door, bowing low with his British accent poured on thick, "M'lady." I can't help but giggle as I get in, scooting over all the way to open his door for him from the inside.

I really appreciate how much Chase and his family pay attention to me. Is the way that the Harper family cares about me the same way that God shows his love? I roll down the truck window in an effort to let the deep thoughts blow away. I just want life to be easy for a little while.

CHAPTER 27

Boyfriend and Girlfriend

Adin

Later that evening, Chase and I are riding to Friday night Youth Group. The wind is blowing softly, and I have my window down, rolling my arm thru the spring breeze.

Chase drives, one arm propped up on his open window. His thumb is drumming the steering wheel along with the Christian song on the radio. He looks lost in thought while he sings along. I just watch him.

I love this boy so much that I might just have to ask him to be my boyfriend. I mean, why do I have to sit back and wait for him to ask me anyways? Maybe he is too shy. No, Chase really isn't shy, but maybe he's never had a girlfriend before, and he doesn't know how to go about it.

We already act like we're together; maybe we are. Maybe I've just made much too big a deal about this whole thing, and he already thinks of us as a couple. Well, I can do that too.

I relax a bit, letting myself believe it all. I want life to be easy, right? Well, it can't be any easier than having Chase as my boyfriend. He parks the truck in the church parking lot, right beneath a light pole that is dimming on. I start to open up the cab door but hold onto the handle when I remember that Chase likes to open the door for me.

I reward him with a big smile when the door slowly opens. He offers his elbow, but I so badly want to interlock our fingers. Maybe he doesn't want his parents to see us holding hands at church; it could seem disrespectful.

Honestly, I don't know what kind of behavior is acceptable or inappropriate at church. Chase asked me if I might be coming to Sunday service this week while we were in between classes today at school. I dodged the question by pretending to look for an important homework assignment that was part of my make-up work. I told him I'd let him know, but I really had to find my Literature sentences or Mrs. Hyde was going to make me stay after school and do it all over again. Thankfully, he let it go.

Chase escorts me inside the church where I can hear the music blaring well before getting anywhere remotely near the youth room. I roll my eyes at Chase when he drops his elbow from mine and begins dancing crazily around the hallway. He does play a mean air guitar though. I laugh at his childish antics and keep walking forward while he lip-sings the lyrics from beside me.

It would almost make a cool under age club, which is the first thought that always enters my mind when I come here. The walls are painted black with all kinds of glow-in-the-dark graffiti marking them. I don't take too much time reading all the Bible verses though, even if they are graffiti. The white Christmas lights hanging up everywhere are pretty awesome, some of them blinking in time with the music. I have no idea how they were able to hook that up.

The youth room is huge, with stairs leading up to a game room that a lot of the teens are already hanging out in. Some are up there playing foosball or pool. Aubrey is standing near the balcony talking with a few girls while simultaneously watching everyone who comes in. She bounces up and down, waving frantically when she catches my eye. I give her a big wave back and can't help the wide grin that spreads out on my own face, realizing that maybe she was watching for me.

Chase is the complete gentleman, never leaving me to myself despite the fact that I've been coming for about two months now. He understands that I don't make friends quickly, but he's never pushed me to be something that I'm not. This has to be the number one reason that I absolutely adore him. He knows that I'm still figuring this whole God thing out, and even though I get that he totally believes in God, neither one of us have asked the other to change who we are or what we believe.

All of these happy thoughts release a tension held in between my shoulders that I didn't even know existed, and I find myself swaying back and forth to the upbeat rhythm still blasting its way across the youth room. Chase grabs my hand and leads me down to the folding chairs set up in front of his dad's lectern.

Usually on Friday nights everyone just chills, maybe videoing some crazy prank or game to post on their social media. So, when Chase motions for me to sit down in the folding chair beside him, I'm guessing it's so we can have some quasi-privacy and talk.

But then more and more teens make their way down to where we are and start filling in all the empty chairs. I raise my eyebrows in question to Chase, but he just shrugs and lifts his eyebrows as if he doesn't really know what's going on either.

"Dad just said to sit down, that God wants him to share something with us tonight," he explains.

"That's fine," I wave my hand to let him know that I'm not bothered in the least. He had let go of my hand when all the other teens started nudging in front of us to get to the empty seats on the other side. I sit my hands on my lap, just in case he decides to brave holding it again.

The music slowly fades out as Pastor Ben walks down from the sound system to his lectern. He has his Bible, but not the usual yellow notepad of notes that accompany him on Wednesday nights when he talks to us.

Maybe he just wants to let us know about some youth event

coming up. *Okay, fine, just get it over with, so I can get back to paying attention to your son.* I shake my head at my own inner bluntness, trying to quiet my mind in an effort to pay attention.

"As you all know, I don't make it a habit to give any kind of message on Friday nights. It's usually the night when we just come together to have fun without getting into too much trouble." He laughs, probably recalling turkey bowling a few Friday's back when some of the turkeys landed on top of the Church shed. By Sunday, Pastor Tim was wondering why cats kept trying to scale the building.

"However, this Friday, God has nudged me, a bit forcefully I might add, to talk to you all about dating." He holds his hands up as if in surrender as he continues, "I am definitely not trying to offend any of you if you have a boyfriend or girlfriend. I'm totally okay with you guys dating, and you know that, but as someone who cares about your heart, there are a few details that I want to make sure all of you are aware of."

My heart picks up with the premonition that somehow, when he's done talking, my entire life will have changed. I lean my head forward, giving Pastor Ben my entire attention.

He continues, "Many of you are jumping into relationships with people that you know don't share the same faith as you do. This is what I call 'missionary dating'. You do this in hopes that you can somehow change the way this person believes. This is not only unfair to you, but it is also unfair to the person that you are showing affection to."

"For a person to come to an understanding of who God is, he or she must first understand that they need the Lord personally. This is not because of a relationship that requires them to believe in God for it to exist, but because they personally need a Saviour. A person's relationship with God should not have anything to do with the person they are dating, other than they are under the same moral code. How many of you have had friends that liked things that you didn't?"

I watch as several teens around me, including Chase, raise their hands. Mine remains numbly on my lap as I continue to look around.

"If you think about it, during the time that you spend with them, you find yourself drawn to their opinions. Now, how many of you have ever lost some of these friends, and in turn no longer agree with their lifestyle choices?"

Again, several people around me nod their heads in agreement to what Pastor Ben says and raise their hands. My heart is pounding so heavy that I'm sure everyone around me can hear it too. I almost feel like all their eyes are inadvertently gazing at me.

I am the outsider here. I am the one here who doesn't necessarily believe in everything they do. My face is hot with shame as Pastor Ben picks up momentum, striking to the core of what he wants to say tonight.

"It is the same thing when we as Christians date people who don't believe the same way we do, feeling that along the span of the relationship we will turn them into what they should already be. It is wrong for us to have this mentality because it is never us that make that change. It is a personal heart change between God and that person, having nothing to do with us."

"In the event that your relationship would end with that person, their view of God is directly associated with you. So, when you leave that relationship, in their eyes, so does God. 2 Corinthians 6:14 reminds us 'Do not be unequally yoked together with unbelievers. For what fellowship has righteousness with lawlessness? And what communion has light with darkness?' I challenge you to stand in the gap for these people that you care about until the day comes when they choose to accept Christ on their own terms, not because they want you to like them or date them."

The entire youth room is quiet in thought. Me? I'm just glad the lights are out so no one can see the humiliation written so plainly on my face. Pastor Ben must have been observing how close Chase and I have gotten, and it's worried him.

I thought that he and Mrs. Kami were different; never once did they give me that wary, side-ways glance while I rode to church with their family. I have felt completely included until right now.

Now, I need a good getaway. I am too embarrassed to even look at

Chase. Most of the teens have gotten down on their knees, propping their heads on their hands in the folding chairs. I just sit in my chair, too dazed to act.

I know that they are praying, but to who? If God can hear them, and for that matter me, then why can't I hear him? With all of their prayers circling around me, finding their way up to him, why can't I hear him answering them? What kind of God remains silent?

The same words from Pastor Ben's message keep taunting me: 'light with darkness'. And I'm the darkness. Because Chase would have to be the light. He is so good and honest. He is so full of light. I just know it.

All of the sudden I feel dirty. I know what has been done to me; why would I ever think that I could have a relationship with Chase? I'm not good enough. I am darkness. I have always been darkness, just like the shadows I hid within in that one-room apartment I shared with a woman that I have to call mother. No wonder those shadows hid me so well: I am a part of them.

I feel responsible for the tears that glisten down Chase's cheeks. I can see them sneak from around his arm. I can't believe I hurt him so deeply. What is wrong with me? If I love him as much as I've told myself, then I've got to leave him alone and let him find a girl that believes just like him, a girl that doesn't second guess the God that he belongs to.

I quietly cry while I create this girl in my mind. Obviously, she is the opposite of me. While my brunette hair is short, this perfect girl has long, silky red hair. While I have average brown eyes, hers are a radiant green like Aubrey's. I search around the youth room until I find Aubrey's red hair among the throng of teenagers.

Aubrey would be perfect for Chase. She never has a bad word to say about anybody. She has a big heart and the most contagious laugh. They should be together, not Chase and me.

I wipe my sweaty hands on my pants and cautiously stand up. My chair is conveniently on the outside of the walkway, so there is no awkward moving around the multitude of people praying. I casually make my way to the exit, and without taking one look back, I open the door and slip right out.

CHAPTER 28

Milk Boy Cafe

Adin

I run away from the church as quickly as I can, crossing the main street to the sidewalk on the other side. I almost feel lucky when I notice plenty of people walking around window shopping.

The church isn't located in a bad part of the city. This is more of a tourist area, with craft and candle shops up and down the streets.

There seem to be an overabundance of young couples drifting by me in their own love stupor. I hate being an audience to the hopefulness in their eyes as they peer up at one another, so I opt to stare at my feet as I mosey along.

Waiting at a crosswalk with a cluster of people for the green man to light up, I hear the hum of a motorcycle before it skids to a stop up ahead. One of the street lights hits the chrome on the front of the bike in just a way that it seems ethereal. I smile to find that it's a woman slinking off of it. So cool. As soon as she takes off her helmet, I am knocked into from a pedestrian behind me.

I can't believe it's her!

"Sorry," I mumble to the person behind me, not really caring at all.

I edge closer to the street, standing sideways behind a light pole, watching her. She unlocks the seat of her motorcycle, taking out a clutch silver sequined purse, and then locks it back up with a tiny key. She puts the purse underneath her arm, still holding the hot pink helmet with her left hand. I can't help just staring at her.

She must feel someone following her because her eyes find mine immediately. She smiles and waves. Before I can camouflage myself among the tourists, she is making her way down the street straight for me.

"Hey, Adin! What's up?" She asks, her voice so light-hearted that I find myself smiling up at her despite my evening.

"Not much, Tiffani." I return. "Just hanging out."

"Oh, cool, well, what are you doing right now?" she asks, looking around me to see if I'm with anyone else.

"Nothing really, just felt like getting out of the house, you know?" I say, hoping that she can't tell I'm lying through my teeth. The words feel all wrong coming out. She loops her arm through mine, just like we've been pals forever, pulling me in the direction I was already going.

"You have to come with me tonight!" she gushes. "I'm going to an open mic night, and I'm completely nervous. I've been praying that God would give me a sign that I wouldn't be alone tonight, even though, I didn't really invite anyone to come, being my first open mic and what not, but He brought you! Oh, Adin, I'm so glad it is you, because I've always felt like you're the kind of girl who wouldn't lie. You'll be nitty-gritty honest with me. If I totally suck, you'll let me know, but in a way that I can laugh it off and love you anyway." Her hair frames her face perfectly, even though she is jumping around excitedly while she talks.

I'm sucked into her monologue, never getting a chance to nod my head in agreement before she's pulling me into some door with neon signs covering the windows. Is this a bar? Because I don't even have a fake ID. Didn't she just mention God in her last sentence? I can't believe I'm at a bar with the pastor's daughter who I just saw in church last Sunday. Does God listen to your prayers after you've hung out in a bar?

After tonight, Miss Tiffani is going to have to answer me some questions. Maybe she just goes to church to make her parents happy. Who cares? I've always thought she was great, and that's not changing now.

"Where's your guitar?" I ask. I thought people always had their own guitar on open mic night. She doesn't give me a verbal answer, just laughs openly and shrugs.

"This is going to be so much fun!" Her exuberance almost contagious.

Tiffani personifies beauty to me. Her hair is all scrunched up in waves. She has dark hair with the same kind of blonde highlights that she gave me, bold silver eye-shadow lines the lower edges of her eyes, and she is wearing black leather pants, my favorite, with a silver sequined tank top that matches her clutch purse. To complete her amazing ensemble are black leather ballet flats. Can one ride a motorcycle in ballet flats? Well, she does.

As my eyes adjust to the soft glow of lamps scattered here and there, I realize that I don't smell any alcohol. This can't be a bar. I look over to the neon sign in the front window, trying to read it backwards. Milk Boy. Huh? I inhale deeply, smelling the roast of coffee beans. Where am I?

"Do you want anything to drink?" Tiffani asks directly into my ear, so that I can hear her over all the mechanical noises from the coffee machines layered by multiple conversations that come with being inside a café filled with people.

"Um, sure, whatever you're having." I say, trying to mimic her volume.

Her eyes light up, and she heads towards a line of people on the other side of the room. Great, now what? It's dark enough in here that I can eyeball the people around me without causing any discomfort. I discover a mosaic of characteristics in attendance and decide that the music coming from the stage really isn't that bad.

It's jazz, and the girl singing up there has got some lungs. She does a little dance number while she's singing, leaving me thoroughly impressed. I clap along with everyone else as she winds down for no other reason than she is amazing. At this point, I'm wondering if this could be some kind of a talent contest, because if so, Tiffani has got her work cut out for her.

"Come on girl, let's get a table near the front." Out of nowhere Tiffani has come up behind me, her hands full of two red foam cups with 'Milk Boy Coffee' scripted on the sides. They don't seem to be steaming, which is a good thing because it isn't exactly cold outside mid-April.

"I think you forgot your helmet somewhere." I say, noting that she no longer has a hand to carry it in.

"Na, I left it behind the coffee bar with Trevor. He's and old friend of mine and offered," she informs me.

"Oh, cool." I continue to follow her through the maze of standing people and pub height tables.

We come to a stop at the very front of the room, right up next to the stage. I look around nervously because there are no empty seats. She turns and hands off both of the drinks to me, making her way over to the left. When she opens up a closet door, I look up to the stage, hoping that we aren't distracting the audience from the next person and find myself relieved that the next act is tuning his guitar with the sound guy.

She comes back holding two folding chairs. Is she allowed to do that? Great, folding chairs, why not. I just love sitting in folding chairs this evening; they've brought nothing but good fortune thus far.

She sets them up to the side of a front table, asking the people sitting there if they mind. They shake their heads no, telling us they'd love for us to join them, and she gifts them with a huge smile.

I sit back and close my eyes, listening to the mellow tune drifting down from the stage. There aren't any lyrics, just the beautiful sound of his strumming. I stretch out my neck from left to right, hearing the cracks.

Then, habitually, begin to crack my knuckles. When I get to my right hand, I stop, all of it reminding me of Chase. That's right, for a moment in time, I forgot how unworthy I am. I wonder if I should even be near Tiffani. I might contaminate her.

During my own personal pity party, she grabs my shoulder in hyped-up anticipation.

"Wish me luck!"

She laughs at my surprised expression and continues, "Just pray that I don't trip over my own feet going up there. Okay?"

"Got it." I reply, giving her a thumbs-up with my free hand.

I take this opportunity to try out my beverage. It's an iced spice chai tea with lots and lots of frothy foam on top. Mmmmm, it is delicious. I take another long chug before turning to where Tiffani is on stage.

She really is spectacular. There is no one else like her that I've ever met. Her diamond Monroe stud glitters in the lighting from the stage, while her sequined top throws off the impression of diamond studs, literally causing her to sparkle. The uniqueness of her tattoos are something else, as if her body is telling a story.

I see her reach into her back pocket and take out a sheet of paper. There is a connection I feel when I realize that we share something in common: she is biting her lower lip while unfolding the paper.

Clearing her throat, she begins, "This is my first night ever on stage here at Milk Boy Cafe, although I hang out here all the time and enjoy everyone else's contributions. Thanks for having me on stage tonight!" Her voice booms across the audience.

I grin when everyone gives her a loud, welcoming hand clap, along with a few whistles of appreciation. I don't think that I could ever get up on a stage in front of people and do anything. I clap louder for her. She winks down at me

"This is a poem that I have written about my own journey in this life. It is a very dear part of me, and I hope that you can share in the hope and joy that I had in living it. It's titled *Jesus's Prayers.*

"When that tear falls down my face,
and drips to the shadows below.
I'll close my eyes and say a prayer,

that I know You'll already know.
When I try to hold back that sob,
that is desperate to escape.
I'll grip my hands thinking of You,
and continue in earnest to pray.
When I can't breathe because of the pain,
I'll fall on my knees in despair.
I'll know in my heart of your intervention,
as I continue these long awaited prayers.
When I feel Satan come near me,
beckoning me to allow him here,
I'll give your angels all authority,
as I scream out your words through my prayers.
I'll cover my ears against his pleas,
as you defeat the sin I've let in.
I'll cry out to you, 'Oh, my precious Savior,'
continuing my prayers within.
When that tear falls down my face,
I'll be thankful that you have always been here.
I could never make it without you, Lord,
and all of my Jesus's prayers."

How could she know? How could she know that just this evening God and I were duking it out over prayer? I know I cried out to him myself many times in life, even when I didn't know who it was that I was crying out to. But he never came.

The roar of clapping surrounding me is minimal compared to the buzzing in my own mind. Tiffani gingerly walks across the stage; I'm sure being careful not to trip. Once she reaches me, she literally picks me up in a tight hug.

"Thank you so much for sharing this moment with me, Adin." Her genuine gratitude shining in her eyes as she stares at me.

My throat is too thick to respond, but I'm sure she saw my nod. I can't get in a good breath of air; I feel like I'm going to suffocate. Just leave me alone already, God. Why can't you just leave me alone!

CHAPTER 29

A Time to Pray

Dave

I turn up the volume on the television when I hear the phone ring. I don't want to get distracted from Matt's baseball game with Joan on the telephone. Literally sitting on the edge of the sofa, I scream, "Come on Matty, you got this guy—he's totally going for the curveball. Fix your stance up buddy, get your shoulder back, that's right! Swing, swing Matt!"

There is no place I'd rather be on a Friday night then in front of the television watching Matt play ball, that is unless I have box tickets right behind the ump. I see Joan's shadow fall across the TV screen as she leans on the wall between the living room and kitchen.

"What is it babe? I'm a little busy." I imagine her grin without actually having to turn around to witness it. As long as she doesn't call me cute or anything mushy like that, there won't be any problems. I hear her sigh, and it is not a good sigh. Immediately, I push mute on the TV remote.

I turn around, giving her my full attention, shooting my eyebrows up in the air, "Joan, honey, what's going on?"

"I just got off of the phone with Kami. Adin left church tonight without telling anyone where she was going. They've been looking for her for almost 45 minutes, but as far as they can tell, she is not on the church property. What if that attacker has been following her, Dave? What if she has been abducted?" I can tell Joan is really worked up the way her last sentence barely sputters out.

I'm up and holding her tight as her body sags against me. If I thought that praying for Matt was a rough road, I was wrong. We have never hit the mountains that loving Adin has required.

"Shhh" I whisper as she cries. "Joan, she has not been abducted. What did they do tonight at church? Did Kami tell you what was going on before she left?"

Lord, please let there be a rational reason to Adin's disappearance. Please let this just be a huge misunderstanding. Everything has been going so great. Lord, I know that you can make sense out of this; bless Joan and me with your wisdom.

"No, I didn't think to ask. I really couldn't even talk. I was so shocked that she wasn't there, that no one knows what happened to her. I feel so bad, Dave, I couldn't even console Kami. She was crying too." She hangs her head down while speaking. I hug her tighter.

"It's going to be okay, honey. I'm sure that something happened at church tonight that set her off, and maybe she's walking home, blowing off steam. We probably need to get her a cell phone. Then, she could've called us. There has to be more to it than you and Kami spoke about. I'm going to give Ben a call and we'll sort it all out."

I guide her to the loveseat in the living room and then run into the kitchen to grab my cell phone off of the island. I punch in Ben's cell phone number and wait for him to pick up.

"Hey, Dave," Ben answers. He sounds out of breath.

"Hey, man," I say, "so, you got any idea why Adin might have left tonight?"

"Maybe. Dave, I am so sorry if this is what caused her to leave. God really laid it on my heart to give a message tonight. I don't know if you know this, but normally Friday nights are just hang-out nights. I don't usually get real deep with the teens. But all day long God kept speaking to me that I needed to cover Christian relationships."

"I'm honestly going to tell you that I don't know who the message was meant for exactly, but a lot of my teens wanted to talk about it after I was done. There were so many questions following the message that I have no idea when she left."

"I don't know exactly where she stands in her relationship with God, and I talked about Christians dating non-Christians and how that is not what God desires. I honestly was not pinpointing her and Chase's relationship; like I said, it was simply what God wanted me to say, and so I obeyed." I can hear the guilt in Ben's voice.

"Ben, this is not your fault. Don't even think that it is, because I certainly don't. I'm betting that she ran out confused about what God expects from her. She is still making baby steps in what she believes. Look, do me a favor, have Chase drive around the normal teen hang-outs in town. I'm going to drive from here to the church the normal route, and you take some back roads in case she decided to walk herself home. I'm sure we'll find her within the hour." I grab my key ring off the hook in the kitchen.

"Definitely, Dave. I'll also tell Kami and the teens that are still here to stay put and pray for her."

"I'd appreciate that, man. Thanks. Talk to you soon." I close my cell phone, filling Joan in on what happened at youth, while also grabbing my jacket.

"I can't just sit here and wait, Dave," she replies defensively.

"Sweetie, you're going to have to in case she comes home. I know that you hate being the one in waiting, but tonight this is where God wants you. Kami and the other teens are staying put at the church and praying. I need you here doing the same thing." I kiss the top of her head before opening the front door and heading out.

"I love you." I remind her before closing the door.

CHAPTER 30

Simple Answers

Adin

"So, let me make sure that I've got it all straight. You have a thing for Chase, have had it bad for a few months, but you're not good enough for him because you don't know how you feel about God. Also, light and darkness are not allowed to mix, and you are too dark for Chase's light? Did I get that all right?" Tiffani asks, trying her best to keep a straight face.

After she figured out that I was angry at the coffee house, she pushed me out the door and down the block to a donut shop. She shoved me into a booth and ordered us both up some hot, glazed donuts. *Comfort food* is what she called it when the waitress brought the steaming, gooey goodness to our table.

"Basically," I respond, feeling like an immature idiot when she puts it all that way.

She tries to hold back laughter, but I can't get angry with her for it when the hand covering her mouth is the one connected to the sleeve tattoo.

"Why do you have that?" I ask, pointing to the bright colors swirling around her arm. I can't even tell if all the pictures make a kind of mural, or if each one is distinct and has its own personal meaning.

"Lots of reasons that have changed multiple times. But, it's me, and I like that," she responds thoughtfully.

"Well, why did you get your first tattoo?" I inquire, not willing to let her off that easy.

"To make my dad angry." She answers without hesitation. If I thought she might want to sugar-coat the truth, I was wrong.

"Wow, how come?" I ask, my mouth full of yummy donut.

"Because I felt hurt by him, and I wanted to hurt him back. I figured with him being the Pastor of a church, he probably wouldn't want me to have any tattoos. I went through a very dramatic phase in my younger years, and, during that time, opted for the extreme more often than not." She takes a huge bite after finishing her explanation.

She really doesn't hold back, and I like it. I hope I can be just as matter-of-fact as her when people question me. She doesn't labor on and on about the right and wrong of the matter; she just puts it out there for me, letting me decide. Continuing to devour the donuts, she allows me to take it all in, not really bothered by the quiet at our table.

"So, then why did you keep getting more? Did he keep making you angry?" I push. I don't know why this is so important, but it is. I meet her eyes when she puts her fork down, wondering if I've pressed her too far.

She smiles at me, almost in a knowing manner, and then responds, "No, of course not. I mean, has my dad made me mad since that first tattoo? Definitely. But, I made myself mad too. For a while after high school, I just got really messed up. See, I'm a PK—that means Pastor's Kid, just so you know. And everyone watches the Pastor's kid, like we're divinely fashioned to be perfect just because our fathers have been called to preach."

"Only we're no more perfect than anyone else, and for people to have that expectation creates a lot of anxiety and stress. I really felt that pressure during my senior year of high school, like everyone expected me to attend some Ivy League college, marry the perfect guy, and never get into any trouble. The problem was that there was no way any person could meet all of those expectations. I just didn't want to let people down. Even more tragic, so much of the entire scenario was my own preconceived ideas of how I thought others wanted to see me, and I could have saved myself so much trouble if I had my focus where it was supposed to be anyways."

"As it was then, I was a time bomb waiting to explode. I went as far away from home as I could: all the way to the University of California. I even went undeclared, so everyone knew I was leaving them, not attending a college so far away for a certain degree. My parents were devastated, but the pain inside of me was so much that it had begun to overflow onto those who stood closest."

I'm sucked right into her story, as if I can see it all, living the memories right beside her. She is really good at describing her life. I sit, hoping she's not done talking.

"While I was at the University of California, I did experiment—too much. It was like I had all this freedom, and I didn't want any stone to go unturned. I was also naive and immature. I tried to adapt to the party scene. It was like I wanted to create a new life for myself, completely erasing any resemblance of who I once was. One night, I partied a little too hard." Pain flashes in her eyes. I scoot closer into her at the table, angling my face towards hers, grasping her hand.

"I must have blacked out because when I woke up I had no idea where I was and no idea what had taken place in the previous 12 hours. I remember showing up to a frat party with some girls from my dorm, but everything after that point became really hazy. I was mortified to find myself lying outside an apartment building all by myself the next morning. It was even worse when I got back to my dorm to discover bruises on my body and the lack of underwear."

Her head jerks up when I gasp out loud. No way. There is no way that something like that happened to a girl like her.

She gives me a half grin before looking down and continuing, "Yep. You're right. After a physical given on campus by the nurse, she told me that I had been sexually active the previous night, but let's be real: I was raped. She wasn't very sympathetic, and her response hurt me because she treated my circumstances like I came into her office with a common cold. She gave me a morning after pill, and after scheduling me to come back in a month for a pregnancy test, sent me on my way. I just held onto that little white pill, feeling thoroughly disgusted with myself."

She opened her arm to show me a few tattoos hidden on the underside. No one would even know they were there unless she wanted them to. There was a skeleton girl hugging herself with tears streaming down her face.

"That's what I felt like at the time, dead inside and full of grief. I never took the morning after pill. I figured if I wound up pregnant then it was my own fault, and I didn't want an innocent life to be taken for my choices. Also, just so we're clear, I'm not big on abortion. It wouldn't have been the baby's fault. I didn't call my parents for help until after my follow-up exam a month later confirming that I was not pregnant. That's when the nurse took a vile of my blood to send off for HIV testing because she forgot to when I came the first time. The shock from that visit floored me, and I called home to my mom admitting everything that I had been doing, leading right up to the rape."

She reaches out and holds my hands in hers, tears beginning to run down her face. I'm completely lost when I see her smiling through the tears. What would there be to smile about? I lean-in even more, my entire body tuned into her explanation.

"Never once did my mom berate me or tell me that it was all my fault. She didn't rub my nose in all my mistakes, like I felt I deserved. She cried with me over the phone and prayed for me before she got off, promising that she would be on the next flight out of Philadelphia to stay with me until the end of the spring semester. When my dad got home later that day, he called my dorm and did the same thing. He thanked God that I was alive and wouldn't stop telling me how much he loved me and how sorry he was that I was all alone. Do you know why my parents were able to forgive me and love me despite all my selfish choices?"

I shake my head no, dumbfounded because truly I don't.

"Because Jesus is reflected in their every choice, Adin. My

parents accepted Christ into their hearts and lives a long time ago, and they make a conscience effort daily to be more like Him and less like this world. They study the Bible because it is the living word of God that can enable them to reflect his characteristics. They loved me all covered in sin and my own disgusting consequences because they had the love of Christ within them. Adin, without that love, I could've never forgiven myself."

And there it was, all the truth that I would ever need said so simply by Tiffani. Monroe-pierced, sleeve-tattooed Tiffani. God love her, and I know He did. This is why Dave and Joan, and even Chase, care about me despite all my junk: because they understand the love of God.

"Thank you," I whisper. I crush my face into her shoulder and cry.

"Let it out, Adin. It needs to get out." She squeezes me in a side-hug, rubbing her hand up and down my arm.

"I'm so sorry. I'm just so sorry for everything I've done," I say, though I don't know if she can translate my words through the sobbing and snot. It's a strangling sadness, completely overwhelming, and if she wasn't holding me up, I don't think that I would have allowed myself to feel it.

"Shhh, none of that, Adin. Jesus died so that every day you are forgiven. You don't have to figure it all out or make amends for it all right this second. It will all come together in His timing. It did for me, and it will for you too."

"How will I know I'm His and not nothing anymore?" I can't even look her in the eye as I give words to my vulnerability.

"You'll know. He'll tell you" she says easily.

Just like that, I believe her. There is no indecision in my trusting her because she's been there. She has been through a horrible experience and came out on the other side, loved by God, and that means that there is hope for me too. I almost ask her if Christian boys still want anything to do with her, but before I can gain enough courage to ask, she pulls me out of the booth and drags me to the door. After we sprint back to her motorcycle, she hands me her hot pink helmet combined with a mischievous grin.

CHAPTER 31

Hot Pink Helmets

Joan

I walk from the island to the living room for the millionth time in the last 30 minutes, peering out the bay window. Nothing new. I scan the driveway for the image of a teenage girl walking herself home. Closing my eyes, I rest my forehead against the outside trim. *Lord, I'm scared. Please don't let her be hurt. I pray a hedge of protection around her, that you will keep her safe. I pray that she comes home.*

I startle at the sound of a motorcycle approaching my driveway. Alarmed, I yank my head back to the window to get a good look. I don't know anyone who drives a motorcycle. I am puzzled when two people swing their legs over the bike, one wearing a hot pink helmet.

Relief warms my body when I recognize Tiffani Isley's face. The pink helmet must be Adin. *Thank you, God!* I hear them giggling as they make their way up the driveway. Running over to the front door, I fling it open and wrap Adin in a hug.

"Joan, are you okay?" Adin asks. Her head is cocked to the side in confusion, but her arms are around me, and that's all I need.

Tears have made their way out of my eyes. I pull back, trying to make a joke, "What, you girls didn't know that when you get to be my age sometimes you leak."

Tiffani snorts out a laugh, sending Adin into a fit of giggles. Tiffani was so great for Sara. Better yet, they always seemed to balance each other out.

"So, Joan, I was wondering..." Adin begins, darting her eyes toward Tiffani, "ummm, just in case you and Dave didn't know what to get me for my birthday. I'd like a motorcycle. Oh, yeah, with a hot pink helmet."

"Hey, don't forget that you have to have your name nicely spray painted on the helmet! See." Tiffani thrusts her helmet at me to inspect, while both girls walk around me into the kitchen.

I hear Adin rummaging through the drink shelf in the laundry room and slit my eyes towards her voice when I hear her telling Tiffani how on April Fool's day she almost disorganized my drink shelves.

My entire body and mind were burdened just two minutes ago. I take a moment to sigh in relief. I should probably call Dave. I am so glad that he made me stay home. I pick up the cordless phone from the receiver on the kitchen wall and dial his cell. I walk back into the living room, making my way up the stairs, but stop before I get to the top. He picks up on the third ring.

"Sorry, babe, I'm at the gas station around the corner asking the cashier if he remembers anyone resembling Adin hanging out here tonight."

I smile realizing how positive he always is. "It's okay. She's home." I answer. I imagine his posture relaxing.

"Good. I knew she'd come home. How did she get there?"

"On the back of Tiffani Isley's motorcycle." I say, waiting for his reaction.

"Nice. I didn't know Tiffani had a motorcycle. Is it a Harley?" I shake my head in amusement at the noticeable change in his voice, taking no time to transfer from anxiety to excitement.

"Dave, you know I don't know anything about bikes. However,

since you're so revved up by it, Adin just let me know that she wants one for her birthday."

"That would be great, and I could get one so that we could cruise together."

I automatically see where this is going. Adin will become a grease monkey and then Dave and she will be working in the garage on their bikes every evening.

"We'll talk about it some other time." I say quickly, knowing full well that he can already tell I'm not all that thrilled with the idea.

He laughs at me, enjoying his moment. "So, you glad I made you stay home?"

And there they are, the words I knew would come out before the end of the conversation. I could be frustrated, but I'm not. I suck it up and admit, "You were right. I'm sorry."

"Can I get that in writing? Possibly, can we end this conversation, you call back and leave that on my voicemail?" I know he's joking around, probably more jovial knowing Adin is safe at home.

"Ha, ha, ha! I love you too! See you soon honey." I hang up immediately, making my way to the kitchen to join the girls.

CHAPTER 32

Adin's Choice

Adin

I sit cross legged on my floor, running my hand over the jeweled journal that Tiffani dropped off this morning. I look down to the right of me at the hot pink Teen Study Bible that had accompanied it.

I had opened the front door with my morning breath and pajamas still intact. I really wouldn't have thought to open the door, except that the knock came while I was descending the stairs towards breakfast. She had shoved them both into my hands, hugged me, and said she was on her way to work.

"Where did you get these so quickly?" I asked as soon as my brain registered what it was I was holding.

She just lifted her eyebrows and said, "It's a mystery that makes life so much more fun. See you Sunday at church!" With a wave she was gone.

After running my fingers over the jewels on the front of the journal, I flip it open. It contains blank pages. Interesting. I love that the Bible is hot pink; I don't know why, but it really is a much more inviting in that color.

What am I supposed to do with them? I feel like tomorrow

morning when I go to church there is this test that I will be expected to pass when I get there. There must be some type of question or something that Tiffani is going to ask me, and I don't want to fail her.

She said I would know when God and I were on talking terms, and I believe her. I just don't know where to start. I could go downstairs and ask Joan or Dave, but I don't want them to get their hopes up. This could be a long process, and besides, I don't want to fail any of their expectations either. Not that I necessarily would even know what those could be.

I look up to my window and think of Chase, remembering that first morning that I woke up in my bedroom, watching him shadow wrestle. He had come by late last night after Tiffani had left, and Dave had come home.

Neither Dave nor Joan had given me the fifth degree about leaving church, and I didn't want to push my luck by asking why. Dave did make the comment that he was going out today to get me my own cell phone, so that I could let them know where I would be when I went out. I thanked him and told him I definitely would in the future.

I knew it was Chase at the door when I came out of the bathroom from washing my face for the night and heard the knock. It doesn't make logical sense that I can feel his presence, but my heart speeds up and my fingertips go all tingly. Dave had answered the door, and once Chase had entered, I was standing at the end of the stairway.

"Let's go out on the front porch to talk." I motion to the door.

He nods his head in agreement and I follow him out. He leans against the porch railing, looking out into the night sky. I follow his gaze, smiling at the twinkling stars, reminding me of Tiffani's sequined tank top. I chuckle to myself, grabbing Chase's attention.

"Sorry," I say, "just thinking about something." I know it's a vague answer, but I don't know where to begin in how this evening has changed everything. I begin to try when he interrupts me.

"I'm glad you're in a good mood." he says solemnly.

"I am now." I hedge, just now understanding that he is mad. The last time I witnessed Chase angry, it was targeted at the guy who attacked me. This time it's my fault. I blink a few times at the realization.

"Okay." he whispers, clearly at his wits end. I have to applaud the boy's self-control, because based on how tightly he's holding on the porch railing, he's his own kind of Hulk angry. The fact that he's even giving me a chance to explain myself shows a noticeable difference between where he is in life and where I'm at.

It would have been easy for me to lash out at him were the tables turned. If he had walked out on me tonight after we had ridden together anywhere, I would have nailed him with the coldest glare. Then I may have followed that with some pretty hurtful words.

I blow out a long breath of air, fisting my hands until my fingernails dig into my palms. I've never done this before, so I hope it comes out right. "Chase, I need to apologize for the way I acted tonight. I shouldn't have walked out of the church without letting you know. I freaked out at some of the stuff that your Dad talked about, and I understand if you don't want to be friends anymore. I'm pretty messed up, and I'm going to start figuring a lot of that out. I think we should give each other some space for a little while." It all came out so fast, too fast, that I'm not sure he heard everything. But I had to; it had to be like ripping off the band aid because while I know I'm saying all the right stuff, it hurts too badly. My heart pounds against my chest, threatening to explode at the possibility of losing Chase.

Surprise registers on his face when he turns to look at me. I don't know if he is shocked at my apology, or the whole *space* comment. My reflexes tell me to look down, but I know he deserves eye contact, so I give that to him too.

He nods his head in agreement, and without saying a word fades into the darkness between our houses. *Breathe, Adin! Breathe!* I finally take in a woosh of air, and then tiny puffs follow. Closing my eyes to this reality, I sit down on the front step and cry, willing the pain out of my body.

When I had awoken this morning, I was hoping that all of it was merely a nightmare that I would never have to share with anyone. But,

I knew it had happened. I knew because waking up, I felt different. I felt like I had purpose.

Yeah, like cracking open this Bible. When I open up the first page, a piece of folded paper falls out. Hidden behind the note is my name written in Tiffani's cursive penmanship on the inside of the Bible right next to the title "Belongs To". And then today's date is written next, directly below my name. This Bible is now my property. I unfold the note and read.

> Adin,
>
> I've actually had this journal and Bible waiting for you since you came to church last Sunday. Yeah, I saw your eyes bug out when you saw me giving my dad a hug! Ha, ha, and I love that you look for the realness in a person. I bet you never saw me as the Pastor's kid. The thing is, no one is real until they know who really created them— God. I would not be any kind of friend to you if I didn't share the love of Christ. Now, that being said, don't you dare get all freaked out by the number of pages in the Bible. Don't even start at page 1. No, I am not crazy (though many have categorized me as such). I want you to find the book of James and read it. You'll love my advice because this book in the Bible is short. Then, as you feel led, read the New Testament. Get to know Jesus. He's the best friend you'll ever have. I'm always here to answer any of your questions. Every day I am praying for you, just like I know Joan, Dave, and Chase are.
>
> Your sister in Christ,
> Tiffani

I reread the letter several times. I am amazed at how well she knows me. Every time I had looked at the Bible this morning, I was overwhelmed with how thick it was and how long it would take me to read any of it. Then, as if all of that weren't enough, the tiny words that covered each page about undid me.

I open up the Bible to the index and run my finger down until I find the book of James. It appears to be near the end of the New Testament. Once I flip the pages of my Bible to get there, I begin reading the first chapter.

I read the first few verses of the first chapter and stop. I read it again and again trying to figure out how in just a few short sentences Tiffani showed me the answer to my life's question. I've always hated God for how hard my life has been, wondering why. Isn't Chase always saying that God is not a god of coincidences, but one who works out all the details in our lives according to His will.

I never quite understood the fullness of that statement until now. I decide to open my journal and copy the verse out onto my very first page. James 1: 2-4: "Consider it pure joy, my brothers, whenever you face trials of many kinds, because you know that the testing of your faith develops perseverance. Perseverance must finish its work so that you may be mature and complete, not lacking anything."

God, ummm, if you feel like listening to me, I'd like to talk to you. I'm not going to expect you to say anything back. I just want you to know that I do believe in you.

A tear runs down my cheek, releasing me to continue.

I'm sorry for all the bad stuff that I've ever done. I'm sorry that I blamed you for all the horrible things that have happened to me. I know that I don't want to live without you. I can see the difference between Joan and my real mom, and I know that it's because Joan has you and my mom doesn't. If I had to choose who I want to be more like, it's definitely Joan. Thank you for bringing me to live with the Baldwin family. Tiffani says I'll know when I'm yours, and so, I guess I'm going to trust her on that. Thanks for her friendship. Please make Chase feel better today. I know that he doesn't deserve all the hurt in his life because of me. Thanks again for giving me his friendship too. A sob comes out as I continue.

I hope one day that I don't feel like darkness. I pray that your light would cover me, maybe even shine through me. Thank you for explaining my life to me. It seems too easy to have read the Bible this morning, and not that much of it really, to have the pain inside of me explained. Help me to have a better understanding of my trials, God. I am yours.

I sit there in the silence of my room overcome with emotion. My heart is racing in expectation. I don't want to open my eyes, fearing that this amazing high will dissolve. My entire body is buzzing, and I can almost see myself emerging from my past like a beautiful butterfly taking flight.

I love you, Adin.

I gasp, knowing that I have heard the voice of God.

CHAPTER 33

Answered Prayers

Adin

"Adin Taylor, what is going on with you?" Mrs. Hollander stops at my desk.

I stop my humming, put down my calligraphy pen, and try to think of a way to express the huge change that has taken place over the weekend. I can't, so I just shrug my shoulders.

"You are glowing today!" she says smiling. "Good for you." She cocks her head to the side, looking down at my poster board. Our final project in her class is to pen a poem or song that means something to us as individuals. Then, we have to cut out all kinds of slogans and pictures from magazines to create a boarder for the outside of the poster; those clippings are meant to be a collaboration of words expressing the artist.

I hadn't figured out what I wanted to pen until on the way to church Sunday morning. Joan and Dave had been stunned when I had bound down the stairs dressed in one of my many new spring dresses, hot pink Bible tucked underneath my arm.

"What?" I had asked in mock innocence, not able to hide the

smile from my lips. I knew they were overjoyed that I was making the decision on my own to accompany them to church.

"Nothing, just a little jealous of your pink Bible there," Dave joked, "wondering if I have time to stop and get me one to match."

I shook my head at his usual antics and held open the front door.

"Well, we don't want to be late do we?" I had asked before heading out.

On our way to church, I just couldn't get Tiffani's poem from Friday night at Milk Boy out of my mind. Her words started this change in me, guiding me closer to accepting Jesus. The poem she read, *Jesus's Prayers,* resonated with me because it was a pivotal moment in changing my perspective. I no longer saw my past as the cruel consequences of being born to a bored God, but now could see traces of his love in every moment that I was saved from the worse that could have happened.

Mrs. Hollander still has of yet to move from my desk even though I have turned around and continued penning Tiffani's poem:

When I feel Satan come near me,
beckoning me to allow him here,
I'll give your angels all authority,
as I scream out your words through my prayers.
I'll cover my ears against his pleas,
as you defeat the sin I've let in.
I'll cry out to you, "Oh, my precious Savior,"
continuing my prayers within.
When that tear falls down my face,
I'll be thankful that you have always been here.
I could never make it without you, Lord,
and all of my Jesus's prayers."

"Did I mess something up?" I ask, suddenly apprehensive to what sits before me.

"No, it's beautiful." she answers quietly. There is a notable difference in her voice, breathy and low. Looking up at her from my desk, there are tears dripping to her chin where a peaceful smile resides. I stand up and give her a hug.

"Mrs. Hollander, are you okay?" I know that her tears are of happiness, but I still don't know how to deal with someone crying on my behalf.

"Adin, I am better than okay. You, my dear, are an answer to prayer."

Mrs. Hollander has been praying for me too? I'm stunned by her confession. There are no other words I can think of to say, so I do the best I can, "Thanks."

I run into Chase leaving her class, which is odd, because I never have before.

"Hey, Adin, wait up!" I hear him shout, when I purposely turned to go in the opposite direction. What am I supposed to say to him? I know he saw me in church. I don't want him to think that I am getting close to God just so I can get close to him. I want him to have more respect for me than that. I want to have more respect for myself.

Conflicted thoughts keep running through my mind, but I still slow down to accommodate him. It would be wrong to just ignore him; he hasn't done anything wrong.

"Hey," he says, a little out of breath.

"Hey," I return, really having no idea how to act. I hang onto the straps of my book bag for support and make occasional eye contact. There's an awkward dance of kind, blue eyes and then black converse sneakers . . . then repeat.

He puts his hand on my shoulder, a friendly gesture meant to put me at ease, but it's like a cruel reminder of what I can't have right now. His closeness has the potential to derail me from getting myself on the right path. Immediately, I back up.

"Sorry." He mumbles, his initial confidence gone. I hate the confusion that explodes in his eyes because it's all my fault.

"No, it's okay, I'm just . . . I don't know how to explain." I admit.

"You don't have to." I wonder if he wants to just be near me. Oh, the hopes of a girl with a crush.

I nod my head, taking deeper breaths as my heart picks up.

Stupid, traitorous heart, I have a brain too, I shout at myself. I need to focus. I must remember that if I truly want a relationship with Chase, I've got to straighten out my own personal mess. I do not want him to have to fix me.

"I just wanted to let you know that I miss you. I didn't really have time to process how I felt Friday night after we couldn't find you at church. While I was driving around looking for you, I kept trying to bargain with God." He stops to shake his head at himself before continuing, "The truth is, Adin, I can't bargain with God. His ways are set in place, and I knew that before I met you, and I know that now."

"I don't want you to be anything that you're not. But I can't lie and tell you that I don't pray every night for you to understand the love of God. To be even more honest, it is not only because I know that it is in His will for you to be His but also because I care about you."

He pauses, staring straight into my eyes while I try to make sense of what he is saying. Then, after an almost too long pause he continues, clearly changing topics with his ornery smile, "The guys at practice are making fun of me, saying that my single-leg takedown is super slow. I'm betting it's become that way since we haven't been practicing together for a while. My first wrestling tournament is in two weeks, and I wanted to let you know that I'm hoping you can come check it out. Also, whenever you're ready, I'll be in the garage, blaring the music and wrestling my shadow."

His nervous laugh throws me off. Doesn't he know that I miss him too? That I feel my heart is squeezed to capacity every time he is near me?

I reach out, take his hand, and quietly say, "I miss you too. I just need to take care of some stuff first. I am working really hard right now on making the right kind of choices, the kind that you can proud of me for. But, I have to make them for me...not so I can be with you. You know?" I ask.

He squeezes my hand, but before he can say anything, the bell rings, signaling the beginning of another class.

Dave

"Ms. Ann, I mean Marge, hey, this is Dave Baldwin. I'm calling because Adin asked me to. She wanted me to schedule an appointment with you for some time this week so that she could come and talk. She told me to tell you it has to do with that recording that she listened to in your office last time she was there." I pause, hoping that this is all making sense to Marge, because although I am more than happy to make this phone call since Adin asked me to, I have no idea what all of it means

"Really, Dave! And she asked you to make this phone call, not Joan! That is great." Marge's enthusiasm makes me smile.

"I know. It is great. I think she might like me or something." I kid, the euphoria kicking in at the realization that Adin's healing is moving forward.

"How about Thursday at 10:30AM?" she asks.

I check my calendar to make sure I don't have an appointment that I would need to reschedule. I'm completely free that day.

"Sounds great." I answer. "See you then."

I hear Ms. Ann reply softly. "Okay then, bye Dave."

"Bye, Ms. Ann; I mean, Marge."

I jump out of my swivel chair and rub my hands together, too excited to stay stationary. *Thank you, God! I have no idea what has happened, but you do. You orchestrated Adin coming into my home, and you laid out the steps to her finding your love. Thank you that she was in a place that she could be open enough to listen.*

In my mind, I imagine satan trying to push against the Lord, trying to snatch Adin back. *Ha, satan, you loser! You can't get her! She is a child of God, and He already whipped your tail.*

I get down low in my football tackle position, pretending to see that old deceiver lined up right in front of me. *You don't want any of this!* I come up and see myself pulverizing the enemy. I dance around in a victory dance, coming to a stop in my Heisman trophy stance. Looking towards my door, I find an audience of freshmen boys gawking at me, the laughter coming in around me all at once. I slap my knee, throw back my head, and join them.

CHAPTER 34

Family

Adin

A calmness that I've never known has cloaked me since I began reading the Bible. I'm still in the book of James but that's because there is so much in it that speaks to me. I refuse to move forward until I dissect it all, matching it up to the illusions that I've allowed myself to believe in until now. My hot pink Bible sits in my lap along with my jeweled journal.

Dave is lip singing to a song playing on the radio, while Joan is leafing through her planner, probably organizing her to-do list. My heart warms thinking of how much I have come to care for both of them. I assume that this is how a child might know his or her parents.

We are on our way to One Park Building. Every other time I would think about entering the doors to the Foster Care System, a lost feeling would come over me that would cause me to get angry. I felt like being a part of Foster Care was like a huge stamp claiming that I wasn't good enough to have a real family. Looking at Joan and Dave now, I would say that this family is much better than my real one.

Thank you, God. I love that I can talk to you wherever I am. I called Tiffani last night and wanted to make sure that I've got all the rules down on how to pray. I bet you were up in Heaven laughing with her, huh?

I was relieved when she told me that there really weren't all that many kinds of weird rules with being a Christian. She explained that your rules are the kind that allow me to be safe and live a happy, fulfilling life.

She also told me how your Bible says we can pray without ceasing; yeah, I had to look that word up. It means stopping. I can pray without stopping. I got a kick out of it when she told me she's been known to pray in the shower.

I love how full I am now that I know you. I know you know all about why I'm going into see Ms. Ann today. Please give me a clear mind to tell the truth. Guide my words, push the fear away. James 5:13 tells me, "Is any one of you in trouble? He should pray." Lord, Mark Roberts is the most amount of trouble that my life has seen since my mom left me in an alley eight years ago. I need you.

It would be a lie to say that I'm not dreading this conversation. However, I know that it is the right thing to do and that is the kind of girl that I want to be. No more running from my past or stuffing it down deep that it only erupts with my Hulk-like anger. I am going to reveal it all and know that no matter what God loves me.

I've come to the conclusion that what I admire most about people is the way in which they deal with life. I admire Dave because he backed off without taking it personal when I didn't want him near me. He gave me the time that I needed to feel comfortable around him. I admire Joan because she never took any of my teenage attitude seriously, loving me in any way that she could until slowly I came around to treating her the right way. She never lost her temper and yelled at me, which could have easily been justified many times. I admire her self-control.

I admire Chase for his compassion, his empathy. There is no reason that he has had to put himself through the emotional tornado that is me, yet he is still in my life. I have not been fair to him in my actions, like running out of Youth last Friday night, but he is a very loyal friend.

I admire Tiffani because she has taken responsibility for her past mistakes and yet still has not allowed them to hold her back from enjoying a life that God created her to live. She apologized and concentrated on making the kind of choices that she could be proud of.

I want to be like all of them. In order to do that, there is one common factor that they all possess. They have accepted Jesus Christ into their lives as their personal Savior.

When I had first come to live with the Baldwins, I thought that the type of people who trusted a God they couldn't see were weak minded. I thought that because they didn't have the confidence to take control of their own lives and make decisions then they were incapable of doing very much. I was wrong. It was me who was scared of relinquishing the facade of control that I had on my own turmoil.

The more that I have been around Tiffani, talking and asking her questions about God, the more she has helped me recognize how tricky satan tries to be. Satan doesn't want me to know God; in his own selfishness, he doesn't want anyone to know the love of Christ. She says that his biggest lie is making people believe that there isn't a God at all.

My first step in making the right kind of choices, the ones that I know God wants me to make, is talking to Ms. Ann about Mark Roberts. My leg begins to shake under my journal and Bible as my thoughts wander back to the time I spent in Mark Robert's home. I had built a nice brick wall up inside myself, keeping every thought of him out. This was my way of controlling any type of pain that tried to sneak in. I know that in my own strength I am incapable of talking about him, but I am no longer alone.

This is why I asked Joan and Dave to come with me today. I want them to be there when I tell Ms. Ann what happened when I lived with the Roberts' family. I want to start letting them in, so that when I'm having a bad day, they will have a better understanding of where all of the moodiness originated.

I also want to start taking steps in being a part of a family. They have already made it known that this is what they want, so the decision has always been mine. I take my seat belt off when Dave pulls up to the curb, letting Joan and I out while he parks the car. I nudge Joan with my shoulder in a playful way while she puts her purse over her shoulder. She nudges me back, and then we just stand together—mother and daughter—waiting for Dave to complete our family.

CHAPTER 35

Demolishing "No Trespassing" Signs

Adin

I inhale the smell of Mrs. Ann's cinnamon candle, enjoying the absence of the familiar mothball scent that I use to link to these offices. Dave and Joan are sitting in chairs on either side of me, their emotional and physical support intensifying my resolve to speak.

"Adin, I'm so glad you wanted to come see me today. It's nice to not always be the one making the appointments to spend time together." Mrs. Ann opens the conversation up for me to continue.

"Yeah, sorry about that." I hesitate, realizing how true her words are. "I came to talk to you about the recording." My fingers tap erratically on my Bible cover, expelling some of the anxious energy wound tight inside of me like a slinky ready to rise up and fall over.

She smiles kindly at my confession. Slowly, she turns to look at Dave and Joan, probably wondering if I had told them what I had heard in her office that day. Dave shrugs his shoulders, gesturing that he has no idea what I'm talking about.

"And you've brought Dave and Joan with you?" Ms. Ann tilts

her head to the side, the same way she did the first day I was in her office. At that time she was trying to get a better look at me, but I was so full of hate.

I hadn't wanted to look her in the eyes then. Today, I square back my shoulders and meet her gaze head on. I want her to understand that I can do this. Without a verbal answer from me, she responds, "Okay then, great. Let's get started. Adin, begin when you're ready." She has the same tape recorder out from the day I came to listen; yet, I know that it will not be playing anyone else's words today but rather recording my own. Good. I want this taped and heard again and again until Mark Roberts is put away forever.

I blow out a long breath, scrunch my eyebrows together, close my eyes, and imagine myself ripping apart the barrier that I erected so long ago. Internally, I had built a sign inside of myself, clearly stating, 'NO TRESPASSING', but today, I'm demolishing every last piece of it. My heart races with fear as I recall Mark Roberts face. I grab Joan and Dave's hands and begin,

"Adin, get me another beer will ya?" Mark shouts from the living room.

Tracy Roberts, his wife, my foster mom as of late, is out grocery shopping with Rusty, Trevor, and Bethany. They are all under five years old, and I like playing with them. I never had any brothers or sisters before; all the other foster kids I had lived with were older than me and didn't want to bond.

I could spend all day giving Rusty a piggy back ride or playing Barbie dolls with Bethany. I love to see them smile. I love to hear their belly laughs. Their happiness is sunshine to the dark thoughts that always seem to cast thick shadows over my life.

Right now, Mark sits on his sofa watching some football game. I opted to sleep in today instead of going on the weekly grocery shop. On my way into the kitchen in search of some breakfast, Mark requests his favorite beverage.

"Sure." I yell back from the kitchen.

Mark and Tracy have been pretty cool so far. I had been staying here for a few months, and they respected my need for space. Tracy

didn't try to be my best friend, but she also didn't ignore me. Mark and I horsed around with the younger kids together, sort of creating an unspoken bond.

I'm hopeful that I can stay put with the Roberts until I'm legal. I like the way they treat me and feel a huge relief that I don't have to fight with other foster kids.

I shuffle into the living room, his beer in one hand, my plate of toaster waffles in the other. He hears me come in and shifts his head to the side, keeping one eye on the game. I toss him the beer and sit down in the recliner chair to the left of the sofa. While eating, I try to focus on the game, even though I don't really understand any of it.

Before I finish eating my waffles, Mark stands up, takes a long swig of his beer, and looks at his watch. I watch him out of my peripheral vision, curious.

"Are you almost done?" he asks, playing with the tab on the top of his beer can; a clicking noise resonating between us every time he pushes and pulls it across the aluminum lid.

"Yep, why?" I keep my eyes on the TV when answering him, trying to decipher his facial expression. His eyes are half-closed, like he's just waking up, and I'm wondering how many beers he's already drank this morning.

"Cuz, I want to show you something," he says easily.

I stand up, dust the waffle crumbs off my lap, and head to the kitchen to throw away my paper plate. When I turn around to put my silverware in the sink, he positions his body right behind mine, boxing me in on either side as he leans on the counter with both arms.

My heart races, not understanding the nearness of him. I've never been this close to boys, especially not older men. My mom has been with plenty of them, but they never talked to me. I don't know how to react, and find myself second guessing my reaction.

"What's up?" I ask, trying to sound as grown-up as I can. I want Mark to like me, because at this point I respect the way he treats me and the other kids. I want his approval because every interaction we've ever had up to this point has been better than any other foster family I've lived with.

Without answering my question, he turns my body around to where I'm facing him. My head hits the bottom of his chin; I know this because he takes another step closer until there isn't any room left between us. Using both of his hands, he slides my body to the right until my entire body is left flush between his and refrigerator. Holding his weight there, his breathing picks up, and I swallow down the waffles that try to erupt at the smell of his beer-stale breath. After a pause, where I'm trying to figure out exactly what this is, he rocks his body against mine. At first, I find myself just observing his actions, as if it isn't even my body he has caged in the kitchen, but rather a bystander trying to reach for the last bit of knowledge that will secure me the answer to this riddle.

Sadly, I am stuck in this in-between illusion, hoping that he's just horsing around with me, like we both do with the younger kids right after supper.

But that's not what he's doing, it isn't that at all....

Joan

My chest burns, there are flames licking their way up into my throat. I try to hold myself together for Adin's sake. I feel so worthless sitting in this chair beside the strongest young woman I have ever met.

I wish, with all that is in me, to take away the story of hurt that she is sharing with us right this second. My stomach continues to roll in nausea, while she forges on in her description of what Mark Roberts had done to her.

Lord, why? I can't put your love and this evil in the same world sometimes. I want to erase this horribleness from Adin's memory. But I can't. I don't know how she is even able to sit here in this office and so patiently describe such terror.

Why wasn't there someone there to save her? Why couldn't Tracy Roberts have come home? Lord, where is your hand in this situation? I love you so much, but why?

Tears run down my face, dripping from my chin, leaving tiny splashes of water all over my lap. I look down as the drops continue to grow in number, feeling her sorrow leak from my own eyes.

My heart feels so heavy inside my chest. I wince as she continues to describe how he beat her, threatening her, that if she ever said a word to anyone it would be much worse.

My whole body is spent, just hearing about this moment in Adin's life. How has she dealt with all of this? I don't think that I would ever be capable of going through what she already has.

I reach out, laying my hand against Adin's arm when she pauses for a moment. Immediately, I feel the Holy Spirit, like touching her has opened my eyes to the power of God within this nightmare. My entire body is tingling with goose bumps; she turns and smiles at me in appreciation.

I swallow down the lump in my dry throat, overcome with love for such a precious girl. She is so unbelievably strong. Her life is a living testimony to the victory of Jesus Christ.

I struggle to take in deep breathes as I come to the understanding that God has had His hand unceasingly upon her life: *Joan, she is aware now that what was done to her is in no way her fault. She has carried guilt for far too long, and because of your Christ-like love, she has found Me. I have never left her, and I never will. Thank you for loving her enough that she can see me. Take joy in this blessing, Joan. I love you, my daughter.*

God illustrates to me yet again the power of his presence in this world. It is unexplainable, the love and mercy my Lord so graciously extends to his children.

Thank you, Father!

I look up in time to notice that my hand is no longer on Adin's shoulder but now enveloped within her own.

Adin

"So I ran—as soon as he finished listing his punishment for telling anyone. I had to wait a few days to heal. My ribs were the worst. I don't think that he actually broke one, but the bruises made it tough to breathe. I hid upstairs in the attic. I don't think Tracy or Mark ever thought to look for me up there. I heard them talking for the two nights that I lay hidden. I must have blacked out a few times because

I awoke the second night to Tracy yelling at Mark. I was really out of it because one moment I remember daylight poking through the shuttered vent on the front of the house, and then I woke up to pitch darkness and Tracy's shrill voice.

"Mark, she's still not here! You were the last one who saw her. I want you to tell me everything that happened that afternoon again. Nothing you have said makes any sense. What am I supposed to tell Rusty, Trevor, and Bethany? They keep asking where Adin is, and I don't know what to say."

I can tell that Tracy is crying because her last sentence comes out in labored spurts. I listen to Mark walk across the room, his steps taunting me with a new fear, as if he knows exactly where I'm hiding. I turn and gag, the smell of stale beer permeating my senses even though he is 10 feet below me.

His voice takes on a paternal patience, like he is explaining some life lesson to a child, "Sweetie, you know foster kids are unpredictable. Adin is a teenage girl, who knows what she was thinking? Every time one of them runs away, we go through this. She's stupid for leaving such a wonderful mom like you, that's for sure."

"I came home from work, she was eating waffles and watching TV. I asked her where everyone was, and she said you had taken the kids to the grocery store. I went to take a shower, and when I got out, she wasn't in the living room anymore."

"I assumed that she had gone upstairs to her room. I was just as surprised as you when we couldn't find her yesterday evening. Tracy, you can't keep blaming yourself every time one of these girls gets flighty. I'll go around town tomorrow after work and ask people if they've seen her. Will that make you feel better? I'm so sorry, honey; I hate how upset these foster kids make you."

"I wanted to run down the attic stairs and bash his lying face in. I wanted Tracy to see the marks all over my body. I wanted her to have to face what Mark had done to me. But I hated myself more than the hate I had for him, because even though I wanted revenge, I was too scared of the confrontation. So I left."

Lowering my head in embarrassment, I purposely avert my eyes for the first time since the conversation began. Sighing deeply, I bite the inside of my lip, trying to decide what to say next.

"Oh Adin," Ms. Ann shakes her head sympathetically, "I'm so sorry. We try to take every precaution to make sure that the 'Mark Roberts' of this world do not make it into the Foster Care System. I would like to think that I could take away what he did, erase it all, but I can't. Thank you for deciding to tell me why you ran away. May I ask, what changed since our last discussion?"

"I discovered that I am not unloved. I am not invisible, and my life has never been an accident." I scrunch my eyebrows together, trying to describe what it is that God had done within me.

"Even in the darkest shadows of my life, it all could've been worse. I know that God has always been there for me, but somehow, I decided to blame Him for being there with me. I don't know if I'm doing a very good job of answering your question, Ms. Ann. A few days ago I accepted Jesus Christ into my heart, and He told me that coming here was the right thing to do."

CHAPTER 36

Victory

<u>*Dave*</u>

I knew it. I knew the moment that Adin wouldn't let me near her that some scumbag hurt her. I've been praying that whatever took place wouldn't have been as bad as she described today, but it was. Actually, I think her story is much worse than I had originally imagined. How many girls have suffered because of this jerk?

"Ms. Ann, uh Marge, how many foster kids have already run away from the Roberts' home?"

"I've already been investigating. I can't disclose much, but I can confirm that each foster child that ran was a girl. When Adin came in to see me last week, she got to hear a testimony from another victim."

Marge turns towards Adin as she continues to speak, "I was hoping that what this other girl had to say would in some way open Adin to sharing too. I still wasn't one hundred percent if it was Mark Roberts who had also hurt Adin, but Adin's reaction to the recording gave me enough reassurance. He has already been detained by the Philadelphia Police and is awaiting trial. Adin, would you be willing to testify against Mark Roberts for what he has done to you?"

I don't want any of this for Adin, but she has already proven how capable she is despite her circumstances. I know that she can do this, but does she really have to? I watch as she closes her eyes and sits perfectly still.

Lord, thank you so much for bringing Adin into our home. Thank you for strengthening her when she needed strength and loving her when she wouldn't allow anyone else to. Thank you for all the people that you've sent into her life along the way to reflect your character.

She knows you because of your faithfulness. I pray that you would wrap your arms around her with your peace and be her refuge as she fights for the ability to climb this mountain.

In my devotional book today, I am reminded of the verse that it spoke about, James 5:13: "Is anyone of you in trouble; he should pray." Thank you for the power of prayer. I have been blessed enough to see you in action in yet another young person's life. I am grateful to watch as your providence ensures the care of your children.

You understand far more about Adin than I ever will; and so with confidence, I know that you will bring her through this. In Jesus's Name I Pray, Amen.

"Yes, I'll testify." Adin is no longer the sarcastic, timid girl that I met five months ago.

She literally ran from me the first morning that she awoke in our home. I had asked her if she wanted to ride with me and check out her new high school, but she had fled up the stairs like she was running for her life. I felt it then, that feeling in my gut that something wasn't right.

Again, it was confirmed when I had casually mentioned giving her a ride to and from school, and she had tried her best to hide the apprehension that was raw on her face. She had hidden in the living room, thinking that Joan and I couldn't feel the tension that emanated from her.

That 'Adin' would have never agreed to sit here with Joan and I listening as she retold such events. That 'Adin' would have sat quietly with her head down, never making eye contact.

I smirk, acknowledging the victory that Jesus has won this week in Adin's life. There is a deep joy when I think of how satan's curse on her has been blown to a million tiny pieces.

All the sudden Adin's previous attack comes to my mind; I abruptly turn my head in her direction. She must sense I'm going to ask her a question because her eyes meet mine.

"Adin, who did you really punch the night you were attacked?"

Adin

It's been two weeks since I sat in Ms. Ann's office, reflecting on and trying to describe the abomination that is Mark Roberts. The week before that, when Ms. Ann had me listen to that recording from an adult woman who had once lived with the Roberts when she was a teen in foster care, detailing what Mark had done to her, I wanted to be anywhere on earth but in that chair having to hear it. The only consolation that day was when Mrs. Ann admitted to me that the little girl who had been in her office before me had not been harmed.

What he had done to her was in much the same way identical to how he had treated me, even if, thank God, it didn't go as far. I know that I would have thrown up in her trash can if I hadn't just dry heaved in the women's restroom beforehand.

I still hadn't been ready to contribute anything. I needed more time to put everything in order or just figure out how to forget.

I had tried to make Chase the center of all my attention. God was quick to slam that door shut. Looking back now, I can see how God was shutting every possible exit route that led me away from turning to Him. I would have made Chase my world had Pastor Ben not spoken about "missionary dating" that Friday night.

I remember feeling like God was completely against me, and it ignited a hate in me towards Him that enabled me to walk right out of church that night without having any idea where I was heading. Thankfully, God was still right there, patiently dealing with my stubbornness.

In fact, He led me straight to the one person I would listen to: Tiffani Isley. When I had watched her get off her motorcycle, glowing in her sequined top, I knew that she had something that I didn't, and I wanted it. Little did I understand that it was a relationship with Jesus Christ.

It's comical to look back and see how God pursued me for so long, but Tiffani has told me that it is also amazing to be loved so deeply by our Creator. It has been overwhelming, but in a good way, to go from feeling so unwanted to completely and unconditionally loved.

Mark Robert's first court date is July 27th, but I don't have to attend. I had to turn in a typed testimony that will be added to the other testimonies Ms. Ann collects. I may not have to appear at all, but Ms. Ann keeps reminding me that God's strength will guide me no matter how it turns out.

I use to think that weak people leaned on the Bible because they couldn't find their own strength to just make a choice. Now, I see how blind I had been all along to the tenacity that it takes to have faith.

I am absolutely not looking forward to ever seeing Mark Roberts' face again, but instead of pretending like the situation doesn't exist, I pray. I give it to God every time satan tries to scare me with the unknown.

I smile, thinking of how proud Dave was of me when he finally figured out that my attacker had been Mark Roberts. Ms. Ann had been monitoring his home since it had been my last foster care residence, and Mark assumed that I had talked. Ms. Ann is still investigating how he figured out who my new foster family was.

I made sure to explain that my original story concerning my attack was all true except for two details. The first, of course, being that the attacker was Mark Roberts. The second detail being the conversation he and I had before he smacked me around, and I got in a good punch.

He told me that some nosy black woman from Social Services had been snooping around his house, and I had better keep my mouth shut. He threatened that he knew where I lived, and he could easily hurt my foster family and the boy next door.

At first, when he had put his hands on me, backing me up against the tree, it was like I was back in his kitchen, cowering in fear, but when he had brought up Dave, Joan, and Chase, I became enraged. The Hulk-anger came quickly, and, for the first time in my life, I fought back.

He had bound my wrists above my head in his own, but thanks to Chase's training I broke his wrist control and then, out of habit, completed a single-leg take down so quick and efficient that he landed hard on his butt, his face frozen in shock. I almost got away right then, but he lunged at me from behind, grabbing my ankle, and taking me to the ground. I tried kicking him off, but it didn't work. He yanked the back of my hair and threw me down, straddling me.

Again, he tried to frighten me, telling stories of how he would hurt the people I had come to love if I didn't get Ms. Ann off his case. After turning me over, he punched me in the face to emphasize his point and then, full of an anger I could feel vibrating from his core, gave me a couple blows to my ribs. When he finally rolled off of me, I scrambled up to my feet, getting into my wrestling stance without a second thought. He must have thought we were done, but I chose that moment to nail him hard with a right hook, pouncing back on my toes, and then sprinted to the end of the street.

Ms. Ann had said that she figured it was Mark Roberts all along, which is why she intensified her surveillance after my attack. Joan was spent, and Dave was, oddly, the complete opposite. He was substantially wound up. He was rocking in his chair like he does when the UFC fights are on the television. I can't pretend that I didn't like the fact that he was proud of me though; because honestly, it meant everything.

EPILOGUE

Adin

School let out last week, and I have no idea what I'm going to do all summer. I asked Dave and Joan if they wanted me to get a job, and they said not yet. They are still a bit overprotective since all the details have come out. I can't blame them, but I cannot possibly stay locked in the house all summer. There isn't even going to be a hot boy outside my window shadow wrestling because he'll be gone a week here and there all summer long at wrestling camps and tournaments.

I crouch down in my wrestling stance in front of the wall length mirror on the outside of my bedroom door and do a quick single-leg takedown. Not bad. I wonder if they have a girl's wrestling team? I don't remember ever seeing any girls in a singlet, so I'm going to say no. I finally stopped calling the boy's wrestling outfits ballet suits but only because Chase put me in a headlock and made me promise to never call it anything but a singlet again.

I really, really miss Chase. It's not like I haven't seen him at Youth Group on Wednesday and Friday nights or at church on Sunday, because I have. I just won't let myself spend any time alone with him yet.

I need to focus on getting to know my new best friend right now: God. And not let anything else take that place. I get around Chase, and it's like my brain shuts off, and I go into sensory mode. I want to have something with Chase that lasts longer than a feeling. In order for any type of relationship between us to work, I've got to focus on me first.

I also miss his family. I use to ride with them to church on Wednesdays and Fridays, but since I called the *break* between Chase and myself, I've just ridden with Dave and Joan. We had Carter ride with us this past Wednesday because he said he missed me. But let's be real, I know I missed him more.

Tiffani says that we must have fellowship. That means that we must have people who understand what we are going through in our life so that we can be encouraged and supported to do the right things, make the better choices. I don't know where I would be without her friendship and our Friday night donut-eating contests.

I'm a little nervous because I'm going to get to meet Sara and Matt on July 4th. Dave and Joan are having a cookout, and they are both coming into town. Tiffani and I have talked at length about my fears involving both of them. Her stories make it seem like I know them better.

The sound of someone running up the stairs in a hurry interrupts my thoughts. There's a sharp knock on my door that continues in an annoying chaotic rhythm. I have to say "Come in" several times before I get a response.

"Adin, you have to come downstairs right now! Okay?!" It's Dave's voice, but almost in a chipmunk squeaky high that garbles all of the words in the sentence into one long impossible word.

"Okay, I'm coming." I open the door and start to make slow, intentional motions meant to portray an attempt to remove my body from the bedroom, which I know is driving him crazy.

He waits for me to get in front of him before he half ushers, half drags me down the stairs into the kitchen. He gestures for me to sit down at the island in front of a rectangular box that is wrapped in hot pink wrapping paper.

Joan is already seated next to me at the island, hands folded patiently in her lap. She has a smile on her face that's got me wondering what exactly could be in said hot pink box.

"Joan?" I say casually.

"Adin?" she mimics.

"What's going on?" I ask purposefully in order to delay opening the box.

She looks over to Dave, who keeps moving back and forth beside me. This guy has had one too many coffee's this morning.

"Open it." Dave states in a faux-calm voice. I want to say he's being encouraging, but the tone is somewhat threatening as well.

"All righty then, I will." I answer.

Slowly I peel the tape off of one crease at the end of the box, knowing that I'm quite literally shaving years off of Dave's life. I hear Joan supress a giggle at what I'm doing. She hides it well by tapping her pointer finger over her lips—it's a good cover.

I look up to see how Dave's doing with my charade, only to find him with his eyes closed, drumming his fingers against the island. He must be praying for patience. I can't help myself. I double over in laughter. I end up falling right out of my seat onto the floor. At which point, Joan loses all control and laughs so hard that there are tears streaming down her face. This only makes me laugh harder.

Dave shakes his head in exasperation. I can see the plea for help in his eyes while Joan and I continue to laugh. It's getting hard to breathe. I bring my knees up to my chest and take a few deep breaths of air.

Standing up, I return to the wrapping paper, only this time I rip into it. I notice the imprint on the outside of the box says "Asics." Why does that seem familiar? I look to Dave.

"Open it!" he says again. This time pointing emphatically at the box.

I lift the lid to find a pair of hot pink wrestling shoes. I'm dumbfounded. When I take them out of the box, there is a piece of paper folded at the bottom of the box. When I open up the paper, I read through a list of wrestling camps and tournaments with summer dates out beside each event. Some of the camps are for girls only while a few are co-ed.

"These are wrestling shoes," I remind Dave, as I hold them up in front of me.

"Duh!" he returns, "They're for the first girl wrestler to attend

Central High. She's going to rock!" He puts his fist out for a bump. We have definitely bonded past the high fives.

I'm shocked. He really thinks that I can do this? I really want to do it. I never figured that it was an option until this very second. I mean, sure, I wanted it to be an option, but never in a million years did I think it could be.

I give Dave a quick hug and then step back. Looking down, before I turn to show Joan my new shoes, I notice that Dave is wearing wrestling shoes too. Thank God they're not hot pink.

COMING SOON!

Their story continues with Tiffani's journey in

Back To the Beginning

Chapter 1: The Beginning

The Call
Now we're back to the beginning
It's just a feeling and no one knows yet,
But just because they can't feel it too
Doesn't mean that you have to forget.
Let your memories grow stronger and stronger,
Until they're before your eyes.
You'll come back when it's over,
No need to say good-bye.
~Regina Spektor~

I tilt my head to the side, walking across the salon, loving the feel of the bouncy curls brushing across my shoulder. I had just finished creating them with my new Curling Wand. I tilt my head to the other side, feeling the same bounce on my left shoulder. I smirk at myself, easily amused with my own behavior, when I meet Rochelle's eyes.

Rochelle is the genius owner of *Curl Up and Dye* where I spend at least twenty-five hours a week. It's not a hard gig to get paid while doing something you love. I remind myself this every time I have to work the early-bird shift. A piece of heaven on earth would be an all-night salon. I cover my mouth as a yawn slips out. Why in the world ten in the morning was invented is beyond me.

"Tiffani, please tell me you are not sashaying across my salon modeling your curls?" Sarcasm oozes from Rochelle's voice.

If anyone had missed my abnormal behavior, they're in on it now. I giggle in reply before turning the corner from the customer area into the back where we keep all of our dyes, towels, extra brushes, combs, scissors, tweezers, and anything else a salon needs to run. It's like a personal Sally's store where I work, which is an extreme bonus in the world of Tiffani Isley.

As I reach up to get some towels for my station, I hear Melissa walk into the back. Melissa and I graduated from Central High School the same year. Sadly, we never spent time together when we both actually attended high school. I spent most of my time at church, or with my best friend Sara. My dad is the pastor of New Hope, one of the biggest churches in Philadelphia.

Melissa spent her fall playing field hockey; I spent mine volunteering with mom at the local Pregnancy Center. Melissa spent her winter cheerleading for the basketball and wrestling teams; I spent my winter practicing for the church Christmas program and singing in the church choir. We really lived on two different planets during high school. Towards the end of my senior year, I dove in to a rebellious stage that about drowned me, but it also allowed me to learn some hard truths about who I am, and for that, I would never take back any of it.

"Hey Tiff, you are so doing my hair later." Melissa grins.

"Thanks! I am in love with the new Curling Wand that Rochelle has out front. I already picked mine out: zebra print. What did you get into last night?" The question part of our normal routine.

"Not much. I stopped in at Milk Boy; there was this amazing new guy who had a set last night. I didn't see anyone I knew, so I jetted after he was done. How about you?"

"Well," I draw out in a high pitched valley girl accent, stopping only when I have her full attention.

Her drawn brow a dead give-away that she's thinking this is going to be good.

I can't suppress my smile when I finally give her an answer, "Nothing. I mean, I did give myself a much needed pedicure and caught up on my *Grey's Anatomy* episodes, but otherwise, a fairly quiet evening."

"Hmmmmm," Melissa begins, "we are going out tonight. I

am so tired of hearing your old lady renditions of a night. You are aware that you are twenty-two years old right? And that we live in a city with a million and one social activities that have the very real possibility of putting you in the orbit of an exceptionally hot guy? You are gorgeous Tiff, but you are lazy." She holds up her hand as I try to get a rebuttal in. "No, no excuses. Shave your legs sweetheart because we are going out. Tonight!"

She puts her fingers in her ears and starts singing "la, la, la" while simultaneously exiting the supplies area. I sigh inwardly. I finger one of my bouncy curls, thinking that this day had started with such promise.

Throwing my keys down on the closest table, I kick my apartment door shut behind me. Immediately, I spit the dry cleaning hangers out of my mouth. They land with a thud on the scratched wood flooring of my foyer. Leaping over the dry cleaning, I dump my purse, Bible, and new free trial shampoos on my already crowded love seat, making a bee line for my refrigerator in hopes that I have some Dr. Pepper. I get happy thinking of the hot bubbles making their way down my dry, scratchy throat.

There is something about riding my motorcycle that makes me thirsty. Thinking about Lucy, my hot-pink Ninja, leaves me with a deep sense of satisfaction. I paid for her out right and spent a better part of a year saving every penny. I even dodged Milk Boy, the best café and coffee in Philadelphia, so I wouldn't be tempted by their Godiva Hot Chocolate. Sometimes a girl just has to flee temptation.

Oh, I wish I could have a Godiva Hot Chocolate right now. Coming back to reality, I notice that I am no longer holding my refrigerator door open, but instead am gazing out the front door of my apartment at the fluorescent lit hallway. I wonder if I'm the only person whose body voluntarily follows a wandering mind. I would get frustrated with myself, but I get some of my best ideas when my mind takes the scenic route. It is as if when I am giving the least to figure out a situation, God directs me. I love it!

Backing up, I shut my front door and catch myself right before tripping on the dry cleaning that I had previously abandoned for a Dr. Pepper. I scoop up the plastic liners and head to my bedroom. My finger flips the light switch on but nothing happens. I continue to flick the switch up and down a few times before conceding that I cannot win this battle.

Where did my phone end up in the chaos of returning home? Scanning the living room, I don't see it. I squint my eyes towards the kitchen, located just behind the living room, but I still don't notice the hot pink crystal case of my beloved cell. These are the times I wish I had a landline. Ninety percent of the usage would be in finding my cell phone. Out of habit, I check my back pocket. There it is!

Unlocking the phone, I hit the button that allows me to take pictures. Rushing around my living room and kitchen, I ensure that every light is on. Good lighting is essential to any audience when viewing a picture; at least I remember highlighting that when Mr. Peters lectured on it in my Photography course.

At the last second, I decide to use elevation for a better representation of what I need, so I push my coffee table to the side of my living room and step up. Clicking the circular button on my phone, I capture the perfect image of my messy home. I post the picture on Facebook with a status that reveals I will be cleaning if anyone wonders why I am not answering my phone. I lose myself in the lyrics of Regina Spektors "The Call" as I undo the mess of my week.

Melissa grabs me on either side of my arms and gives a slight shake.

"What are you doing here?" I ask, almost jumping out of my skin.

As soon as the question is out of my mouth, I remember. "Never mind that question." I get out before she can speak. "It will only take me five minutes to get ready."

"I am picking out your outfit; go get in the shower. Men are not attracted to the smell of bleach."

I sigh quietly, heading towards my newly clean bathroom. Rotating the shower knob to hot, I grab my new Tangerine Body Wash.

After rushing through my shower, I notice that Melissa has already brought in my outfit: canary yellow skinny jeans with a white cropped, v-neck cable sweater. I'm going to have to straighten my hair, curling it will take too long. Melissa brings me my black short belted boots as I finish up.

"Looking good, girl!" Her smile reflected in the mirror.

"Thanks, just trying to keep up with you," I wink.

I grab one of my perfumes off the shelf and spray a fruity scent into the air as I walk through the door.

"Where to?" I ask Melissa as she ushers me out the front door.

"Milk Boy," we say in unison.

"Jinx," I squeal! "You owe me a Godiva Hot Chocolate."

The strong smell of ground coffee beans envelopes Melissa and I as we transfer ourselves from the bustling city street into the creative energy flowing throughout Milk Boy. I inhale deeply, allowing the simple aroma to fill my body with an invisible high. I can taste excitement while my eyes wander around the tables of men and women laughing and chitchatting. I don't care to hear the details; I thrive living in the thick of it all.

"There's the smile I've been waiting for." Smugly, Melissa strides to the counter, no doubt purchasing two Godiva Hot Chocolates.

Milk Boy is a cutting edge coffee house. It has open mic nights twice a week, bringing in local and out of town talent. Trevor opened the doors four years ago and is a good friend from high school. There have been bands that have played here since it opened that have gone on to make it big. I finger the signed pictures of one such band, *Rush*, taken before they signed with MTV and went on to win countless vocal awards.

The lamps in the room throw light in pools of energy, leaving sections in complete darkness. Unless you are sitting at one of the pub height tables, there is no candlelight to break up these fragments of seclusion. I enjoy hiding within them. Just to watch, sometimes just to pretend, taking on the persona of one person and then another.

Once you enter the front doors, there is a long counter where people place their drink order. The counter only takes up about half of the entryway though, and large groups can easily maneuver to the left of it to get a seat at the tables. On the far wall behind the counter, beyond the tables, is the stage. The stage isn't huge like I remember from our high school plays, but big enough that a band can set up and move about. The overhead lights throw sporadic color throughout the seated guests, dramatizing their faces as they immerse in their company.

I am just getting myself comfortable to watch tonight's artist when I hear the soft strum of the guitarist on stage, and then a whisper of a song begins. My heart goes from a steady, constant beat to that of a thousand motorcycles gunning to life all at once inside my chest.

"Oh no…" I'm lost in the lyrics and deep voice of my past.

Closing my eyes, I try to picture the European Geography study guide of the Mediterranean countries as Mrs. Lowe takes attendance. I have got to ace this quiz, or I'll be bringing home a "C" on my progress report.

"Spain, Portugal,…" I whisper out loud, moving my finger over an imaginary study guide.

"How's that working out for you?" Gabe asks.

The rhythm of my heart completely changes with his question. Normal, Tiff, keep it together. Just be cool here. I hope my inner dialogue reveals a confidence that I realistically lack.

I squint my right eye open to make eye contact without looking down at the imaginary answers.

"So far, so good. What's your secret?" There. My voice is normal. I don't spit on him when I talk. High five, Tiffani.

"What do you mean, 'my secret'?" he asks curiously, turning his whole body my direction, clearly holding in a laugh at my expense while watching my imaginary study game.

"You get a hundred on every one of these, Gabe." I huff, trying not to let my complete failure in Geography squeak through my voice.

"How do you know I'm not cheating?" He leans in closer, mouth tight and askew at my obvious observation of his grades. I find myself holding my breath because I can't figure out if this face means that he is curious or angry. Why doesn't he make this face more often?

Here's what I do know: he is only asking to see my take on his bad-boy image. We've been in school together since junior high, and I've noticed him since day one. He's the tough guy, the kind of boy who isn't afraid to stand up to a teacher that he doesn't agree with; the kind of boy who has lost his temper once or twice on school property when aggression is frowned upon, even though every single time I've been audience to such high tense displays, he's really just called out someone in authority on their misuse of it.

Anyone else in the class probably assumes he's failing. Our peers seem to think that the teachers pass him because they don't want the headache of him back next year. No, I know he is brilliant. Of course, I've spent more time than I should watching him.

"Because I'm smart. Of course you're not cheating. You fly through the quiz in less than a minute. Okay, maybe an exaggeration, but still, super-fast. I barely have my name on the paper and figure out what is a body of water and what is a country before you are already walking to the front, laying it on Mrs. Lowe's desk with a smug grin." I look up during my monologue and catch his eyebrows raise, combined with that smug grin, all of which causes my heart to change gears once again.

"My smug grin, huh?" I don't like how pleased he looks with that comment; there's a glint in his eye now and an easiness in his smile.

Is that all he got from my ranting?

"Do not deflect! How are you so good at this, and why am I such a

failure? I'm hanging on for dear life here man, throw me a bone!" My voice rises a little towards the end of my hyperbolic meltdown.

Usually, I don't get so bent out of shape about schoolwork. I'm not a brainiac, but I hold my own. However, when it comes to Geography maps, I've got nothing.

He scoots his desk closer to mine, leaning over, creating a tiny world that includes just the two of us. "I pretend I'm taking a trip. Right now, today, it's to back- pack around Mediterranean Europe. So, I got to figure out where I'm starting and which direction I'm going. I even imagine what kind of food I'll be getting or someplace I want to stop. It makes learning all that trivial pursuit information in the book easier too. Then I'm off. It doesn't seem like homework anymore. It's more of an adventure. Do you want to come with me?" His last sentence is asked in a serious tone, which has me guessing at his intent— genuine or overly sarcastic?

I'm pretty sure that my heart just stopped beating altogether because it is not humanly possible for it to hold a beat pattern necessary for Gabe Riddick to be sitting this close to me, whispering into my ear.

"Yes." I barely say, because talking is all of a sudden a foreign concept under such duress.

He leans back, smiling, right before Mrs. Lowe lays down a quiz on his desk. She taps his desk and points to the left, signaling that our desks are too close together. He moves back over, covering the chair imprints that he had let breathe for a short time at the expense of my own oxygen intake.

I can feel all the blood rushing back into my heart, once again taking up residency inside my chest. I flip my quiz over, writing my name and the date at the top. Just when I locate Spain, Gabe slips out of his seat. He stops in front of my desk for a split second, not long enough for anyone else to give notice, as they too are deciphering between a body of water and a landmass.

"Wish you could have been there this time..."His voice giving away a longing that I pray isn't a part of my over-active imagination.

I put my head down in an effort to appear busy, but as he returns to his seat, I whisper down to my paper, "Me too."

I wipe the tear away before Melissa begins a mantra of never ending questions that cause me to unwillingly admit information that I just don't want to talk about. I don't even want to think about why I am still not ready to talk about it. I pretend to pick something up off of the floor, allowing the time that it takes for me to bend over and stand up to wipe my face. In any case, if my face is red, I can blame it on the fact that I was upside down for a few seconds. A stretch for the truth, I know, but at least I have something.

"Is it heads or tails?" Melissa asks.

"What?" completely bewildered by her comment, I give her a dumbfounded look.

"What do you mean, 'what'? What else would you have been down on the floor for so long?"

Oh, she just offered me an out.

"No, I don't know what I was looking for. I thought I saw something, and then...... it was gone." I clench my teeth as soon as the words are out of my mouth.

I haven't lied in so long; it's awkward. I can't believe it only takes Gabe to be within my perimeter for old habits to resurface. I don't like myself in this moment.

"Okay, you have inhaled way too much bleach this evening. We need to find seats. I think you need to sit down."

I allow Melissa to escort me out of my concealed shadow into the mass of life that congregates around each table. I'm so thankful that she's letting me off the hook about before that it doesn't register in my mind that with every step we take I come closer to a piece of my life that has the very real possibility of turning me inside out. Looking up, I catch Gabe strumming his guitar, eyes closed.

Melissa finds us a couple of seats at an already crowded table close to the stage. I nod my head in thanks to a few familiar faces and scoot my chair behind the tallest guy. There is no way Gabe will be able to see me here.

"This is the same guy that was playing here last night! He must be good for Trevor to have booked him two sets in the same week. What do you think, Tiff?"

I think that I am going to vomit. I think that my legs cannot possibly run as fast as necessary to get me on the perimeter of such desolation. I think that I cannot think anymore or my head will explode.

There are murmurs of agreement from among the group we've settled with, so instead of verbally giving my opinions, I nod my head relaying an overly-fake enthusiastic yes. My teeth come out, biting down hard on my lower lip, hoping that pain can anchor me back to reality instead of allowing my heart to rise up and cry out to Gabe's presence.

I am an adult now; so much has happened between now and then. I can get through this. I am okay.

Lord, I know that you are here with me. Father, why is Gabe back? It was five years ago. Five years is more than enough time to heal. I am so different from who I was back then. He probably is too. Lord, I pray that he found you. I pray that he loves you with all of his amazing energy. He was such a huge part of why I am here today, but I have no idea of knowing if that is reciprocated. I just need you to take over because I can't do this. I would like to think that I have grown past this, this...well, you know what this is better than I do, but obviously not. Please come, Lord. I need you. Amen

I lift my head from conversing with God in time to hear Melissa's signature laugh, snort and all. I watch as she leans into Paul, a new guy from our church. Now I know why we are sitting at this table. Paul is sitting at this table.

A real smile forms when I think about how much Melissa deserves a great guy. I peek around the tall guy that I have camouflaged myself behind, hoping to appease my heart's desire for a quick glance at the only boy who has owned real estate in my heart. When I do, I wish I could take time's hand and skip backward. Eyes closed, fingers working the guitar, body relaxed as he leans on the stool, Gabe is handsome and full of peace entertaining the crowd. I don't want to process all of the emotion that goes along with him tonight. So, I close my eyes and make a deal with my heart that we'll listen instead.

CPSIA information can be obtained
at www.ICGtesting.com
Printed in the USA
BVHW031943070719
552810BV00015B/12/P

9 781512 794144